IRON PRISON

PRISONER SERIES: BOOK TWO

M.J. THOMPSON

Crystal Eye®
Absolutely Unprofessional®

© 2023 Imagination, creation and publication by Crystal Eye® in partnership with Absolutely Unprofessional.® All rights held onto by M.J. Thompson through Crystal Eye and Absolutely Unprofessional. This book may not be reproduced, recreated, rewritten or reused in any manner beyond the authors intended purpose hind-or-henceforth without written permission and personal autograph by those personally and vocationally responsible for the content and the creation of Iron Prison©, namely, M.J. Thompson.

However, portions of Iron Prison© will be allowed for the use of brief quotations in a book review, scholarly journal, blog, website, magazine, newspaper, family holiday newsletter or personal poem to loved ones.

Cover and interior layout and design by Absolutely Unprofessional.

Print and distribution through IngramSpark at ingramspark.com.

Paperback Printing: 2023
ISBN 979-8-9879116-2-4
Crystal Eye®
crystaleyepub2022@gmail.com
Absolutely Unprofessional®
absolutelyunprofessional.com

What a journey!
This one goes out to all my friends whose support after the
release of *Glass Prison* truly gave me the encouragement to
keep going on this writing adventure.
Book two was a vastly different experience than book one
and my loving husband and children gave me the solitude and
support to keep writing... even when it meant they were on their
own for a meal or two.
R. J Dyson, who took care of the book layout and design, and
who is also a co-publisher, really got tossed into the ring on this
one. I could not be more thankful to have him in my corner.
To my readers, Thank You!
Your joyful partnership fills my heart.

Prologue
Run!

"**D**octor, they're coming. They've breached the door."

Dr. Harold knew this moment was coming. His team knew what to do, but getting the girls out was going to be difficult. "Do you know who it is?"

"A Tactical Firearms Unit out of London."

He nodded. "Okay. Get them out. I'll be right behind." Racing to his office, he grabbed his files and the hard drive containing videos of each session with the eight girls he'd been experimenting with inside the old hospital.

The commander of his security detail burst through the door. "Sir, we have to leave. Now!"

Handing two Pelican cases off to the commander and dragging two more behind, they ran down the hall to the freight elevator.

"Stop!" A TFU officer in black fatigues rounded the corner. Dr. Harold put his hands in the air as the elevator doors opened. He knew it would take several seconds for the officer to reach him. Giving a nod to his security detail, he jumped into the elevator as several bullets screamed past. His own man fired back, though he took several hits in the exchange. As the metal doors closed, he watched the man take his last breath while blood pooled beneath his body.

Exiting on the third floor, he was met by the second in command. "Sir, we have them safely secured in a van just over the footbridge. Waiting on you."

Dr. Harold handed the two cases off as he pictured the remaining two cases in the hallway beside the body of the deceased commander. Putting his hands on the cold metal elevator doors that had just closed, he pinched his eyes shut, knowing there was no way to get back up there.

"Sir?" The nervous timber of the man's voice pulled him back to the moment.

Slamming his hand on the door, the doctor spun around and, in a hushed but direct voice, said, "Alright, let's go." They ran over the footbridge to the parking deck where a black van awaited them.

"You'll never get out of here, doctor!" A disembodied voice filled his ears from behind. "There's nowhere you can go with all those children!" the TFU officer shouted.

Dr. Harold stopped, turning back to confront the voice.

"Do not get in that vehicle, sir. We will be forced to open fire."

Flicking his eyes over his shoulder, he saw that some of

the children were still awake. The anesthesia never seemed to last very long on them. Just one more thing he still had yet to understand. Taking a slow step back toward the open van door, he was met with a final threat.

"Don't do it. Stay where you are." Taking a step toward the doctor, the TFU agent knew he couldn't take a shot with the target standing directly in front of the van. The risk of striking a child was too high.

Taking a deep breath, Dr. Harold threw himself into the vehicle as the crack of a handgun echoed in his ears.

The door slammed shut and the van squealed away.

"Doctor? Doctor! You need to sit back." The nurse's words didn't register

as His adrenaline compelled him to verify that all the girls were safe.

No one seemed to be following them as they skidded out of the garage onto a one-way street. Snaking through back roads, they made their way to a remote airfield.

"Harold!" The sound of his name finally caught his attention. "Sit back. I need to stop the bleeding." Her words sunk in just as the pain in his leg hit him like a ton of bricks.

Staring down at his thigh, he saw thick red blood soaking into his pant leg. As she worked to staunch the flow, his face went pale. "How far out are we?"

"Three minutes," barked Sergeant Long, the new officer in command.

"Long, is the pilot ready?"

"Yes, sir. Everything's prepped. It's a fourteen-hour flight to Helmand Province, Afghanistan."

"Let's make sure our man over there knows to expect us. I

left the clinic stocked the last time I returned to the States. With any luck, it hasn't been ransacked or destroyed over the past year."

"You're sure this is the safest place to take them?" Long had his doubts. He'd spent several deployments out there; his last was where he'd met Dr. Harold. He'd lost many friends, brothers, and sisters on those missions, and his sense of purpose waned with every loss. Jaded was an understatement. When Dr. Harold reached out about his plan, it seemed the perfect time to abandon the military in service of a higher purpose.

Dr. Harold left Long's question hanging. With fearless conviction, he said, "What we're about to learn from these girls will change the world."

Chapter 1
Blindsided

"I thought you said this was supposed to be an *exciting* experience. Where again is the exciting part, Addie?" Joanna pushed a wayward branch out of her face as she stepped across the mossy ground. They were nearing the Harris Power Plant and her sister Adeline insisted they put on their masks. Sweat immediately began trickling down her face. August in North Carolina was no joke.

The rumor was that whatever had caused the world to go dark seven years earlier had taken shape in those woods, but at the moment, Joanna didn't really care, she just wanted to throw the mask to the ground and smash it under her boot.

"We're not there yet, Anna. Patience!" Addie couldn't stand being bored, which had gotten the two of them into trouble throughout the years. After the power grid failed across the majority of the world, they'd heard from travelers that a power plant near Sanford, North Carolina was the origin of the outages across the U.S. Granted, it was a telephone game kind of story that had wound its way up to their city of North Canton, Ohio. A lot could have been misconstrued—especially the part about a little girl having caused it. Once Addie heard about it, she was like a dog with a bone, and Joanna knew they would end up down there whether she liked it or not.

"There's no way a little girl did this. I can't believe we came down here," said Joanna, breathing deep in her pained chest after the night they'd both had. Somehow neither slept well, plagued with night terrors rabid enough to leave them exhausted and oddly sore that morning. She prayed they weren't getting sick.

Joanna was tired. She just wanted to find a lovely, abandoned mansion that roving bands of apocalyptic drifters had overlooked, move in, and live their lives in peace. Unfortunately, Addie couldn't sit still long enough to sprout weeds, let alone grow roots. They were only twenty-three and twenty-four, Irish twins, as their mother used to say. She'd barely had Joanna when she became pregnant with Addie. As kids, they'd fought over who got to play games first on their mother's iPad on the way to school. Now, the idea of an iPad seemed like a science-fiction born dream.

Addie sat on a fallen tree emptying her boot from an annoying pebble. "I know. It's wild. But you know every myth came from some sort of truth."

"How long does a rumor have to live to become a myth?"

"Jerk. You know what I mean," Addie shot back, giving Joanna the side-eye as she worked to free the pebble.

"Uh-huh. I'm going to guess that a family lived nearby and that a little girl died during whatever caused the power to go out. I mean, we're in the backwoods. Maybe they were squatters?" Joanna said as she moved a prickly vine out of her way.

"That's just mean. Maybe they lived out here for the quiet solitude. Maybe they were millionaires that worked from home on nuclear power research." Addie's eyes sparked as if she'd just solved the world's hunger problem. "That's it!" she shouted, jumping to her feet like a fire had been lit under her butt. "That's it! They were out here pretending to be a normal family living off the grid, but *really* they were testing out some kind of alternative power." Hunched over and creeping toward Joanna with her arms in the air, in her best scary movie voice, she said, "*And something went wrong.*"

Joanna watched as her sister figured out the answer to the most infamous question in history. "Sure," she said, with one eye cocked, "a little girl got caught in the blast of her parents' diabolical scheme. Or maybe she was a witch and used her powers to ignite an electrical rebellion because she'd rather live without a hot shower… forever. Or maybe she was an alien! Aliens can have powers, right?" Her mock seriousness fell away as she broke out in laughter. Her first good laugh in a while and it felt nice.

Addie threw a twig at her. "Shut up, nerd," she mumbled, turning her back on her sister to step over the log she'd been sitting on. Not the most graceful, she was known to trip over invisible cracks, non-existent steps, and imaginary holes in the ground. In this case, though, the branch was very real and she completely failed to step over it.

Joanna didn't bat an eye at seeing her sister sprawled out in the dirt. However, the destructive path Addie caused on her way down had her mouth gaping open.

"What the—" grumbled Addie as she landed on her elbow with a twist and a grunt.

"Addie?" Joanna's voice caught in her throat.

"Dang, I twisted my arm. What—"

"Addie, what is that?" Joanna asked, pointing at the tree her sister attempted to grab on her way to the ground. The exterior half inch or so of bark had turned to ash at some point and the portion Addie hit had disintegrated and was now floating through the air, leaving a perfectly cylindrical section of bare tree beneath. With a curious look, she reached up and began wiping away at more blackened ash. Reaching over, she helped her sister to a sitting position before continuing to investigate the tree trunk.

"Do you think this was from the explosion? That was years ago," Joanna asked, scrutinizing the debris billowing in the air. She followed it back to where a perfect silhouette of Addie remained on the ground in dusty ash. Her forehead scrunched as she moved closer to her sister's outline.

"What?" said Addie at Joanna's expression. She rose to her knees and turned around to get a better look. The brush she'd fallen into had turned to dust, and glowing through the remnants was the brightest green she'd ever seen on a plant outside a coloring book. Or, maybe it was just the contrast of the dead trees and disintegrating ashen leaves that made it more pronounced.

"Is that grass?" Joanna pointed at the ground by Addie's knee. As her sister pushed more of the debris away, they saw the ground brimming with life beneath. While life always seems to find a way, Joanna was convinced that colors this bright and crisp should only exist in the Amazon.

"This is strange—"

"Hey!" echoed a distinctly male voice. Joanna instinctively threw her arms out to shield her sister. "You shouldn't be out here," he said, pushing his way through the briars they'd just maneuvered past minutes before.

"Stop!" Joanna shouted, planting her feet firmly in the dirt.

Wide-eyed, he paused, slowly raising his hands, saying, "I'm sorry. Hey, I'm sorry, but this isn't the best area to be in."

"And who are you? The park ranger?" Addie's smart mouth piped up from behind her sister's legs.

"No, no. This is just not a good part of the woods. How did you even get out here?"

"Why do you care?" quipped Addie, sassy as ever before Joanna flashed her a warning.

"Are we trespassing? It didn't seem like anyone would own these woods, considering...." Considering no one owned anything that they hadn't forcefully taken from someone else. "Who are you?" demanded Joanna.

He put his hands down slowly and braced them between two small trees at his sides. "I'm sorry. My name's Brandon. I hike around here most days, but I don't usually see people wandering through."

"Is there something wrong with these woods?" Addie pushed herself off the ground, slapping black soot from her knees while internally cringing at the obviously ridiculous question. Ignoring her own words, she said, "We heard this is where it happened. Where all things electric died." Her sarcasm thick as she swiped the soot from her good hand, doing little more than smearing it into her clothes.

"Yeah, well, I'm not sure about that, but it's definitely not the safest environment." His tone seemed slightly earnest. Stepping over the same log Addie tripped over, he walked past them a few feet and gently brushed the ground with his boot uncovering more of the unusual green grass beneath the now airborne ash. His eyes squinted and lips pursed as he bent down to touch some new growth. Pulling a few blades of greenery out of the ground, he stood up to inspect it further.

"Is that grass?" Joanna questioned.

"It looks like it." Brandon crumbled it between his fingers, then held it to his nose.

"I've never seen grass like that. Is it native to this area or something?"

Staring at the plant, he took his time to answer. "Not that I've seen," he said, nodding back over his shoulder. "This area hasn't had any fresh growth since the power plant blew. Strange."

Stuffing the grass into his pocket, he ignored their cocked eyes and curious expressions. "Obviously it's not safe with all this burnt material floating around. You're wearing masks, so I'm guessing you already knew that. Look, if you need somewhere to stay, I have a place a few miles east of here. You can get a hot meal and some sleep tonight if you'd like."

Both women somewhat embarrassingly tugged their masks down below their chin. "Uh, as in follow a stranger we know nothing about back to his private lair?" said Addie.

"Shut it." Joanna shot back under her breath.

"Well, you don't have to, but it's going to be excessively muggy tonight. You weren't planning on camping here, were you? And anywhere else around here means lots of bugs. You know, mosquitos. Spiders. Not to mention your backpacks look heavy, and that one," he gave a slight nod toward Addie, "injured her arm and could probably use some attention. It's up to you." Lifting an eyebrow and smirking, he made a show of not caring one way or the other, but he also didn't move from his position between them and the woods leading further into the burnt domain.

Joanna put her hand under Addie's bad arm, her expression said *we are definitely getting out of the woods.*

Addie planted her feet in refusal.

Joanna turned her attention back to Brandon. "We'll come with you. We could really do with some good sleep. But if you try anything, well... I mean... death, and... we have weapons!" Her attempt at being fierce fell flat.

Slowly, he looked her up and down, trying to imagine these two hurting anything more than themselves. Grinning, he shot back, "Sure, sounds fair."

Addie elbowed her sister, "You should leave the threats to me. That was just sad." Cradling her arm, she moved to the side to let Brandon pass.

They let him get several feet ahead before Joanna whispered, "Maybe... maybe you're right. We shouldn't be following him. We have no idea who he is."

"Yeah. That's why I told him we weren't following him back to his murder house, but you didn't listen."

"Is that the vibe you're getting?" Joanna said, anxiously tripping over her own feet.

Addie sighed, then shrugged. "Nah. I don't get a creeper vibe from him. Maybe a shade dark." She cocked her head. "He's harmless." Noting Joanna's concern, she said, "We'll be fine. We're tough, and we can sleep in shifts."

"If he's fine, then why are we sleeping shifts? You gave him a lot of crap when he showed up."

"Well, we still don't know the guy," Addie replied. "We have to *look* like we can take care of ourselves. Which you ruined, by the way."

Joanna knew full well Addie had another reason for not wanting to follow him and continued staring her sister down until she gave in.

"Okay, fine!" Addie growled. "I wanted to go in there and see what we could find. We're so close!"

Joanna rolled her eyes, "You're an id—"

"Crap! I dropped my notebook. I forgot I was holding it when I went over that log."

"I'll go get—"

"No. I got it," said Addie, having already turned back.

Joanna stopped to wait for her while keeping an eye on where Brandon was heading. After about thirty seconds, he glanced back and did a double-take. He looked left, right, then directly at her, "Where's the other one?"

Cupping her mouth, Joanna shouted, "She dropped her book back there. She's just going to grab it." Immediately he began heading back toward her. "What are you—"

"Which way? Which direction *exactly*? I don't see her," he said, only a few feet in front of Joanna.

The sound of metal on metal and the sight of his body hitting the ground hard scared her. Stumbling back, she watched leaves and debris scatter as he screeched in pain. "Addie! Come back!" she yelled over her shoulder.

Pushing brush aside and stepping forward, Joanna froze

at the sight. His pants were soaked with blood. "Holy—okay, don't move. Don't touch it."

"Hadn't planned on it" he groaned, his teeth grinding with each word. Holding his leg with both hands just above where the iron bear trap bit into his calf, he growled, "Go get your sister."

"What? No, she'll be here in two seconds. I can't just leave you like this."

Grabbing her wrist with a strength that surpassed his pain, he pulled her close.

"Ow, stop!" Trying to pull her arm away only tightened his hold.

"Listen. Listen to me! Go get her right now and bring her back. There are people in these woods that take girls like you two. I'm not going anywhere. Go!"

Her heart was racing as she scrambled away. The sound of a muted scream came from behind her and she twisted around looking for its source. In the distance a dark figure loomed over Adeline, pushing her face into the ground and tying her hands.

Joanna half shouted, half croaked, "Hey! Stop! Get off her!" She took two steps in their direction when the figure stood and stared at her. She could barely make out his features from the distance.

Addie got to her knees while he was distracted and pushed herself off the ground into his back before he could go after Joanna.

"No, don't!" Brandon's booming voice preceded his grip on Joanna's ankle.

"What are you doing? Let go!" she demanded, jerking her leg.

Adrenaline fueled Joanna's body, and with a final kick at his knuckles with her free foot his hold dislodged. He yelled, "No! Wait! If you go, they'll take you too."

Ignoring him she screamed, "Addie!" Her voice echoed through the trees as she scoured the horizon.

Off in the distance shapes and shadows moved through the forest. Without hesitation and with eyes on her sister, she took off through the brush. Frantic and running hard, Joanna didn't get far when her foot caught on a root. Pulling her hard to the ground she skid across the dirt, slamming into the base of a tree and splitting open a sizable section of her scalp just above her ear. The forest spun as she pulled herself up from the ground gripping the tree tight.

With blurred vision and her hearing muffled from the crash she yelled as loud as she could. Her voice painfully reverberated through her skull and the edges of her sight darkened. Though she had no idea which direction to go, Joanna stumbled forward, ignoring the warm tickle of blood sliding down her neck. Miraculously reaching the area Addie was last seen, the ground dropped from beneath her just as a hand grabbed hold of her from behind.

Brandon's grip on the back of her shirt narrowly kept her from tumbling head-first over a hidden ridge. Though the scene was blurred, she could see the forest drop nearly twenty feet straight down.

Swiveling her head to see who rescued her, she was startled by the pallor of Brandon's skin and blood smeared across his face; her stomach twisted and heaved before she could stop it.

Joanna dropped to her knees right there on the rocky ridgeline. It took several moments before she could get her bearings. *Where is she?* "Where is she? Addie!" *She should be down there. She would've fallen off this cliff.* She went this way, right? Her mind spun along with her vision.

She looked again at the empty ground below. Then turned back to Brandon. He looked almost unrecognizable from the blend of rage and unbearable pain. Barely noticing his blood-soaked leg, she looked over the drop once more. "Where is she?"

He didn't respond.

"We have to get down there." Joanna started to kick her legs over the side when Brandon's arm shot out and grabbed hers. The dizziness left her with little strength to resist. "What are you doing? My sister's down there."

"No, she's not." His teeth clenched together while spit formed on his lips.

"What? She's got to be. She was just here!"

"She's not!" he yelled, pulling her down. "We have to leave right now."

"Let go of me. I'm not going anywhere without Adeline!"

"I can promise you we will not find her here. They're gone." His voice dropped to a whisper.

"What? Wait, what? Did you do this?" she asked, pushing him away. "Who was the person chasing her? They can't be gone. I just saw her." Her petite frame shook with anger. "What happened to my sister?"

"I didn't do this," he said, narrowing his eyes before looking away. "You shouldn't have come out here. No one should be out here. This is a dangerous place. We need to go."

"*Where* is my *sister?*"

"When people come into these woods, they disappear. Especially women."

Her eyes grew wide. "I'm not leaving," she said as her chest heaved, "without Adeline." Joanna reached down to the rocks.

"Okay. OKAY! Stop. Just stop."

Her head lifted but she didn't stand up.

"I've been coming out here almost every day for years." He held her gaze. "People, specifically women, seem to disappear in these woods. Most often, it happens when they cross into the ash zone, you know, where your sister hurt her arm. I don't know what's going on, but I've worked hard to keep people away."

Desperate for more information but trying to play the calm card, she said, "They can't be far. If we go now, maybe we can follow their trail." He shook his head. Joanna's attempt at calm was short-lived. "Why aren't you doing anything? If you're out here protecting strangers, why aren't you helping me? Help me!"

"Fine!" He took several deep breaths before looking into her eyes. "Look down."

"What?"

"Look down."

She peered at the brush and rocks below. "What am I looking at?"

"Do you see anything on the ground down there? Broken limbs, displaced leaves, any sign of people leaping over the edge and scurrying across the forest floor?"

Kneeling on the edge, she took stock of what he was saying. Her eyes, still fuzzy, made it difficult to focus. "I can't... I'm not sure."

Brandon crawled to the edge and looked for himself. Scanning the ground around them, he looked for any sign of a trail they could've left. A guttural sound left his lips as his hand hit the ground hard, scaring Joanna into falling back from him.

"I don't understand," she whispered, dropping her shoulders.

"There's no sign." Brandon took a few deep breaths and then looked directly into her eyes. "I don't know where they went, but they're gone, and we won't find them here."

Chapter 2
It's All a Dream

Scorching pain swelled within Zuri, so ferociously all-consuming that it stretched from abdomen to eyelids. Tears tickled her face as they made their way down into her ears. Aside from the gentle tickle, she hadn't even noticed she was crying until an unrecognizable moan escaped her lips.

Agonizing jolts just beneath her ribcage shot straight to her back. There was nothing to compare the pain to. Nothing she'd ever felt before. Desperate to ease it, she tried to move, to adjust her position, anything that might help.

Breathe.

But each breath reignited the unbearable flame, causing her to choke on grit filling her mouth and lungs.

She couldn't feel anything or anyone around her. Nothing

but the searing pain within. Between blinks, her vision only seemed to blur more and more.

Help me.

Where am I?

The ringing in her ears muffled the voices around her. Zuri couldn't fight it. Darkness began to settle in. She yearned for it.

Make it stop.

Make it stop.

Someone, help me.

Make it stop.

"Zuri?" Lexi gently touched her sister's shoulder. She could tell Zuri was trapped in a nightmare and wanted to shake her free, but Zuri's injuries made touching her difficult. And with Madison, her newfound sister and once captor, sleeping nearby, Lexi wanted to remain as quiet as possible. Granted, they weren't sisters by blood, but certainly in ways she had yet to grasp.

"Zuri, you're safe. You're alright." Lexi kissed her forehead.

Madison roused from sleep, her eyes flickering around the room. "Lexi?"

Catching one another's eyes, Madison stood and placed her hand on Lexi's shoulder creating an unexpected yet familiar tingle.

They shared a comforting smile before turning their attention back toward Zuri. She was mulling over the reaction her skin had with Madison's touch. It was a sensation Lexi never had with anyone other than her baby sister.

With Madison's touch on her arm and the look in her emerald eyes, Lexi instinctively knew Zuri would be alright.

"She's been through a lot of trauma, and so have you," said Madison, pointedly looking at Lexi's empty bed.

"I hear you. I just don't want to leave her."

"You're not. Besides, I'll be here to keep an eye on her while you rest." Madison knew that wasn't what Lexi meant. After all, the two had only just found each other after having spent years apart, tortured in ways Madison couldn't fathom.

Lexi gave a weak smile but didn't move as their eyes locked. She tried to reconcile the strangeness of this instant familial bond with the very woman who had kept her captive for so many years.

"I'm sorry," said Madison before quickly looking away.

Lexi didn't just hear the words. She felt them. Madison's heartache was genuine.

Their heightened emotions acted like an antenna, enabling Lexi to feel further out around her. Not just picking up on the others in the building but outward to their fourth sister. It was as if she could see Zoey's thoughts. Zoey had been injured almost as much as Zuri out in that field during the shooting. She, too, seemed to be reliving her nightmare if what Lexi could feel was any indication. Despite their intense connection and all Madison had shared about her, Lexi and Zoey still had not met face-to-face. This woman who had felt her pain for so long remained a mystery.

"Do you feel that?" Madison said, pulling away from Lexi.

Just before she moved her hand, Lexi thought she saw or felt something like a shadow.

"I'm not sure. What did you feel?"

"I don't know. It was like there was someone else here," she whispered, her forehead wrinkled and her eyes shifting back and forth as she attempted to explain. "Like a… um… almost painful feeling, only not so heavy. Not my pain, someone else's."

"Zoey?"

"No." She had a far-off look in her eyes for a moment before the connection broke. Her eyes flicked around the room as if that *someone* was there with them.

"Are you okay?"

Madison gently nodded her head. "Yeah. Yes. Sorry. I'm not sure what that was."

Despite needing the rest, both girls talked for hours knowing Zoey would arrive post-surgery soon enough. Madison told her about the world as it was now and, to the best of her knowledge, what happened after the power grid failed. Lexi and Zuri had missed all of the fallout and it was nearly impossible for her to comprehend.

Lexi stayed at Zuri's side, realizing that as long as she touched her sister, Zuri seemed to be in less pain. Despite their efforts to stay awake, Lexi pulled Zuri into her arms and snuggled tight. Warmth moved through her to Zuri, and when Madison reached over to touch her arm, the hum between them amplified.

"Oh!" Lexi said. "What is that?" she whispered.

Madison's voice caught in her throat. She'd done this over the years, touched a person and felt a warm vibration push into them, creating a sense of calm. This, however, felt much stronger than any past experience.

"I…."

Lexi waited for her to speak, but no words came. "Is this something you're doing?"

"Yes," she breathed out. "This will sound strange, but,"

her explanation was slow and jumbled. She'd never put it into words before. "I've always been able to help others stay calm, especially in highly emotional situations. I'm not exactly sure how, but just now," her voice dropped even lower, "this is stronger than I've ever felt. I think we're doing it together."

Looking down at Zuri, Lexi could tell her pain was significantly eased. Even the strain in her own arm was diminishing. She felt stronger as the pain faded.

Before they could wrap their minds around it, Lexi's eyes cut to the door.

She could feel her. Just before she came into the room, Lexi could *feel* her approach. It was like the air in her lungs froze, though not uncomfortably, and the blood flowing through her body seemed to pause. It only lasted a moment and no one else seemed to notice, though Lexi could tell that *she* did. Zoey felt it too.

Carefully repositioning Zuri back on her pillows, Lexi maneuvered her legs off the bed and sat motionless as the door opened. Zoey, wrapped in blankets and covered in wires, entered on a hospital bed. She was awake, and as her sight landed on Lexi, she whispered something that sounded like the ocean.

Their eyes locked. The shock was palpable. They'd witnessed life through one another's eyes but never saw this— mirror images. The same deep purple and mahogany vines sprawled perfectly on the opposite sides of their faces.

Neither one had seen the other's face in their dreams.

The unexplainable pulling sensation between them was extreme.

How is this possible? She wasn't in that prison. How did those lines get there? Zoey? Madison? Are there others? Lexi's mind raced. So many unanswered questions.

Every eye in the room was wide. Slowly and simultaneously, they visually traced the spider-web-like maze trailing up each of their necklines, spanning their mirrored faces, as if a perfect line was drawn from their chins up the creases in the center of their lips. A straight line between their eyes and into their hairlines. The two women were not identical in any other way, but there was no mistaking their connection.

Lexi stood and, as if gravity had shifted, took slow and airy steps toward Zoey. Zoey felt it too. Her injuries, however, made it impossible for her to sit up. Instead, wincing as she extended her arm, she reached for Lexi to take hold of her hand.

A current of electricity raced up their arms as their fingers touched. Warmth flowed through their veins.

"Oh!" Zuri and Madison exclaimed. Madison leaped to her feet. And Zuri, now wide awake, was breathing quick, shallow breaths, confused by the electrical pulse that woke her.

Madison laid her hand on Zuri's, then placed her other hand on Lexi's shoulder.

As soon as they connected, darkness settled over their eyes and a crystal-clear memory unfolded for each to witness.

"Hold on. Tight as you can, okay?" The woman's whispered words calmed Lexi, allowing her muscles to relax for the first time in so long. What should've been a scary moment was instead magical. The men around them were large and carried guns. They crept in the shadows snatching the girls one by one. Yet, somehow, Lexi knew these men were there to help, not harm.

Zoey watched as the woman picked up Lexi. Feeling a pinch

on her arm, Zoey, too, was being hoisted up into the arms of a giant. "It's okay. Don't cry, okay?" he whispered into her ear. She knew he was safe as her eyes drifted shut.

"Zoey?" Lexi exhaled, noting that for the first time she was saying her name from a place of personal knowledge and not simply told to her by someone else. They were sisters. All of them. Not by birth, but sisters from a past they'd forgotten.

"Yes, sisters." Zoey's hoarse voice forced the words. She knew Lexi's thoughts without her having to speak them. "I remember you," she said, shaking loose the cobwebs from her mind and coughing with a heavy dose of pain. "We were all there. A dark room, somewhere." Her gaze flitted around the cramped space, now seeing the others through the eyes of that small child back then. She recalled Lexi's blond hair whipping in the blowing sand, arms around Zuri, trying to protect her from the sting of it. And two other girls, holding onto one another, with hair and eyes like magic.

Lexi turned her head so quickly that the room continued to spin. Before she could steady her vision, she felt the settling touch of Madison's hand gently squeezing her upper arm.

Muted emeralds glowed beneath contacts, not quite strong enough to cover the light reflecting off the prisms in Madison's eyes. Zoey froze, then choked out, "She's one of us?" Her hand squeezed Lexi's so tight her knuckles turned white. "But how… here? How are we all here?" Memories of whispers in the night, each sharing their name, huddling close, and comforting one another in those first few days of terror flooded her mind. As she looked into those green eyes, she knew. "Madison?"

Tears fell from Madison's face. All she could do was nod.

Clouded by the pain medicine coursing through her body, Zuri shifted her gaze to Zoey, unsure of who Zoey was referring to, and asked in a weak voice, "One of us?"

Madison stepped to Zuri's bedside, tilted her head forward, and removed a contact from her eye. Zuri gasped as a crystalline glow burst forth beneath the missing contact. "It's a lot to take in," Madison said, placing her hand on the young woman's forearm to provide comfort.

Lexi crouched down beside Zoey's bed. "You are the girl I could… feel. I knew you were with me," she said, her voice soft and high and full of wonder. "I knew that Madison," nodding in her direction, "was the woman I could see when I was allowed to open my eyes, but you—" her breath hitched, grateful that Zoey was truly real, "you were with me." Reaching out with trembling fingers, she lightly traced the lines on Zoey's face. "And you suffered too."

Taking in the spiderweb lines, Lexi, usually steadfast, began to sob. Her tears were a blend of joy at the reality of Zoey's existence but also tinged with anguish, knowing that she'd endured the same torture Lexi herself felt all those years.

Madison had also been part of that torture. That horror. Yet living free while they'd been trapped. Lexi's heart and mind battled over those thoughts—that painful reality. And now, with these connections coming to light, something else began to race through her mind. Another feeling reverberated deep inside.

That's when the door began to crack open… to their memories.

Chapter 3
Elevator

VISP | August 11, 2029 | 4:45 p.m.

"Where were you, Gavin?" Maria was heartbroken. After Justin and the others had been taken, she was devastated. In total shock for the previous twenty-four hours. *What if the soldiers returned for them? Were Justin and the others even still alive?* "Where were you?" she demanded.

Taking a deep breath, he spoke softly. "Honestly, I was flat-out angry." His chest heaved as he shifted his legs to lean back against the wall. "I saw Jones' key card in his shirt pocket. I wanted to hurt him, and without a second thought, I grabbed it when I let go of his shirt. Like I said, I was mad, so I took off to the center elevator. Mainly just wanting his smug red face to suffer by having to take the stairs. But when the elevator was between the 13th and 14th floors, it shut down."

Instantly, she felt terrible. The power had gone out. She knew what he was going to say next, so she said it for him. "You were trapped." Studying her hands, she regretted all the not-so-nice thoughts she'd had about him.

He nodded slowly. "I was there several hours. At first, I assumed maintenance would get it running again, so I waited. When that didn't happen, I started yelling and kicking, pounding the walls. Tried to get someone to hear me, but there was no one. It was just silent." Shifting again, he sighed, then cleared his throat.

"It took me a while to get the door cracked enough to see where I was between floors. By the time I'd gotten that far there wasn't enough space to shimmy through." Standing up straight, he began to pace. "Eventually, I got through the top of the elevator and climbed the inside wall ladder to the next floor. At that point, it was obvious everyone was gone. I went to your rooms, but you weren't there. Ran down to twelve to find Jones. Empty."

Maria's eyes followed his pacing.

"I had planned to pack some essentials, then race to the lab. I was only in my room for a few minutes when I heard someone coming." His glossy eyes held Maria's.

"So…" she said, exhaling relief. "You *didn't* just leave us." Her heart rate climbed, realizing she had been angry with him for no reason. He hadn't left them. "Gavin, I'm sorry," she said, wiping her eyes and shaking her head.

"What? No! No, no, no. Why would you be sorry? I'm the one that took off just as everything went to hell." He pulled her into his arms and she buried her face in his chest. This time the cry was more a welcome release.

Sniffling, she looked into his eyes. "Well, I do, in fact, owe you an apology."

"I don't understand. What for?"

"For all the nasty thoughts I had about you after I thought you'd left us… not to mention the few I might have said out loud."

After an awkward silence, a broad smile spread across his face and he started laughing from deep in his belly. The shock of his response got her laughing along with him. Both felt the tension deep in their souls ease.

"Okay then, I accept. On one condition."

"Oh yeah?"

The glint in his eye made his condition pretty obvious.

Tilting her head back, her smile was lost as their first, non-stress-induced kiss drew them together.

They sat holding onto each other for some time. It had been nearly a decade since either had someone to wrap their arms around.

Maria, her mind pleasantly blank as she snuggled in peace, noticed the corner of a box sticking out of Gavin's bag. Suddenly, she remembered it from his room.

"It's none of my business—"

"When has that ever stopped you?" Gavin whispered, his lips brushed the top of her head.

She gave him a soft elbow to the ribs. "That box in your bag. You went back for it before I broke my ankle. Can I ask what it is?"

Feeling his breath pause and his heart skip a beat, he cleared the lump from his throat and said, "It's old photos and trinkets. Things from my life before all this."

After a pause, Maria gently pressed further, "It just seemed more important than that for you to run back up for it in the middle of the chaos we were in."

He knew she was right, but he hadn't talked about this with anyone before. "You're right. I guess I was afraid something would keep me from going back for it."

Maria held her tongue. She could tell he needed to work out his thoughts without her harassing him.

Gavin took a deep breath and released her from his arms. There was no reason not to tell her. After all, they may never make it out of there alive, and at least one person would finally know. "I had a sister a long time ago, before the fall of the grid. I was just a kid when she was taken."

Maria pulled herself upright, shoulder to shoulder.

"It was late at night. A noise from the kitchen woke me. Without hesitation, I left my room assuming it was my mom. None of the lights were on. When I got to the living room I could see someone in the kitchen. It was suddenly obvious that it wasn't either of my parents. Honestly, at the time, I thought it was a monster. I guess, in hindsight, it really was.

"Then he started coming toward the living room, so I ducked behind the couch. There was gunfire and screaming. I sat there with my hands covering my ears, paralyzed. Not sure how long I sat like that, but eventually a police officer scooped me up." He paused, staring off as if it were all playing out in front of him.

Maria, not one for hiding her emotions, looked horrified. Her heart raced, envisioning his scared little face.

"My father didn't make it," he choked in quiet bursts, "but my mom did. It took a long time for her to recover. They never found my sister, though."

She leaned toward him, putting her hand on his. "You've carried that around with you all these years. I'm so sorry."

He couldn't quite meet her eyes. "Well, I suppose it's not something easily forgotten."

"Can I see?"

He'd never shown anyone before and he hesitated.

"You don't have to." Her usual sass had been replaced by compassion.

Blinking a few times, he realized that showing pictures would probably be the healthiest thing he could do. Share his loss with someone else. He nodded and, with a half smile, grabbed the corner of his bag, trying to hide his shaking hands.

Setting the box in her lap, he let her open it. Inside were a few photos of a dark-haired toddler laughing. A hospital bracelet, probably from when she was born. There were a few trinkets and a delicate-looking gold chain necklace with a russet-colored stone.

"She's beautiful," Maria whispered.

"She was," he breathed, smiling at the sound of another person speaking so tenderly about his sister.

"What was her name?"

His throat tightened, though not as much as it used to. Sharing this with Maria was the first time he didn't solely feel pain at the memory of his sister. "Macie," he said. "I remember my mom had wanted to call her Kelly, so right before her due date, we bought these wooden letters to hang on her bedroom door. Painted them different colors and hung them up." He laughed, "But then, the day she was born, Mom changed her mind and told my dad her name needed to be Macie instead. So before they brought her home, he and I frantically took down the name Kelly and raced to the store for new letters. He had me paint them while he put the car seat in the car, which, by the way, took him forever. He ended up having one of the nurses at the hospital do it for him."

Maria stared at Macie's picture, imagining the joy of welcoming her life into their home.

"He hung the letters on the door before they'd dried. When we got home with Macie, the paint had dripped down the door. Something out of a horror movie," he said, laughing while picturing the moment his mom saw the mess. "To her credit and my feelings, she didn't say a word. Just looked down and smiled, pulled me to her side, and said she loved me."

Maria held his hand as he spoke but kept her mouth closed.

After a few deep breaths, his smile faded.

"Is all of that the reason you came here?" She prompted when he seemed to be in a far-off place.

Gavin shrugged. "When I got older, maybe thirteen, my mom shared something that seemed a little crazy. Even as a baby, my mom knew Macie was unique. She said her eyes looked like little coffee colored-diamonds.

"She said there were times when rocking Macie to sleep she could almost feel a gentle sort of purring."

Maria squinted, not sure what to make of these particular memories.

"Not like a cat, but this little hum and a radiating warmth my mom could feel in her bones. Then there were times when Macie would get mad, like crying in her chair for food, and things around the kitchen would fall to the floor."

Maria sat up straighter.

"I know, it sounds ridiculous."

"Well, not after what we witnessed from Zuri." Just saying her name caused Maria's heart to palpitate while her mind spun all sorts of ideas. As random puzzle pieces connected in her mind, one burning question burst from her lips. "So, did you think Zuri was your sister?"

"I don't know. My mom and I had long talks when I was a teenager. Her stories about my sister were why I went into neurology. I just wanted to know if the brain or body could actually do things like that.

"I guess, yeah, I thought that if the rumors were true, then I wanted to be where I had the best chance of finding her. If she were still alive."

He glanced at the hospital bracelet in Maria's hand and released a defeated breath. "Zuri wasn't Macie. I knew it the moment I walked in on my first day." Gavin's eyes finally found Maria's as he shared his worst fear. "I don't think she's still alive, or if she is, she most likely doesn't know who she is. I mean, she was taken so young, you know?"

Maria wanted desperately to offer hope, tell him she'd help find Macie or anything that would wipe the defeated look from his face. Of course, she knew that words wouldn't help, so she leaned in only inches from his face, looked into his eyes, then let their kiss offer what words couldn't.

Chapter 4
Iron Bars

"Get up!" the deep voice growled, startling Addie awake. Pain exploded on her right side as a dirty gray boot left its mark. Gasping in shock, she groaned as the air burned within her lungs.

"I said get up!"

Wincing and disoriented, the ground dropped out from under her. Forced onto her feet, then shoved from behind, Addie was left vulnerable to the iron pole only inches from her face.

Fireworks burst behind her eyes and a crunching sound filled her ears. Excruciating pain reverberated throughout her body, distracting her from the sting of her knees smashing into the ground.

"Dammit, look what you did," he barked, grabbing the back

of her shirt, choking her with its collar. "You'll be cleaning that blood up when we're done."

She could sense the disgusting grin stretching across his face as she felt his hot foul breath on the back of her neck.

Addie leaned her head forward until it almost touched the ground. Visualizing his dark form hovering behind her, she shoved herself back, hard and fast, until she felt the crushing bone of the man's face impact the back of her skull.

The only sound he made was his body hitting the floor.

Addie, slowly opening her lids despite the immense pressure expanding in her brain, had no idea where she was or if anyone else was with her. Turning her head despite the wave of nausea, she saw something typically reserved for nightmares.

Women.

Many women.

Broken and battered.

All leaning away from her.

Afraid.

They were all different, yet, all the same. Same dirty clothes. Same shaved heads. All brutally abused and young. Seemingly the same age.

Her age.

Before she could make any sense of it, she picked up two deep male voices and a rush of movement in her direction. The compression in her head muffled the sound as a mix of swirling lights played in front of her eyes. Unable to see the men from where she knelt on the ground, panic pierced every fiber of her body. As disorienting lights and sounds danced in her mind, she instinctively knew their hands were reaching toward her. Spinning around on her knees, she met them face to face.

No longer in control, a blinding white light stole what little vision she had while a fierce heat spread throughout her body like lightning. The last thing she saw was their fingertips only inches from her face, then nothing.

Ringing. The piercing hum in her ears blocked all other sounds. The heat that rushed through her had dissipated as fast as it came. Now all she felt was the cool concrete of the floor on her cheek.

Slowly, voices seeped into the ringing as careful hands touched her arms and face. Her chest slowed its rapid heaving as her heart rate dropped. There was nothing she wanted more than to let sleep take over, yet something was off.

She could hear the awestruck whispers around her. "Are they dead… Is she alive… Untie her…." The whispers stopped. There was a shuffling and she could feel the space around her open up. No more careful hands.

A high pitched metal creak cut through the ring in her ears. Addie never saw it coming. Another rush of movement. An atmospheric blast of fury.

I can't stop it this time. They're shattered. I can feel the bones are shattered.

The warmth of her blood oozed between her teeth.

A disembodied voice hovered close to her ears. An almost familiar timber. "Stop! Don't kill her. I have a good feeling about this one. Pick her up and bring her to the practice room."

Darkness was her only release.

LIMIT      6:45 p.m.

Slipping out of her chair onto the floor, Madison curled into

39

a ball. She grabbed her side with one hand and her head with the other. The pain was just too much.

"Madison?" Zoey was the first to see her fall. Trying to sit up, she was met with a sharp pain pulsing in her chest. Gasping, she choked out, "Lexi!"

Lexi's eyes flashed open. Getting her bearings, she saw Zoey pointing toward the floor. "Madison!" Lexi yelled, slipping to the ground and touching her shoulder. Immediately Lexi could feel the shadow Madison had described earlier. Only this time it was much more than a shadow.

"Madison? Maddy? Can you hear me? I'm right here." She couldn't feel Madison's pain, but she understood the torment her new sister was experiencing. "Zoey, something's wrong."

"I know. I feel it too," Zoey whispered, her voice hoarse from all the pain medication.

Without warning, it stopped. Madison sprawled out on the floor, eyes closed and breathing hard. Minutes ticked by before the anxiety of the moment eased and she was able to open her eyes.

"Is this what you went through?" Madison's eyes met Lexi's, then shifted over to Zoey's.

"What do you mean?" Lexi asked.

"Yes," Zoey said, fully in tune with Madison's realization. She knew what was going on the moment Madison started writhing on the floor in pain. "When Lexi was being crushed, that's what it felt like. Her pain was my pain."

Without moving from his perch in the far corner of the room, Joe added, "I don't think you four are the only ones out there."

Chapter 5
What Do We Do?

"So what do we do now?" Joanna sat beside the fire with her arms tightly wrapped around her knees. She'd held in her tears since they stopped looking for Addie, but now, in the deep quiet of the night, they were pushing at the corners of her eyes.

Despite Brandon's warnings, she still climbed down the steep rock and ran in every direction for over an hour. Joanna knew he was right but didn't concede until she saw how pale he'd become.

His leg made it impossible to walk any distance, especially in the dark, so they set up camp about two hundred yards from the spot he was injured. Joanna cleaned and wrapped his leg the best she could with her small medical pack. Even with the heat of the summer night and the fire by her side, her body still shook from a cold deep inside.

Her eyes unwillingly flickered toward Brandon more often than she cared to admit. She couldn't help but wonder how he managed to pull the bear trap off in time to rescue her. However, she'd been too incensed with the toxic mix of adrenaline and anxiety to ask.

"Tomorrow morning, we'll walk back to my place, clean up my leg thoroughly, and resupply. Then…" he grunted, trying to lift his leg onto his bag, "we'll talk to a few people I know and see if we can get any information."

His face was so ashen Joanna considered offering him some water or a granola bar. Instead, she let her anger burn, choosing to remain seated next to the fire. She didn't know him. This could be his fault.

They took the wrong sister. If Addie were out here, she'd survive this better. She'd make a plan. What if they're torturing her? She'd be fearless until she found me. How can I save her? I can't even save myself.

Sighing, she laid her head on her knees. Clearly, she was going to need Brandon more than she wanted, and obviously, he couldn't help her if he was dead.

Even if he is a bad guy, if he leads me to Addie, she'd have a plan to escape together. She always had a plan.

Brandon, struggling on the other side of the fire, unintelligibly murmured in pain. If there was one thing Joanna couldn't do, it was not to help when help was needed.

Resigning herself, she pulled a water bottle out of her bag and handed it to him. "Here. Take it."

His eyes stayed closed as she placed it in his hand. A very

quiet "thank you" came from his lips as she plunked back down, folding her legs into her chest.

The scene rolled through Joanna's mind on a loop. *How did this happen? How did I not get to Addie in time? How had someone physically taken her in the middle of the woods, in daylight, with nowhere to go?* It didn't make sense. The whole ordeal turned her stomach.

Her eyes landed back on Brandon. Lips parted, she leaned in ready to ask a question but her voice caught in her throat. Slumped over, with his bloody leg propped up, she took note of his sleeping features. He'd seemed older under the sun. All high and mighty as he tried to get them to leave the forest. Older and angry when they'd lost Adeline. Now, chin to chest, one arm resting on his stomach while the other dangled by his side, she put him at no more than thirty. The elements had hardened him.

Why would someone spend so much time, years, living out here? Alone.

Chapter 6
The Replay

Madison quietly scanned the room, momentarily holding her gaze on each of the battered women. She hadn't cried in years and had even convinced herself nothing could make her. Yet, there she was, rivers streaming down her cheeks, and more so in the past forty-eight hours than she thought humanly possible.

As the door to their makeshift bedroom opened, she quickly wiped at the wayward tears. It was Phil, Jahnsen's second in command at LIMIT. When he finally saw her, he whispered, "Got a minute?"

Nodding, she made her way through the maze of hospital beds. Zoey, Zuri, and Lexi were gathered in the middle of the room, along with the cot she'd brought to be near them. Justin,

Joe, and Aidan had beds off to the side. All in all, they were packed in. None of them seemed to want to leave each other, like an incredibly odd yet emotional family reunion.

Outside the room, Phil took in her exhausted appearance. "Madison, you look like hell."

"Ah, thanks, Phil."

He paused before asking, "How did you get out of the building with Lexi? What happened in there?" Phil was never one for small talk.

"I… a lot. A lot happened. I haven't had much time to think about it, but I'll send an after-action report to you and Jahnsen by tomorrow."

"Look, I'm not worried about all that right now. We've been rewatching the video feeds, and I'm just trying to figure out how the rest of them ended up out in that field, but somehow you and Rose… er, Lexi, made it out unnoticed." His face puckered as he stared her in the eyes.

"I never saw them. I gave Jones the date. August 10th. Everything went haywire with Lexi the night before. As for Zoey and the other two—they never showed up."

"That just doesn't make sense." Crossing his arms, he wanted to believe her. Had no reason not to, but the pieces weren't fitting. Madison, Jahnsen, and Phil worked together for several years before she got affiliated with VISP. Jones became the middle-man, feeding information to Jahnsen at LIMIT once she was pulled in since she had no direct contact with them from the inside.

"After the glass around Lexi shattered, we were knocked unconscious. When I came to, the others in my lab, Grant and Gray, they…" she shuddered at the memory of Gray trying to kill Lexi, "they weren't moving, and neither was Lexi. I ran out to find help but the place was empty."

"Wait. What do you mean empty?"

"There was no one. Everyone in the building was just gone. By the time I ran back to the lab, Lexi was gone. There was blood smeared on the floor, so I followed it. When I found her, she was running down the hall." Madison skipped over the part where Lexi knocked her down with an unexplainable force. Not to mention her own mysterious outburst. "I caught up to her just as she fell down the stairs. Luckily we were only a few floors from the internal stairwell hidden between the exterior walls."

"How did you get her out though?"

"She's not that heavy. I just threw her over my shoulders, you know, fireman style."

Phil's eyes were wide, staring off, trying to imagine the scene as it unfolded. "Impressive. Wait, what hidden stairwell?"

"Seriously? As part of our emergency protocol there is a secured stairwell inside the western wall of the building. We were told from day one that should anything happen out of our control, we were to utilize those stairs."

"Do you know where they lead?"

She shook her head. "Supposedly, there would be guards in there to guide us, but Jones gave me different instructions. Said there was a hall leading to a back door behind the hidden stairwell on the first floor. Your guys were supposed to be waiting for us when we opened it. He said if you weren't there, to take..." she began to say but looked away, realizing the importance of her words.

"Take what?"

She pulled her eyes back to his as incredulous laughter burst from her lips. "He was so in-depth with a backup plan, leaving a map with a highlighted exit route in a vehicle outside that door. He knew the team wouldn't be there."

"But that doesn't make sense. We could've gotten both girls out if we'd known about them." He stepped back and shifted his weight. "Why wouldn't he tell us?"

This was the question she needed answers to. "I don't know." Her head shook, trying to put the pieces together, but she was at a loss. "What about the bird? How did you not see us when we left the building? The feed should've picked us up, right?"

"I'm not sure. I'll check the tape again. Maybe the drone was on the south side of its flight path when you left the building. That would be the most likely position for you to have avoided detection. The back of the building faces North. It could've shielded you."

It was a reasonable assumption, but shockingly lousy timing if it was. "What I don't understand is where you sent Zoey. What intel did Jones' give you?"

"He directed us to D4."

Madison stepped back. "D4? But those floors are just storage facilities. Food and supplies."

Phil didn't have to give a response. It was clear there was a lot even she didn't know.

"I need to see what data he gave you for Zuri's rescue."

Taking a breath and rubbing his forehead, Phil wanted to tell her to get some rest, but he knew better. "I'll get it for you. In fact, we all need to sit down and review the timeline from the beginning. Jahnsen and the team are dealing with the fallout. Rewatching the videos to figure out how Zuri was hit so many times with gunfire."

Madison, clearing her throat, felt a new wave of moisture dampen her eyes.

Phil pretended not to notice. "Are you sure you don't want to grab some rest? We'll all meet up in the operations cell after lunch."

"No. I need to see the footage. I've been preoccupied for too long. I need to know what would cause our guys to aim at her like that." She gave Phil that *don't look at me like that* stare, then said, "I'll be fine."

He smiled, jiggling the keys in his pocket, then nodded toward the operations hub. He'd known Madison a long time. After all, he was one of the operators that rescued her all those years ago. Saw firsthand what these women could do. She was young, 2011 was a long time ago, and he hadn't witnessed much more from her since then. He had no idea what bringing them together might stir up.

"Maddy…"

"I'll be right in," she said, turning away. "I just need a minute." With that, she jogged down the hall to the bathroom. Phil stood watching the door after it closed, sighed, then hurried back to the operations cell.

As he walked into the room, his blood pressure skyrocketed. The scene on the big screen showed dust clearing around five bodies on the ground. Jahnsen was rewatching the event for the twentieth time. He had extensive knowledge of three of the individuals on screen: Joey, Aidan, and Zoey. They were the small insurgent team LIMIT sent in to retrieve Lexi. In the process, they'd found someone that no one could've guessed would be there, her sister, Calla Lily, or Zuri, as they were now aware.

They strongly suspected Zoey was another of the girls but didn't have concrete evidence until now. Together with Madison, that made four. Four of the six. The fact that four of them were still alive after all these years was more than they could've hoped for.

The third man lying prone was initially an unknown. Phil watched as he slowly crawled across the dirt toward the fifth person, a girl who wasn't moving. The unexpected target.

Phil's commander, Rice Jahnsen, was the reason they were all there. His vision for the future started it all. Jahnsen managed to pull together three groups of people to make his vision a reality. One, a combat squad, who could be seen on the feed standing around the target; two, a team of support technicians working diligently alongside him inside the joint operations cell; and three, an extraction team: Zoey, Aidan, and Joey. The final team could be seen in the replay, lying amidst the bullet-scarred ground he was viewing from the safety of his protected underground bunker.

Currently, all five were in LIMIT's underground facility in Ohio, recovering from various wounds and injuries from a scene that should never have played out. Popping an antacid, Phil shook his head as the horror unfolded again on the screen.

The support team worked endlessly to connect the dots. With all their inside intel, only one of the girls had ever been made known. At least that's the intel they received from Jones—the Director of VISP, their inside source beyond Madison.

Jahnsen, catching Phil shaking his head, motioned him to his station.

"It just doesn't make sense. I can't see anything that shows the men were aiming for her."

"I know." Phil's voice fell away at the sight. Dust cleared, showing a blood-spattered ground around the group. Pools of black splotches spread out from their bodies. They watched as the man they now knew as Justin wrapped his arms around a young woman, shielding her with his body.

Jahnsen's voice was low, keeping their conversation semi-private. "Jones knew. He knew they were both in there. Why wouldn't he provide us with that information?"

Phil shook his head. "I was just talking to Madison about that. She's just as confused."

"We need her and the others to share what they know. It's impossible to put this together otherwise."

"Where was the bird when the attack happened?"

Jahnsen looked at him blankly.

"I'm trying to figure out how Madison got Lexi out without being seen. She said there's a hidden stairwell on the west side of the building that leads to an exit on the north side."

Jahnsen's brows furrowed as his face flushed. "There was never any indication a door was located on the backside. The whole building is a SCIF, a giant safe. Only one way in and out."

"I know. Another piece of information Jones failed to mention."

Putting his fingers to his keyboard, Jahnsen left the video feed playing on the main screen as he pulled up the FalconView data on only his computer. FalconView tracked any aircraft at any given moment. He pulled up the history files. It was easy to pick up their lone bird in Pennsylvania with the lack of aircraft flying.

Both men scanned the data and saw it at the same time. "It

was at 190°," Jahnsen said.

Turning their attention back to the screen, they could see their three-man team sprawled out in the dirt. The view on the monitor came from the south-southwest side of the building. "No one should've been shooting," Jahnsen murmured.

At the time of the assault, the image had been zoomed in significantly to see if the targets were moving. It showed pocked dirt depicting where bullets had missed their targets. Blood depicting where they hadn't. The building in the background was barely visible on the screen.

Phil listened intently as the Team Commander on the ground spoke.

"...moving. Repeat, only one moving. Permission to move in and obtain the target?"

Jahnsen listened to his own voice responding. *"Move in. Resuscitate as necessary. We didn't come here to lose anyone. Bring them all back."*

"There." Phil pointed at the top center of the screen.

"What?"

"Go back ten seconds and watch the top of the image as the back side of the building comes into view."

Jahnsen pulled the slide bar beneath the frame back several seconds.

As the video of the ground below the bird played, a sliver of imagery behind the building came into view. Jahnsen saw it. The edge of a bumper could be seen pulling away. With all the commotion on screen, it was easily missed. A blip of evidence, but it was there.

They knew Madison was more than capable, but she single-handedly saved Lexi. All the while, just around the corner, their combat operatives nearly killed the five people they were tasked to rescue.

Chapter 7
An Old Friend

"**F**ound it!" yelled Gavin, squeezing his radio.

"You did?" Maria threw her arms up in victory, spinning in her office chair. She could hear him bounding down the stairs and smiled as he burst through the cafeteria door triumphantly.

Maria put her finger to her lips to shush him.

"Why are you shushing me?"

"I…" she said, looking around, "have no idea." It had been three days since everything had unfolded. Being quiet in a corporate setting used to make sense. It probably no longer mattered.

When Gavin was within arms reach, she stuck out her hand. "Gimme, gimme, gimme."

He laughed as she dug through her bag, pulling everything out until she found her treasure. "Ah, my old friend!" Her expression priceless as she threw her hand up in the air, holding two little glass bottles.

"It's five o'clock somewhere," Gavin joined in, his voice echoing throughout the stale, empty room.

Maria picked up one of the two glasses she'd found in the kitchen. Pouring the golden liquid into each, she handed one to him.

"What are we toasting?" he asked.

Her smile faltered as her eyes earnestly searched for a reason. "I think this one is to our friends, who are not lost, not gone, and who we will most definitely find again."

They clinked glasses and tipped them back.

A minute of silence took over. Not because they were pondering the fate of everyone they cared about but because the burn hit their throats so hard they struggled to breathe.

Nudging his shoulder, Maria whispered, "You're still… weak," before pouring round two.

"Only two, Maria! Only two. I have no tolerance."

"Shocker," she said with a smile. "Alright, fine. This time you make the toast."

Gavin took a deep breath, preparing for the burn. So painful, yet the heat was decidedly a welcome one. "Alright. This is to not being alone."

Their eyes locked, recognizing how awful it would have been if either of them had been abandoned in the tomb of VISP.

Maria nodded.

Gavin tipped his glass and, without hesitation, sprayed the drink out like a broken sprinkler, coughing in bursts.

Maria's chair went sideways as tears dripped from her eyes in deep belly laughter.

"It… burns… I told… you…."

Catching their breath, she poured half an inch into their glasses for one last hurrah. They sat silently, soaking in their own worlds, letting their thoughts replay the last several days. That first day after Justin, Zuri, and the others were taken, all they could do was grieve. They held onto one another, not knowing if their friends were alive, mystified as to how an entire compound of personnel could vanish.

Maria was the first to break the silence. "Where would they be?"

Gavin stared at the floor, tracing the lines of the tiles. "I wish I knew. It turns out, after all this, I don't know that much about anything, apparently."

"You know that's not true."

"Should I list the ways—"

"No. You've been in this building for years, Gav—"

"Exactly why I should've had some clue as to where everyone in the building could've gone. Shoot, for all the years around Zuri, I knew nothing about what she could do. I'm a neurologist, but for all the good I did here, I might as well have been her babysitter."

"That makes three of us," she said, placing her hand on his with a somber smile. "Let's be proactive." Letting go of his hand, she leaned over, grabbed some paper and a pen, and said, "I do better when I'm focused on a problem and it turns out we have plenty of those. So let's do what we do and figure it out. Grab those blueprints and see if anything looks off. I'm going to write down everything I remember about the events leading up to and after Zuri woke up. Something will give, Gavin."

He tossed back his remaining drink, grunted, winked, and said, "Yes, ma'am." She'd never really seen this side of him. It was endearing.

They sat for several hours, reviewing maps, taking notes, and occasionally making those grunting noises people make when something catches their attention.

Maria's leg was wrapped in a brace and propped up on a chair. The cafeteria had become their main living space since it all went down. After all, it was the logical choice with food and a nearby bathroom. Gavin, now the official human golden retriever, spent his time running between the cafeteria and their D4 lab grabbing blueprints, maps, and all the data printouts from Zuri's coma breakout. He also made trips up to their rooms for personal effects. He felt so much guilt over Zuri the least he could do was climb stairs as a form of weak punishment. Beating his body through service was the least he could do. Or at least a decent distraction.

Taking a deep breath, he finally broke the silence. "Alright, here's what we know: One, everyone in the building—"

"Compound," she corrected.

"Eh, compound… logically still has to be here because they didn't leave via any kind of transport." Maria nodded in agreement. "The only place that makes sense is the bunkers, even though they're sealed shut with concrete, so far as I'm aware."

"From the outside," Maria pointed out.

"Correct again. You're reading my mind."

"Joey and Aidan said they saw everyone, like literally everyone, come into *our* building."

"So the access point has to be here, right?" he asked, swiveling from map to blueprint for any clue.

"Wait!" she yelled, wide-eyed. "Okay, so when we came up from D4, Justin said they'd found fresh blood on the platform of floor sixteen."

His head snapped up. "Blood?"

"Yes. Blood. Can't believe I forgot about that. Zuri was certain it was her sister Lexi's, but when Justin and Aidan got up there, they couldn't trace it to or from anywhere. But if," she continued in a low voice, her speech slowed as she processed her thoughts, "if she was there and somehow exited or was taken out of the building, there has to be another access somewhere near that point of the building. If she'd left through the front door, Justin, or anyone of us, would have seen her, right? So there's another possible exit to explore."

"Or, the obvious… that they're still in the building. Just hiding like everyone else."

"I don't think so," Maria shot back, playing it over again in her mind's eye. "After Justin returned from the stairwell and said they couldn't find anyone, Zuri said she couldn't feel her sister anymore."

"Feel her?"

"Yes. Both she and Zoey, the one you saw running, said they could *feel* her at first and then all of a sudden, they couldn't," she clarified, looking through Gavin as she spoke.

"But it could also mean her sister—"

"Nope." Her tone made it clear they weren't going there.

Gavin understood her unwillingness to accept the words he didn't say more than she knew. "Okay. Well, wouldn't I have seen something if they did get out? I didn't see anyone other than the five of them and the guys with guns."

"You weren't necessarily looking for anyone else either."

"True," said Gavin, leaning back in his chair to stretch. "Essentially, there's no way to know. If she's still here, then she's missing with the rest of VISP."

Maria didn't want that to be true. Of all the possibilities, she hoped Lexi got away from the chaos safe and sound.

Gavin squinted, deep in thought, as he processed the options. "But…" shifting his view back to the blueprints, his fingertips started errantly tapping on the paper, "I bet you're right. There's another access to this building."

Maria leaned forward, willing to consider anything at this point.

With a burst of energy, Gavin bent down so close to the blueprints his nose grazed the paper. "See these two places here?" He sat up and pointed to the far outside wall of the main building by the stairs on the west side, followed by the same place on the eastern wall.

"What am I looking at?"

"Nothing."

"No, tell me your idea."

"I am. There's nothing here."

"I can't read your mind!" She would've punched him if her arms were long enough.

"Look at these side walls." He tapped on the same two places. "Compare them. There's a gap." His eyes were bright now. A sliver of a smile creased his lips.

"Space." The air released from her lungs in comprehension. "That means—"

"It could be a passageway," he cut in as a wide grin swept

across his face. Sliding over, he squeezed, then kissed her with just as much passion.

Breaking his embrace, she locked eyes and said, "Go find them."

As if timed, the radio on the table next to Maria went off. "Gavin, Maria, this is Rice Jahnsen with LIMIT."

They froze.

"If you can hear this, please respond. Your friends are alive and well. We've treated them, they're in recovery, and now, if you're there, we want to help."

Gavin reached for the radio.

"No!" Maria shouted, swatting at his hand. "Don't answer."

"What if they're telling the truth? How else are we going to find out if they're alive or not?"

"We know you're in there and just want to help. You have nothing to worry about. If you can hear this message, please respond."

"Why would they hurt us at this point? We have to do something, don't we?"

"What was their reason for hurting everyone else? I think we need to stay invisible, at least until my ankle has healed enough to run if we have to. We have everything we need right here."

"Eventually, though, we won't. Plus, the rest of VISP could show up at any time, and who knows what mood they'll be in when they do. Shouldn't we leave before that happens?"

"I don't… but they're the devil we know, right?" Her eyes bore into his, pleading.

With a deep breath, he placed the radio back on the table, then said, "Do we, though? Know this devil?"

She blinked, recognizing he was right. They really didn't

know anything about VISP. All the years spent behind closed doors, everyone quietly working their own job, forbidden from discussing their part. With so little cross-interaction, was anything really being accomplished?

"Alright. Cover me. I'm going in," he said without conviction.

"Sorry, I'd go with you, but…" her eyes drifted to her leg.

"Excuses, excuses," he muttered, his smile shaking off some of their frustration. "You said pool of blood, right?" She nodded. "Okay then, keep your radio on."

"I'll try to pay attention," she said with a wink. "Oh! While you're up there, can you grab that book off my nightstand? And also under my bathroom cabinet is a bag of nail polish. Grab that too, please."

Gavin stared at her.

"What? A girl needs to maintain."

Shaking his head, he smirked. "Got it, Boss." With that, he turned and made his way up the stairwell.

As soon as he hit the landing on floor sixteen, he saw it. Bent over and breathing hard, he examined the dark, dry blood pool. "Found it," he relayed into the radio.

"Can you tell which way it goes? Any smears or droplets?"

He looked up and down the stairs. "I don't see—"

A loud crash sounded above him. Gavin slammed his back against the wall and crouched down. Holding his breath, he listened so intently that his ears rang.

"Gavin?" Startled by Maria's voice, he dropped the radio. Swearing and snatching it up, he pulled it to his chest, desperately trying to turn it off before Maria could say anything else.

After enough time had passed without another sound, he

flicked the radio back on and immediately hit the call button so she couldn't respond. "Maria," he whispered, barely audible. "I think there's someone else here. There was a crash on a floor above. Listen, I'm going to investigate, but I'm locking the mic so you can hear what's happening." Clipping the radio onto his belt, he pulled the gun from his bag and white-knuckled it with hands shaking.

His heartbeat pounded in his ears as he crept up the stairs. A cursory look through the doors on platforms seventeen and eighteen showed no discernable signs of movement. The door on the nineteenth floor, however, could only be opened with a keycard. Pulling his out, it proved fruitless as the LED rapidly blinked red.

"I'm on nineteen. My card doesn't work."

Pausing outside the door, his chest heaved as he considered whether or not the noise was an accident or from an actual person. *Maybe I already passed them on seventeen or eighteen? Maybe they're further up? Maybe it was just a poorly stacked pile of boxes finally tipping over after the rush?* He knew the symptoms of hyperventilating, but this was the first he'd experienced it.

Calm down, you idiot! Halfway up to twenty, he hesitated long enough to look up over the platform. The door leading onto the twentieth floor was wide open. It was definitely a keycard entry door, he could see the keypad, but there was no illuminated LED, red or green.

Once again, his heart beat distractingly loud, only this time accompanied by heavier breathing and sweat dripping into his eyes.

"I'm inside the hall on twenty. Something unmistakably

similar to the events with Zuri happened up here." Tiptoeing down the hall, he peeked inside any room with an open door. "There's blood smeared on the floor. It looks like shattered glass as well. I'm coming to the far end and—" his voice cut off as he looked inside the last room. Despite the damage and chaos, it was clear that someone had been held in a replica of the glass prison Zuri had been kept in. What was left of it sat center mass in the room. Glass was blown corner to corner. Desks and debris littered the space. Blood was on the wall inside the room not far from where he stood. "I don't think there's any question. Lexi was here."

Something or someone may have died in here. The putrid smell assaulted his senses.

Moving slowly, he saw graphs identical to the ones they'd used. From what he could tell, their output lines were far beyond what Zuri's had been. Gavin walked to the side of an overturned desk, then stumbled back as a leg came into view.

The hair on his arms stood up but quickly settled as he realized where the smell was coming from. Based on his attire, the man must have been one of the doctors in the lab.

"Okay, I need to get out of here."

Out in the hall he placed his hands on his knees then pulled in a deep breath. "Whatever happened, she's not here—" His head snapped up at the sound of footsteps only a few doors down. Suddenly another crash broke the silence. He watched as a hand hit the ground outside the doorway.

"Who's over there?" Gavin cried out, his voice cracked. "I have a gun!"

The hand didn't move.

"I can see you!" His gun was up, aimed directly at the hand.

"I don't want to hurt you!"

Pressed against the wall, he slowly made his way forward. At the doorway, he carefully eased his head around the door frame until he saw the body of a man wearing a white lab coat covered in blood and ripped in patches. He lay on his back with his eyes closed.

"Crap. Please be alive." Gavin growled, checking for a pulse. Finding one, he rolled the man over. As he did, a pained groan escaped the stranger's lips.

"Hey, what's your name? What happened up here?"

The man struggled to breathe, his eyes wide as he gasped. Finally, whispering in a panic, he said, "Lexi? Where's Lexi?"

Gavin's heart skipped and his face flushed. "You know Lexi?"

Shaking him as his eyes rolled back and his breathing shallowed, Gavin asked, "Did you have Lexi up here? Hey, I need you to wake up. Can you hear me?" Noticing the name tag on his coat, he calmly asked, "Grant? Is your name Grant?"

Grant nodded. His eyes rolled until they met Gavin's. "Did Lexi kill Madison?"

"What? Who's Madison?" Shaking him again, Gavin could see he was losing him. With a burst of adrenaline, Gavin managed to pull Grant's arms up around his neck, draping him over his back.

"Maria, I'm bringing him down. He's in pretty bad shape," groaned Gavin, trying to shift the man's weight on his back. "If you can stand to move, grab a med kit or two… he's gonna need it."

Chapter 8
The Wait

"**B**randon?" Joanna poked her head in through the crack of his bedroom door. He'd been asleep since they arrived at his cabin three days prior. It was a slow march back, and as soon as they arrived, he fell face down on his bed and hadn't moved since.

She'd barely slept, but last night her emotions caught up with her. A migraine like a hangover consumed her. When he didn't respond, she quietly avoided looking at him as she walked past his bed to the only bathroom in search of Tylenol.

Not one second had passed that she wasn't internally panicking about where Addie might be. Her thoughts often paralyzed her with fear, eating and drinking little, feeling trapped inside a strange home in a strange place. Screaming and sweating, nightmares routinely woke her without, apparently, affecting the only person who could help her.

Albeit a little terrified, she knew his wound needed cleaning. The day they arrived, she bandaged his leg with supplies found in his bathroom while he slept. However, she hadn't been able to get him to wake up beyond a few disorienting grunts and groans for some water and painkillers she'd discovered under his sink.

"Brandon? Are you up?" Trying again as she peeked her head around the bathroom door frame. She saw his form sprawled out on the bed. When her eyes adjusted to the dark, she noticed he wasn't wearing a shirt. Her sister's voice popped into her head. *Not a bad thing to wake up to in the morning.* Joanna smirked, imagining Addie waggling her eyebrows with a devious smile. As quickly as the thought caused her to smile, it squeezed the air out of her lungs.

Shaking off the unwelcome fear, she moved closer. The rise and fall of his chest seemed irregular. Too fast with shallow breaths. Squinting, she could see sweat pooling in the crevice of his collarbone. The sheets around him were dark with moisture. Touching his leg, she called his name louder this time, but he didn't flinch.

Pressing the heel of her hands into her eyes, she thought, *You can do this Anna. You've got this. Just wake him up.* Kneeling on the bed, she gripped his shoulders tight. "Hey! Wake up! Brandon, time to wake up." Attempting to pull him upright, she tumbled backward as her hands slipped from his sweaty skin.

"No, no, no, no, no, no! This isn't happening." Moving closer to his ear, in a motherly voice, she whispered, "Brandon, hey, I need you to wake up now. You've had plenty of rest. You don't even have to help me. Just tell me which way to go. Brandon?"

Not even a flicker of consciousness. Walking around his injured leg, she began pulling off the blood-soaked bandages. Awake or not, she needed him to live. When she got to the skin, she pulled as carefully as she could. The infection was evident even before she saw it. As the top layer of skin pulled off with the bandage, Brandon jerked upright, groaning like a zombie with the smell to match.

"Okay! Okay! I'm sorry." Jumping back, her fear caused her to freeze in place. Her sister was gone. She might be hurt or worse. And the only person that might know how to find her was a half-conscious, zombie man with an infection she didn't have medicine to fix.

Joanna had tried to pay attention on their way back to his house but found herself lost in thought too many times. Not to mention the hum of a gong resonating in her brain from her altercation with the tree. She was stuck. On her own, she would never find the location they'd lost Addie.

Pull it together! she urged herself, physically trying to brush the fear from her hands and shoulders. Hurrying into the bathroom, she scanned for anything that could help.

On her first day at his house, a small prayer of thankfulness left her lips when she reached for the faucet. Well water. Small favors.

She grabbed a clean rag from a stack on top of the toilet, ran it under the water, and found an old tube of Neosporin in a drawer, along with an almost empty plastic bottle of alcohol under the sink.

"You are not going to die on me. Do you understand? Brandon, are you listening? No one dies today." Steadying her breathing, she braced his foot between her knees and finished unraveling the bandage. A few moans escaped him and some minor resistance, but his eyes stayed closed.

With a clear look at the wound, and a plan forming, she surveyed the floor for anything, a bowl or towel, something she could place under his leg to catch the fluids. The narrow edge of a brown rug poked out from under his bed. With bare toes, she positioned it as evenly as she could beneath his ankle now hanging not quite far enough off the edge of the bed.

"Brandon, I need you to scootch down a bit. I need to clean all the way around your calf. You've gotta move for me just a little, okay?" No response. After a brief pause, Joanna gingerly wrapped her hands around his foot and pulled. Not an inch. Tugging at his leg was like pulling a tank.

Stealing herself a moment to devise a new plan, she braced her right foot against the bed frame, grabbed both of his ankles tight, then whispered, "Here goes nothing," before yanking as hard as she could while leaning back and gritting her teeth.

"God, you're like a bag of cement." Wiping her forehead, she took off the sweatshirt she'd thrown on before collapsing on the couch the night prior.

Stretching in preparation for another go at it, she noticed a strange look on his face.

"Brandon?" Gently placing his legs back down, she took a step forward.

His eyelid peeked open.

"What the—are you awake?" she asked with pursed lips.

With a gravelly voice, he uttered, "No." Despite his obvious pain, the corner of his mouth kicked up. "Do I get dinner and a movie first?"

"Aaaaghh!" Stomping into the bathroom, yelling, cursing,

and swinging wildly at the shower curtain, Joanna momentarily declared him dead to her. After more than a few deep breaths, she walked back in and picked up the wet rag she had placed on the bed. "Here, wipe your forehead," she said, dropping the rag onto his face. After wiping himself down, she used the back of her hand to check his temperature.

"Is it bad?"

"It's pretty bad, yeah."

"How long have I been out?" He tried to blink his eyes open, but they were swollen, probably from his blood pressure being so high.

"Three days. It's like nine in the morning. How do you feel?"

"Cold."

"Makes sense. You have a wicked fever, and we need to find a way to bring it down. Do you have anything stronger than Tylenol?"

"Wicked?"

"Fever!"

He gave a half-hearted grunt. "Did you try under the sink? I'm… not sure." His words slurred. She didn't think he'd be awake much longer.

"I need to clean your leg, but first, I need you to tell me something. How do I find my sister? How do I find Addie?"

His breathing was shallow, but he cracked his eyes open again. Staring at her through blurred vision, his mind swirled, slow to comprehend her request until the events in the woods came back to him. "I don't know," he whispered, his words abrasive and short.

"What does that mean? You said you've lived out here for

years. You must have an idea or a… theory... something."

Her heart raced, unsure if he was even with it enough to answer her when he said, "I've been looking for my friend, Kristine, for years. I thought—" Pain washed over his features as his stomach turned.

"You thought? Thought what? Hey!" she shouted, leaning over to touch his face. Her hand was cool, and he leaned into it. "Brandon, you thought what? What were you about to say?"

"I thought I'd found a lead a while back but couldn't make anything of it." He groaned louder this time.

"Okay, well, tell me what it was, point me in a direction. Just give me something!" Smacking his cheek, she struggled to keep him with it. He was fading fast.

Changing tactics, she quickly began to clean his wounds. If she could stop him from passing out, even if it meant torturing him by cleaning up the infected area, maybe he'd stay with her long enough to offer better information.

"Real quick... real quick here. I need you to move down a little to get your leg off the bed."

He groaned in response, more like a sound of fear than pain, which she hadn't heard from a man before.

"Don't be a baby, just a few inches."

"I… can't move… please…" he barely got the word out before rolling onto his side and vomiting on his sheets.

"Well, that's unfortunate, but luckily for you, that movement gave me enough room to work." She placed the cool rag open on top of his face. Her mother used to do that when she was young—just drape the rag across her face. Somehow it always seemed to settle her nausea. It must have worked for him because his whole body seemed to relax.

Here we go, she said to herself, *you can do this Anna.* Running back into the bathroom, she snatched a second rag off the stack, got it sopping wet, then brought it back to the bed.

Once again, she braced his leg between her knees and squeezed the rag over his wounds to rinse some of the muck she'd missed the first time. He only flinched when he felt the cool water hit his leg.

Grabbing the alcohol, she took two steadying breaths and held the last. Her left hand held his leg at the knee and began to tilt the bottle with her right hand.

"Crap!" *I can't waste it all in one pour.* "Think, Anna, think." Reattacking the situation, she filled up the bottle cap instead and, getting as close to the wound as possible, poured just a few drops into each puncture.

The first one, Brandon bucked so hard she lost her grip, nearly dropping the entire bottle. Before she could even scold him, he was out.

Passing out was not the plan, but at least it made it easier for her to clean out his wounds. Once finished, she cut a clean shirt into squares, not wanting to waste the whole thing by wrapping it. She was used to scrimping and saving, so the extra work didn't bother her. After finding another ankle wrap under the sink, she secured the handmade bandages.

Walking outside, Joanna took as much air into her lungs as she could and shook out her arms. They had stayed steady through the process but were now spasming uncontrollably.

What if he stays sick too long? she said to herself, shaking and massaging her spasming arms while taking deep, cool breaths outside. *What if we don't get to Addie in time? What if he dies in that room and I have to find my way out of here? How will I find her?* Dropping to the dirt, Joanna collapsed into full-out wracking sobs, the sort of ugly crying she hated to see, let alone give in to. She couldn't help but think how unattractive she probably looked especially considering how long it had been since she'd taken a shower.

Seriously? What am I thinking? What is wrong with me? My sister might be dying or dead somewhere, and I care about what I look like? What he thinks! Laughing, her sobs turned into hysterics as her thoughts swung wildly through memories, confusion, and feeling helpless.

Amid her personal meltdown, she felt something else well up within her. A type of pain. Not physical. It was as if the hurt wasn't her own. With each passing second, the sensation became stronger. Visions of her sister lying on a dirt-covered concrete floor came to her in flashes. She knew without question that what she was seeing and feeling wasn't a dream.

Her sister needed her. Now.

Where are you?

Where are you, Addie!

Help me! Tell me!

Sucking in air, she screamed louder than she'd ever screamed. It was the only word that meant anything. "ADELINE!"

Chapter 9
Connected

Madison slipped into the room, not wanting to hinder the conversation between Jahnsen, Phil, and a few others. Standing behind Phil, the room began to spin. Trying to be discreet, she brushed her forehead and blinked several times, long and slow. The dizziness quickly turned to shortness of breath as a muffled moan escaped her lips, catching Phil's attention just enough for him to glance back.

Before he could say a word, she had folded in half from the piercing pain and dropped to her knees.

"Madison?" he shouted, squatting next to her and placing his arm on her back just as a convulsion turned her body rigid. "What the—help! Medic! We need help over here." He sat on the floor with his arms wrapped around her upper body to keep her still. As she seized, her strength multiplied, making it impossible for him to keep hold of her.

"Madis—*Madison*, what is going on?"

It was surreal. She knew that whatever was happening wasn't actually happening to her, yet she was utterly helpless to stop it.

The medic leaped over his desk and slid across the smooth vinyl floor to her. "We need to put something in her mouth so she doesn't break her teeth," he barked, searching for anything within reach when someone tossed him a t-shirt hanging from a chair. Twisting it lengthwise, he wedged it between her teeth.

With Phil holding her arms tight to her body and the medic bracing her head, Madison relaxed. Her wide-open eyes slowly fluttered closed.

"She's out," Phil said. "Should we move her?" Madison could hear every word but had no way to let them know she was still coherent. They maneuvered her body safely to the floor and placed the t-shirt beneath her neck and head for support as she tried to process what had just happened. Problem was, there was no way to process it. She was more lost and confused than ever inside her own skin.

After a brief examination and some back and forth with Phil, the medic said, "She's out and might be for a while. Let's move her to the back room so the doctor can thoroughly assess what's happened."

"What in the hell is happening around here?" Jahnsen protested as he assisted Phil and a few others with picking her up and whisking her out of the room.

"Does anyone else feel that?" Aidan sat up in bed, immediately wincing at the burn in his neck, realizing he'd moved too fast.

Joe lifted his head and looked at the girls. Zoey and Lexi were sitting up, wide-eyed. His body felt heavy as he got out of bed. Ignoring his crutches, he limped over to Zoey's side. He could see they were both in some sort of trance—off in another place. Physically there, but not really there. "Zoe? What's going on?" he said, touching her shoulder. Immediately her eyes blinked clear.

"Joe?" she responded, as if surprised to find him beside her. She looked around the room and saw the others still deep in a similar trance. Reaching over, her fingertips grazed Lexi's arm. Instantly she knew.

Lexi's quiet voice hauntingly cut through the silence. "Madison. I can feel her—"

"And she's in pain." Zoey cut in. "We have to find her. Where's Madison?"

As if on cue, with the loud kick of a boot, the door flew open and Madison was rushed in by Phil and the others.

Lexi was on her feet. "Madison!" Helping them put her down on a bed, she grasped her hand. "Maddy? Are you ok?"

"We don't know what happened. Thinking it was a seizure. She just collapsed," Phil said, out of breath.

"She's connected," said Zuri, her quiet voice barely audible from across the room. Though her gunshot wounds were healing more quickly than should have been possible, she was still too weak to walk to Madison's side.

"To who, Zuri?" Lexi twisted around, straining to see her sister work to share her thoughts through the haze of painkillers.

"To the girl with shadow eyes."

No one could make sense of her message.

Aidan had slowly maneuvered his way across the room. By the time he reached Zuri, he could barely stand. Without hesitation, he plopped onto her bed and swung his feet up. After laying back on the pillow beside her, he grabbed her hand and attempted to translate. "She's saying there's another one of you guys… uh, another girl out there with black, onyx crystal eyes. Somehow all of you are reaching out to one another simultaneously. It's like when the first domino fell—Zoey feeling Lexi—the rest began to fall." Pausing, he glanced around the room. "I'm pretty good at this, don't you think?" he bragged, to no applause. "Any chance you guys know how many of you there are? Cause it would be nice to know how many young ladies we're going to have to rescue."

Their mouths dropped open. A grin spread across Zuri's face though her eyes remained closed.

After a few uncomfortable moments, leaving even Jahnsen speechless, Aidan said, "What? I know things."

Chapter 10
Trail of Blood

"Why don't you bring me up there? I can help you look. Oh, c'mon! Second set of eyes!" Maria pouted, only now it was Gavin's turn to shush her—and for good reason.

"Did you just shush me? Really?"

"Grant's still asleep."

"Uh-huh, and it's about time he woke up too. We need answers."

"I know. We'll wake him when I get back."

All they knew about the man was that he was their twin. Lexi had been held on the twentieth floor, confirming their suspicions. However, after tending to Grant's injuries, he'd fallen asleep, only conscious enough to sip water and relieve himself. As it was, they'd learned nothing new.

Gearing up to search for a blood trail, Gavin filled a backpack with supplies, including a keycard he'd found in Jones' office that was completely different from his and the security staff's fobs.

"Okay, well, bring me with. I'm losing my mind just sitting here."

"And how do you suggest we do that, Maria? I'd carry you on my back, but I might die before we reach the tenth floor." He wasn't being facetious, just stating the obvious, which made her crazy.

"So I'm too heavy to carry that short little distance, is what you're saying?" Her hand-on-hip sass made her look all that more imposing yet adorable. Without another word, he walked over, wrapped his arms beneath her arms and legs, and lifted her off the chair.

Looking deep into her eyes, there was so much he wanted to say—*He adored her. She was the yin to his yang. That he was in love with her....*

She knew by his gaze how he felt. This was the moment— she could feel it. He was finally going to say what was on his heart.

"Maria, I just need you to know...." His pause gave her goosebumps. "I would die carrying a ten-pound baby up twenty flights of stairs. Let alone you."

Gasping, she cried, "Seriously!" Feigning anger, she smacked his arm. "Put me down!" In truth, she was shocked at how real he was becoming—cracking jokes and smiling at her like she was his whole world. In all fairness, and despite the pain in their hearts, they were both becoming real people again.

"Well, if you're not going to bring me with you, then I have another idea."

"Shoot."

"In the medical ward is a blacklight type thingy."

"Very technical."

Her stare spoke volumes. "Go grab it, then bring it with you. When you get to floor sixteen, shine it up and down and see if any clues pop up.

"Huh. Okay, yeah. Brilliant."

"Obviously," she said with a sparkle, "it was my idea." Laughing, he turned to head to the medical bay. "Ahem." Hearing her clear her throat, Gavin looked back to see his supply bag in her hand. "Need this?"

"Yup. That might help."

His bag was packed with flashlights, batteries, radio, snacks—thanks to Maria, a few other essential pieces of equipment, and his gun.

The blacklight was an excellent addition, and carrying it up to floor fifteen only made him think of Maria all the more. Once there, he turned it on, aimed it at the floor, and followed the flight of stairs upward. There were interesting splotches on the stairs, but nothing that jumped out at him. At sixteen, he settled the light over the dried blood pool so he could gauge the color of it and, with any luck, find other droplets to follow. There was nothing like it heading downward, so he went up. On the edge of several steps, he saw tiny drips of the same color.

"I'm on seventeen. There are more droplets on the stairs, but they don't seem to trail inside the doors on any particular floor. I'm going to do a quick check." Gavin pushed the door open to find remnants of clothing and other personal effects.

"Only apartments on this floor."

"Okay. Keep going."

"Yes, ma'am," he replied, as a cockeyed smile formed at the corner of his mouth. He wasn't looking for these kinds of details the day he'd found Grant. Just anything that would've made a loud crashing noise. This time he was searching for anything that would tell him where Lexi might have gone.

"Dang!" He'd just pushed through the door on the eighteenth floor. "It's like a café. Not quite the cafeteria on two. And the back half is more like a research center. Books lining the walls, tables with docking stations for laptops."

"You sound a little jealous." Her smirk could be felt through the speaker.

"I am! What's the deal? It's like we were the B Team or something."

"Sounds like the trade-off is real food down here." When he didn't respond, she followed up by saying, "Oh, stop scoffing, Gavin."

"I'm not," he scoffed, rolling his eyes. "I'm climbing the stairs up to nineteen." He was breathing hard, regretting not spending time in the gym like he kept saying he would.

"What do you see?"

"This is the level my keycard wouldn't open."

"Did you try Jones'?" Maria asked, just as the green LED began to flash.

"Yup," he responded as a subtle click was heard at the handle. Pushing it open, he froze, squinting and studying the room. "It's a mirror image."

"What?"

He blinked a few times, shook his head, and said, "It's D3.

This whole floor is laid out like the one above ours. It's where we'd send our bio and neuro tests."

"Lexi." Maria's voice was somber and the radio went silent for a moment before adding, "That's wild. To be in the same building the whole time."

"I mean, I never sent anything up here related to Zuri."

"I take it no one's up there now, right?"

"Nope. Ghost town." He shined his light on the floor and around the walls and doors, but there were no blood droplets that he could see. "I'm going to head up to twenty."

"Alright. Be careful. For all we know, another doppelganger could be up there."

Gavin laughed at her use of doppelganger. "Noted."

There were only two drops on the stairs going up, but it was enough to give him the confidence to keep going. At the top platform, he flashed the light at the doorway, the walls, and even the ceiling. Nothing.

"It's strange. The main pool of blood is on sixteen. So if she was being held up on twenty, that would mean she somehow got down to that floor and then came back up." Turning in circles at the top stairwell his eyes caught a black smear on the wall in front of him. Holding up the light, he could see it was a smudged fingerprint. The same color as the blood on the floor down below.

"Maybe she was running from something and got hurt. Or *someone* hurt her," said Maria trying to follow his thought pattern.

Getting closer to inspect it, he saw an indentation in the wall where the dried blood was. Putting his finger to it, he tried pushing. When nothing happened, he started feeling for a door line, anything that might offer a clue. As he pressed his fingers into the indent once again, he felt a little round bump. He put pressure on it, but nothing happened.

"Anything of interest?"

"Lots," he said with a jump at the sound of her voice.

"What does that mean?"

"It means there's what looks like a bloody fingerprint on the wall across from the door to twenty. It's out of place, but—"

"But what?" Maria's impatience oozed through his radio.

"I'm coming down. We need to wake up Grant."

Chapter 11
She's a Witch

Iron Prison | August 16, 2029 | 11:23 a.m.

"*Iron bars, iron fists, the eight remain, she'll bring them back. Iron bars, iron fists, the eight remain, she'll bring them back. Iron bars, iron fists, the....*"

"Why does she keep repeating that?" whispered Addie, with minimal movement of her jaw. Her eyes were still shut due to the pain rolling in waves throughout her body. She wasn't sure exactly who she was speaking to, only that a woman was sitting next to her holding her hand. The woman sat there, gently attentive each time Addie was lucid enough to acknowledge her whereabouts. At first, there was no response to her question, so she cracked open her slightly less-swollen right eye to catch a view of her personal aide. "Why does she keep—"

"Oh! You *are* awake." The woman's voice was wispy and

slightly high-pitched but very quiet. "I'm sorry, I thought you were dreaming again." Adjusting her position away from the wall, she leaned in so she could more readily look Addie in the face. "It's going to be a while before you can really move about."

Addie didn't need to see herself to understand why. She could tell right off there were more broken bones in her body than she could count. Despite all that, she still wanted to know. "Why does she?"

With dim light filtering through her barely opened eye, she caught a glimpse of the woman repeating herself over and over again with a sadness Addie could feel.

"She never says anything else. Just repeats that phrase again and again. None of us know what she's talking about besides the iron bars, I s'pose." Her gaze traveled around the room as if taking notice of them for the first time in a while. "Don't have a clue who the eight girls are. There are more than eight of us here."

Addie attempted to push herself up from the ground but found it to be an impossible request of her body. The woman noticed her attempt and grabbed her under the arms, clumsily helping her into a sitting position. The agony forced Addie's halfway decent eye to open to its fullest extent. The pain would have made her scream in a more familiar setting, but she choked it down, releasing only a moan. Tears slid down her face as she settled in place.

"I'm so sorry. I'm trying to be gentle, but I have little strength and brittle bones." Her apology was genuine. Once Addie was able to take a breath, she realized the woman's arms were bent at odd angles as if they'd been broken time and time again, healing in a new position after each break.

Thoughts of torture immediately consumed her mind.

The woman looked down at her arms. "I know. Not pretty, I guess." She tucked them under her filthy brown shirt. The smell wafting past Addie's nose had finally registered in her swollen brain. Without her permission, her stomach began to heave, which had the effect of sending what felt like an electric shock into the base of her head. *This is torture*, she thought.

"Oh, girl." The woman got onto her knees and wrapped her arms around Addie's midsection. Addie expected the pain to increase and had no strength to fight her off, but the woman did so with practiced experience. Somewhere in a small space in her mind she realized the woman was holding her ribs and organs steady while she heaved up nothing but bile. "It's okay. Janice will take care of you. Janice is here."

Where is here? How did I get here? Where's my sister? Who's Janice?

Her heaving began to subside and she was able to straighten her back. Searching through blurred vision, Addie could see they were in a cage. Iron bars framed the entire room. Beyond the bars was nothing but dirt. Like being in a cave. The ceiling, the walls—all dirt. The floor was cold concrete, but even it was covered in dirt and patches of mud. There was only one actual wall covered with drywall. It was the inside wall. The wall the girls dreaded—where the monsters entered from.

As her vision cleared, Addie saw a black hole on the back side of the room. The bars formed a door, but she could see the lock. It looked like a hallway of sorts.

Janice was repositioning herself against the wall when Addie asked, "Did anyone else come in with me? Another girl? My sister?" Her intensity got Janice's attention.

"Well, no. No one new but you. The first in years, actually. You were a surprise for all of us a few days ago."

"Days?" Addie's head swam. She began to lean as vertigo rocked her. "I got here days ago? How many" Then to herself, *Joanna, oh my god, where's Joanna?*

"Is that your sister? Joanna?" She placed her hand gently on Addie's shoulder. "There's no one else here with that name." She patted Addie's arm and said, "That's a *good* thing. You don't want her in here."

Everything was so fuzzy. She tried holding to a single line of thought, but there were just too many floating through like wisps of smoke in and out of her mind.

The room started a slow spin that grew faster and faster. Addie felt the cool, dirty concrete as it rose up to meet the side of her face. Darkness consumed her, thankfully taking the pain with it.

"Long's coming," one of the women closest to the door whispered. Immediately, like a well-rehearsed game of telephone, the information passed through hushed voices until it reached Janice along the back wall. She had been trying to cover Addie with a tattered blanket, but upon hearing the news, she used her body to block as much of her as possible instead.

"Where's she at!" Long's slurred voice rang through the room. His face was swollen and crusted blood smeared the side where Addie had split his lip and nose open with the back of her head. All the women pushed back against the walls, grabbing onto one another. Of all the guards, he was the most heinous. Most violent. They knew he wasn't there for them, but they didn't want to end up in the crossfire either.

"Right now! Someone better tell me where she's—ah, there

she is." He walked toward Janice with rage and excitement gleaming from glossy and puffed-up purple eyes. His nose was contorted at an impossible angle. And he was walking off-kilter as if dizzy from the effort. But his focus was pinpointed enough to push him through.

"No, wait. Please. If you take her now, you'll never get anything from her." Janice begged, fully aware that he had no intention of listening to her.

"Move, *witch*!" Grabbing her outstretched hand, he yanked Janice's arm from the socket, flinging her out of the way like a helpless child.

Bending down over Adeline, he looked over her unconscious form. "Get up!" he bellowed before smacking her face in a way that would've woken the whole room if she had, in fact, simply been asleep. Instead, her body remained limp. She was completely oblivious. "Fine. Have it your way." With a perverted grin, he grabbed her hair, using it to drag her across the floor behind him and out through the door.

Janice's only redeeming hope was that soon enough the monster wouldn't be able to drag her in that way again once they shaved her head. And that Addie would never have to remember the abuse.

Harris Lake Woods   12:15 p.m.

"Oh, god," the words barely passed through his cracked lips. Brandon's eyes parted just enough for daylight to blind him. *Where are my curtains?*

With arms like weights, he slowly lifted his hands to rub his dry eyes. Aside from a bit of morning crust, his face felt strangely clean. Snippets of recent memories flooded his mind with each passing second: his injured leg, waking up freezing or burning so hot it was like being inside a furnace. A glimpse now and then of an angel over him mumbling in a voice so sweet it was like flowing honey. He even remembered feeling calm whenever he would wake long enough to hear her muttering to herself.

"Oh, god—" he uttered as the memory of getting sick came back to him.

When his vision cleared, he saw, then felt, nothing but clean sheets. *Maybe it was a dream. But why would I dream about puking?* He knew that was unlikely, which meant his unintentional house guest had cleaned it up however long ago it happened. The groan that left his throat this time was deeper and more from embarrassment than anything related to pain.

Hearing movement in the other room, she was clearly coming his way. Sprawled across the bed, he attempted to get to his feet when he realized he was adorning nothing more than well-worn underwear.

"Hey, you're alive," Joanna said from the doorway, her voice still scratchy from another fitful night of sleep.

"Uh, yeah," he mumbled, trying not to make eye contact while feeling around for pants, shorts, or anything he could use to cover himself up.

"Forget it. I've seen it all." She walked in, picked his blanket up from where it fell off the side of the bed, and handed it to him. Joanna had long since overcome her fear of him and was well beyond the pleasantries of being a stranger.

She'd seen him in his birthday suit. Strangers, they were not.

"Uh, thanks." Brandon considered cracking a joke about her seeing him naked but couldn't get past her nonchalance about it. He made awkward sounds trying to think of what to say before simply asking, "How many hours have I been out?" Pulling the blanket around his waist, he moved over to the side of his bed before gingerly applying weight to his injured leg. When she didn't respond, he paused to look in her direction. "Has it been that long? Are you counting—"

"Five days. I think."

No! "Five days?" he choked out louder than intended. "Your… your sister." His words fumbled, and she could see he was internally scolding himself. It wasn't the reaction she'd seen playing out in her mind.

"Your leg was infected. Was touch-and-go there for a while, I think, but I tried to keep it clean and change out the bandages. Food-wise, you didn't have much for soups. Luckily you have a lot of mushrooms around here. I was able to cook up and create a sort of earthy-herbal stew. I don't know much about mushrooms. Fed you first," she said with a smirk. "When you didn't die, I went ahead and ate some myself."

"Thanks, I think. I can't believe you did all that." He caught her eyes and saw the strangest shimmer of cinnamon light looking back at him. It was mesmerizing. Neither moved a muscle until a squawking bird outside the window broke the silence. "Ahem. 'Scuse me. I'll just go get cleaned up, then we'll make a plan and leave." His eyes took in each corner of the room, looking for something. Turning back, he started to say, "Have you seen my—"

"Pants?" Joanna held them out.

"Thanks." Watching her walk away, he wondered again if

he wasn't still dreaming. He hadn't had more than a passing wave with a woman in years since he took up staying in his cabin full-time. Now all of a sudden, there was one living in his house, and apparently, no longer concerned he might be a threat. And not unattractive at that.

Frustrated by the reality of the new arrangement, he groaned once again. He didn't need or want someone else to take care of. No matter how caring at the moment. Limping his way to the bathroom, he was grateful his granddad had never gotten rid of the place. Even a cold shower was still a shower.

He was in the bathroom for about thirty minutes. The moment he walked out, still wearing a towel, she began firing questions at him.

After ten minutes of his short, monosyllabic replies, Joanna paused before saying, "Seems you're new to this whole conversation thing, so I'll just recap if you don't mind. This Thomas character knows where she might be?"

"Not sure."

"Then why are we seeing him? Isn't there someone with more information? Someone else that knows those woods?"

"No one knows them better than me," he said bluntly. Her attractive warmth had worn off with the barrage of questions he didn't yet have answers to. And so had his cordial demeanor.

"Then how do you not know where they could've gone?" Joanna said, crossing her arms and leaning forward. After sitting in silence for days, walking as far as she dared into the woods by his house before risking getting lost, she knew she couldn't go anywhere without him. She had had plenty of time to consider what she had control over and what she didn't. The only thing she could control was trying to make him better. So that was her sole focus, pushing everything else to the background. Paralysis through worry would not help her or her sister.

But now Brandon was awake, and she was feeling her feelings again, and she just wanted to move. His slow movement flared her anger. Staring at him, she let her mind entertain her impatient fury. Soon her thoughts quickly derailed.

Maybe he is a bad guy. Maybe that's why he's so silent. He has remorse for what he's got to do to me after I nursed him back to health.

She tried to recall what Addie had said about Brandon before she was taken. Her sister had a knack for reading people, often joking about seeing a person's aura and discovering what kind of person they were. She started using the term aura after a sixth-grade sleepover with a friend who swore she was descended from witches in Salem. The friend had brought a book called *The Spell Book For New Witches*. One of the chapters was about auras, so from then on, Addie decided that was what she could see. It stuck.

Laughing most of the night while trying to cast spells showed them their friend had zero percent witch-like abilities, but it was fun just the same. Addie once said years later that it wasn't colors or even auras but shades of light she would glimpse around a person. The brighter the hues, the more pure or genuine a person turned out to be. The darker the light didn't necessarily mean they weren't genuine, just that they were carrying more weight in and through them. Of course, it sometimes meant the person wasn't good, but most of the time, it just meant they were suffering.

Joanna thought back to when Brandon first walked up. *What did Addie say? Something about darkness?* She took a deep breath to settle her thoughts, remembering that flash of a moment before Addie ran back to get her book.

I don't get a creeper vibe from him. Maybe a little dark. He's harmless. Dark. She said *dark*. But also harmless. She would never have left me with him if she'd thought there was anything sinister about him.

Joanna struggled to hold onto her derailed thoughts and emotions, tasting them like an addict looking for a hit, but couldn't make the thoughts stick. She had witnessed him at his worst and even heard some of his more coherent, subconscious thoughts as he dreamt. Several she wanted to know more about, but clearly he wasn't a big talker. Her only priority now was to find Addie and get the hell out of North Carolina.

He sat down, gingerly pulled his pant leg over her carefully placed bandages, popped a few Motrin he'd forgotten were hiding in his nightstand, and said, "Put your boots on."

She froze mid-disparaging thought. "Are we going to find Addie?" Without another word, Joanna snatched up her sweatshirt, grabbed her boots, and immediately deflated.

"I won't make it that far."

A loud thud from her boot hitting the ground startled him into sitting up too fast. "Gah! What was that?"

Ignoring his question, she asked her own, "Why am I putting my boots on then? You could just give me directions, draw me a map, or point your finger in the right direction! Anything so I can look for her at my own pace!"

"*You* won't make it that far. You'd end up disappearing right along with her. What good will that do your sister… or anyone for that matter?" Brandon was mad, not necessarily at her, but at the entire situation. Unfortunately, she was the only one there to take it out on.

"I don't care! It's been too long already. At least I'd be with her, and we could figure it out together."

"Or die. Do you understand that? Or you both could die."

"And if she's already dead, then it doesn't matter, does it? If she's dead, I might as well be too!"

Her words stunned him into silence. His anger dissipated as her desperation pierced his heart. After a few moments breathing heavily and red-faced, he gently said, "We will find her. I promise—"

"Don't make promises you can't keep." Her voice cracked, but she held her tears in like a warrior on a mission.

"I was going to say, I promise we won't stop looking for her."

Their eyes locked again, this time with an intensity she'd never felt before. If she knew nothing else about him, she believed, for whatever reason, that he was telling her the truth.

"So, remind me, why am I putting my boots on then?"

"Because my mouth tastes like mushrooms and dirt. We need provisions."

Chapter 12
The Wake-Up

"**W**here are my waffles?" Maria whisper-yelled. "I made dinner last night." Gavin's calm voice was sing-songy.

"And you know that's not how this works. You *offered* to make dinner. I didn't ask you to. Breakfast is your gig, remember!" It wasn't a question.

"I guess getting any sleep with you two around is going to be a bit tough," Grant added from behind them.

"Whoa!" Gavin's hand hit the table with a bang. "Warning next time!"

"Good thing I'm not one of the bad guys or you'd be toast," said Grant, smiling.

"The jury's still out," Maria shot back with a wink.

"How are you feeling?" Gavin asked, pulling a chair over for Grant.

"Surprisingly better. Although starving."

Maria smiled and slid a muffin in front of him. "Well, you've been asleep for about four days, so I'd say you're a little peckish."

Grant's hands stilled on the table. "Days?"

Gavin cleared his throat and then spoke a little softer. "It's been four days since I found you. We were surprised you were still alive after examining you. Covered in bruising, we expected you to have internal bleeding, but if you had—"

"I'd have died well before you found me."

Gavin nodded, not wanting to agree with him out loud. "Do you remember that first day?"

Grant shook his head slowly, trying to clear the cobwebs.

"You never told us how you survived or how exactly you ended up like this," said Maria, never one to beat around the bush.

Taking a larger-than-average bite of his muffin, it took some work before he could swallow and speak. "It's hard to explain or even believe, I guess."

Gavin and Maria locked eyes. "I don't think we'll have trouble keeping up. Believability has a wider range in our world," Maria said, smiling at him with a nod to go on.

Grant, searching for a place to begin, looked lost, maybe frustrated, so Gavin jumped in first by giving him the short version of their own experience.

His muffin forgotten, Grant didn't ask one question. The shock on his face told them he had no idea another team existed to study and contain another young woman.

"I take it this is the first you're hearing about Zuri?"

Grant's face morphed from shock to anger, then finally to defeat. "I just can't believe all that was happening so close, and yet I never knew."

"You're not the only one, my friend." Maria slid him a glass of orange juice.

"Thanks." Grant stared at the table, lost in a whole new world of thoughts.

After a few moments of grace, Gavin pulled him back to the present. "Before you passed out, you told us a few things about what happened to you. Like the glass around Lexi shattering after she woke up. And that two other doctors worked with you, Madison and Gray?"

He nodded as memories blurred his vision. "When I came too from the surprise glass explosion, I wasn't badly injured. Just stunned. I saw Lexi getting up and I tried to get to the lab door to find help, but there was this rage in her eyes." He paused, recalling each detail. "I tried to tell her who I was, but she was so incensed… it looked like… I mean, she was just enraged. She swept her arms in front of her. I didn't understand what she was doing, but I suppose I didn't really have time to because I was immediately thrown back against the wall."

Maria and Gavin leaned in, hanging on his every word.

"I woke up shortly after. As I tried to get myself to the medical bay, I found her in the hallway. Madison was there too. Both lay on the floor as if some invisible force had also knocked them out. Thankfully they were breathing. I didn't have much strength, but I decided to grab Lexi and drag her to the medical bay with me."

"Why not Madison?"

He knew that question was coming. "I guess I thought if I could get Lexi to the med bay and put her back to sleep then no one else would get hurt, including her."

"Did she ever wake up?"

"Yes. And when she did, she was actually pretty calm. Confused, yes, but she wasn't angry anymore."

"Was she hurt?" Maria wondered, looking off, trying to imagine the scene.

"Not critically. The toxicity from the Cease Protocol made her skin feel like it was on fire, not to mention the glass cut her up pretty bad too, but otherwise, she seemed okay. I gave her an injection to ease the pain of the side effects. Once that was done, my own injuries took me down." He shook his head as if trying to remember what happened next. "I don't have a lot of clarity after that. I do know that at one point I woke up and my head was on her lap. She was bent over me, tears falling down her cheeks. There was this…." His voice became a whisper as if trying to come up with the right words.

Maria leaned forward even more.

"It was like a vibration? Like an electrical pulse. I could feel it spread through my body."

"Coming from her?" Gavin asked. His eyes skirted to Maria. He could see on her face she too was thinking about the story Gavin's mother shared about his sister.

"I mean, I was pretty out of it, but yeah. I think so." He looked up at Gavin. "All I know is after that, every pain in my body eased and I must've blacked out. When I woke up, she was gone."

"Any idea where she went?" Maria knew the answer.

"Wish I did. It's not like she would've known where she

was or where to go. But she was gone," he said, looking down at the muffin. "When my eyes finally opened, I regretted waking up, the pain was so bad. I managed to slide over to a drawer where the staff kept snacks. And there was water at the sink, only I must've passed out after every attempt because I'd wake up in different parts of the room not knowing how I got there. At least, until I heard a man's voice from out in the hall." He raised his eyebrows at Gavin.

"That would be me."

"I'd been lying on a cot, sore and disoriented when I decided to get up. Fortunately, I accidentally knocked over the IV machine. No doubt you heard that. Standing up made me dizzy and I ended up on my knees, out of sight. I heard you go past the room, so I tried to reach the door. I only remember you hoisting me up after that."

Gavin stood, pacing the cafeteria floor. Maria watched as he internally analyzed all the new information through his manic walking marathon. She didn't want to interrupt, but he was making her dizzy circling the tables.

She started to open her mouth when he finally launched his initial thoughts, "So Lexi's alive, somewhere and somehow. You, a woman named Madison, and another guy named Gray have been watching over her all these years the same way we have." He looked at Gavin for confirmation. When Gavin nodded, he continued, "Madison, she was still here when everyone else had left?"

"Yes. The last I saw her, she was lying in the hallway, but since you haven't seen yer, I have to believe she either got out with Lexi , or is still somewhere in this building."

"Or with the rest of VISP who are missing," Maria offered.

Gavin nodded, then changed direction again. "So, Lexi had been moving on her own, or capable of it for how long?"

"At least a year. We had to force her body not to move to keep Jones from making us…." Grant's voice trailed off, remembering those final moments. "The intense pressure of keeping her still in that containment unit was doing something to her physically. We didn't notice right away because it started around her abdomen, which was covered by her gown."

"What do you mean?" Maria asked.

"Hard to explain. And we didn't notice until it began spreading above her neckline." Maria shifted in her seat. She had a feeling she knew where this was going.

"These purple lines were spreading from her stomach like—"

"Vines?"

His eyes caught hers in question. "Yeah. How did you know?"

Maria looked at Gavin, then back to Grant. "Zoey. Zoey had the same thing, only it stopped as if a perfect line had been vertically drawn down the center of her body. None of the vines went past that point."

Grant's mouth hung open.

"It was only on her right side," Maria noted. "I remember Zuri saying that Zoey was looking for the woman with ocean eyes."

"That's Lexi. Lexi's eyes are the brightest blue you've ever seen. The vines were only on her left side. Same thing. Perfect line. Ocean eyes."

"What would cause something like that?" Gavin wasn't looking at them when he asked. He was inside his own head. "I mean. They weren't related, and," he shifted his sight to Maria, "Zoey wasn't in here, right? We know that for sure?"

"No, she came in with two other men, Joe and Aidan. And to be fair, we don't actually know they aren't related, do we?" Maria stated.

"True," Gavin paused long enough to consider her point before continuing his marathon pace.

He offered no more insight, just continued walking until Grant asked, "So you haven't heard from your friends since they were taken?"

With a deep sigh, Maria sat back in her chair and said, "The people that took them, or at least we believe they're the same people, have reached out to us several times over the radio."

"So they're alive?"

"We don't know. We haven't responded. Until Maria's ankle is a little more stable, we don't want to be put in a position where she can't escape."

Grant gently nodded, then shook his head left to right as if suddenly realizing that understanding the scope of this was well beyond what his groggy mind could handle.

After a few moments of silence, Maria asked, "Grant, you guys were on the top floor, right? Why would they have given you a protocol to end her life when you clearly had less security than we had? It doesn't sound like they thought she was as much of a threat as Zuri."

Before Grant could answer, Gavin cut in, "Fear. Control." He stopped pacing and looked at them. "Maria, we never had to use the pressure that way with Zuri. She didn't remotely pose any threat of movement until she was physically standing upright. And at that point, it just happened."

"Based on your timeline, it sounds like Zuri woke up when Gray locked in the cease switch."

"You mean he tried to murder her?" growled Maria.

Grant couldn't deny it. He also hated his fellow coworker for it, but her words made him flinch as if she were accusing him.

Gavin put his hand on her shoulder and asked, "Zuri… she just knew then? I mean, how?"

"I don't know, but that has to be what happened."

Maria's head jerked up, "There wasn't any catalyst for it inside our lab, Gavin. One minute she was unconscious. The next standing upright."

Grant's injuries were making his hands shake involuntarily. "Think of it like this. Twins had been studied for years before the grid failed. Research showed countless instances where twins were able to *feel* when their sibling was in trouble, hurt, or needed them. Like a mother's instinct, right? There are many unexplainable scenarios where it should not have been possible for one person to know what another is going through, yet it's happened."

"So, we're saying they had these *instincts*, just in a more heightened state."

"Yeah. I believe so," Grant agreed. "After all, we know that their brainwaves function on a higher plane, at a higher caliber than the rest of us."

"Think about the brainwave monitors," Maria said, turning to Gavin. "We would see spikes on the output as if she was running a mental marathon, yet nothing but her eyelids would be moving."

Gavin continued to pace, half listening when suddenly he

switched gears. "Everyone in the building. You said you don't know where they went?" His words were almost accusatory.

"No," Grant replied, shifting positions to ease the growing pain. "Most likely, they used the extension stairwell because that was our protocol should we lose control of Rose, eh, Lexi."

"Extension stairwell?" Gavin's eyes almost popped out of his head.

Grant raised an eyebrow and tilted his head. "Yes?"

Gavin twisted back to Maria and shouted, "I knew it! I knew there was a hidden stairwell."

"Well, yeah. That's the protocol. Though, I've never been in it, considering it was only to be used in an emergency."

"How come his team had that plan and we didn't?" Maria couldn't believe they gave his team a way out as a fail-safe, and she, Gavin, and Justin were left for dead.

"They had to believe Zuri was more dangerous. Look at the facts. We were underground, buried in the furthest reaches of the compound. Our security was triple what Grant's was, yet we weren't given an out. But why?"

"Where was Zuri found?" Grant asked. "You know, before she was brought here?"

"Supposedly at a nuclear power plant in North Carolina," Maria offered.

Grant's eyes popped open. "So was Lexi. Do you know where she was at the plant?"

Gavin grabbed hold of a chair and leaned forward. "She was outside the facility, blown about twenty yards back from the building. Lexi?"

"Inside, but there was an untouched circle around her that the blast didn't touch." His breathing was shallow.

"Wouldn't that make her stronger than Zuri? Having survived inside the blast itself?" Maria wondered aloud.

"Unless they believed Zuri was the one that protected her," Gavin answered.

Then, in unison, Gavin and Maria said, "Justin."

"Justin?"

"He was the other doctor on our team we told you about. He had known the girls personally before they ever arrived here. Maybe he had more influence over the program with Jones than we knew."

"Good Lord, I need a drink. This is a lot to process," muttered Grant, leaning back in his chair and gingerly rocking in thought.

Maria leaned over, pulled a bottle from her bag, and lifted it high. "To ease your brain pain," she declared before pouring him a finger of it as he stared at the glass in amazement.

"You've got to be kidding."

The corner of Gavin's mouth kicked up. "Yeah, she does that."

Bringing the conversation back around, Gavin said, "So you've never been in the extension stairwell?"

"No," choked Grant, trying to handle the heat of the liquor like a big boy.

"Yesterday, I saw a bloody fingerprint on the wall across from the twentieth-floor door. There's an indent in the wall but I couldn't figure out its purpose."

"I only know there should be a small button. You have to hold it in for so many seconds for it to trigger."

Gavin breathed out a sigh of frustration. He knew he felt a button, only nothing happened when he pressed it.

"Wait, is the twentieth floor the only access?" asked Maria.

"Honestly, I don't know. It was our access point, but it would make sense there'd have to be more, right?"

"Do you know where it leads?" asked Gavin.

He shook his head. "We asked that question early on and were told the details weren't of consequence. Just that the guards would guide us to a safe zone when the time arrived."

"Dammit, Jones!" Maria's voice echoed through the cafeteria, causing both men to jump.

Gavin put his hand on her shoulder as she expressed what he was already thinking. "The man kept more secrets than Al Pacino in *The Godfather*."

"Okay, I'm going back up," said Gavin. "We don't know if or when the people who took Justin might return for us. We need answers and options."

Grant started to stand up.

"Nope." Maria put her hand out to stop him. "You're more broke than I am. You're staying put."

Grant froze, surprised by her forceful tone.

"She's right. You won't be any good to me if I have to carry you again." His body was still sore from the last expedition. "Just stay on the radio. I'll keep you posted as I go."

Gavin hugged Maria. "I'm finding us some answers today."

Grabbing his bag, Gavin took off out the door. Before climbing the stairs, he looked at the wall across from the stairwell door on level two. Remembering roughly where the fingerprint was on the wall on twenty, he felt around, searching for anything out of place. Nothing.

Climbing to three, then four, he still couldn't see or feel anything out of place. "Ugh! Talk about ridiculous," he growled.

The twentieth floor cannot be the only access. That seems an incredibly illogical place for the only access to an escape route.

As he climbed, he thought about floor twelve. *It would have to have an opening, right? After all, that's where all the bigwigs reside.*

Encouraged by the thought of a secret entrance on twelve, he maneuvered the platform at level five with only a passing glance at the wall. As he climbed onto the first step toward floor six, his mind registered something slightly off.

Stepping back down, he assessed the wall.

There it was.

A subtle shadow, but he could see it. Calmly, he swiped his hand across the wall and sure enough there was a small indent with a button that no one passing by would ever notice. It was the same color as the wall, flat, with a matte white, unreflective paint, and only about as round as a BB.

When he pushed it in this time, he held his finger there for five long seconds. His heart rate climbed as beads of sweat formed on his forehead. Then it happened. His wish was granted with a high-pitched, pneumatic hissing sound.

The entire wall section separated itself inward before sliding sideways on a rail. Standing motionless for several long seconds, he listened for anything out of the ordinary: voices, movement, anything. Nothing.

Poking his head in, he saw a slender stairwell that mirrored the one he'd just come up. He'd believed Grant, but seeing it in person vindicated his previous thoughts. Maybe they would find everyone after all.

Turning down the volume on his radio, he whispered, "Maria, do you read me?"

"What did you find? Did you find anyone?"

"Not yet, but I found the stairwell. Grant was right. Looks like it goes all the way to the main floor on up to twenty."

"Why are you whispering?" she whispered.

"Because I don't know what to expect here. Why are you whispering?"

"Cause you are! Alright. Don't go any further. Come get me and we'll check it out together. I don't want you going by yourself."

"Uh, yeah, no. Listen, I'm currently on the fifth floor. From here I'll work my way down. I'll let you know what I find. If you don't hear from me in fifteen, yeah, there might be a problem."

"Fine. But if anything looks sketchy, come back immediately!"

Rolling his eyes, he whispered, "Yes, ma'am."

"Don't roll your eyes at me!"

He stared at his radio. *How does she do that?*

Clipping the radio to his belt, he pulled out his flashlight. There were low lights spread out along the stairwell, only bright enough to see where your feet should go. He flashed his light up into the corners of the ceiling, looking for cameras or any sort of security that would give him away. It didn't take long. A camera in the far corner registered him the moment the door had opened. Secret agent, he was not. It was too late to step out of view, so instead, he got closer to inspect. There were no obvious LEDs to clue him in on their current status, and, besides, no doubt the door would have triggered an alarm somewhere. After a minor inspection, he decided to press on.

Gavin stopped at every landing on his way down to listen. It wasn't until he was on the main floor that he found the mechanisms for another door to open directly back into the main stairwell. Another escape point.

Looking around from his position, there were two options. The first was a hallway wrapping behind the staircase and down the side of the building. He followed until he got to the corner where it turned. After another fifteen feet, the hall ended, and his light beam showed a door on the exterior wall. Giving it a hefty push, daylight flooded over him.

Okay, so at least we have an alternate way out.

Turning back, he jogged along the hallway to the stairs. His second option was a set of stairs that wound below the main floor, though it was difficult to see how far.

"I haven't heard a peep out of you," said Maria, her irritated voice crackling over the line.

Instead of responding, he pushed a glowing button on the wall. Immediately the door hissed and shifted in towards him, then rolled to the side. He took one step into the main floor stairwell landing and opened the door to the ground floor foyer.

A cursory look around told him the foyer was just as empty as it had been the day before. And the day before that. He picked up his radio and broke the silence. "I'm on the main floor, but the stairs continue downward. I'm going to see how far they go."

"Like hell you are!" Maria's voice punched through his radio. "Absolutely not! I gave you your time. Come get me right now!"

He looked around the quiet foyer, then down the silent stairwell. "There's no one here, Maria. It's a ghost town. I'm only going to check it out. I'll keep you posted."

After a long pause, Grant responded, "Just so you know, she

slapped the radio into my hand and is currently hobbling toward the stairwell. I don't know whether to be scared for me or you."

"Oh geez. Stop her, please!" Gavin considered returning but opted to give Grant a chance. Whether now or later, he knew full well the wrath of the dragon would be waiting for him.

Gavin had just begun to move when her barely refrained rage came through the radio, "Fine. According to Grant, we're too broken to keep up, and for as many days as we've been here without another human being to consider… if you even… if that… when you get…." He could hear the deep breathing technique she used when she was irritated coming through the speaker. "Ahem, I have decided to allow you this opportunity to explore free of distraction."

There were so many ways he considered responding, but he chose the least likely to get him maimed later. "Yes, ma'am."

The mirror design of the hidden staircase was a bit disorienting, fostering a heavy sense of deja vu. At each of the D floor landings was a hidden door access. His personal key card opened none of them, but Jones' did. On the D4 platform, his eyes followed the stairwell continuing beyond what should've been the final floor.

He put his radio to his lips and said quietly, "There's a fifth subfloor."

"A what?" she said, standing up so quickly that her chair rolled away from her.

"As in a D5 level."

"How would we not know that? How would anyone even get there?"

"I guess through this stairwell. Unless…" he hesitated, thinking it over. "Unless Jones' elevator was able to reach D5, maybe? None of the regular stairwells descend this far.”

Gavin's radio crackled again before going quiet.

“Gavin? Are you able to enter D5?

“No. It's not opening the same way as the others,” he said, sounding winded. After several more deep breaths, he said, “I'm coming up. There's got to be another way in.”

Chapter 13
The Four of Us

Jahnsen and Phil stood just outside the room where Madison and the others were bunking. They didn't want to disturb what was happening within, but in truth, hoped to catch any part of the conversation inside.

"Seems like the more time they're together, the less they're telling us," whispered Phil, his arms crossed over his chest with his head angled toward the door.

"Even Madison. She's hardly said a word." Heat climbed Jahnsen's neck as his heel thudded to the ground in frustration. "Jones had ulterior motives for giving us Zuri's information instead of Rose's—"

"Lexi," Phil cut in.

Jahnsen's eyes ticked up at his longtime friend and

teammate. "Right. Lexi."

"We can't stay here...."

"Our apartment...."

"What if...."

"No! There's no time...."

Both men froze as snippets of breathy whispers seemed to intensify.

Phil shifted his weight from foot to foot. He had just opened his mouth when it happened.

The vibration. The hum. It was years ago, but a sensation they'd never forgotten.

"It's them." Turning, Jahnsen grabbed the handle and, in two swift steps, was inside the room with Phil on his heels.

All four girls turned their crystalline eyes toward their interruption.

Justin sat holding Lexi's hand with Aidan and Joe standing nearby when the door whipped open. Getting to his feet, Justin and the other two instinctively formed a human wall in front of the girls.

Jahnsen stepped forward, though no one else moved a muscle. "What's going on? Is everything okay in here?" The question lingered awkwardly for a moment. No one spoke.

"Yeah. We're good," said Madison, clearing her throat. "Just catching up, I guess you could say."

Jahnsen, fed up with the silent treatment, didn't relent. After all, he'd saved them. All of them. And the pressure in the room made it clear they weren't just catching up. "Maddy, what's going on? It's been a week. We need to sit down and talk. All of us."

"Good point. Very true," said Justin, holding firm. "However, my friends are still in that building. Why haven't they been rescued? Why does it seem like you're not telling us what's really happening in there?"

Jahnsen's cheeks grew a deeper shade of red as he shook his head at the accusatory tone in Justin's voice. "Look, we can't get them to answer. We've tried all different frequencies. My men haven't been able to breach the doors and—"

"So blow it open."

"*Aaand* we only want to use explosives as a last resort."

"Okay, well then, have someone bring me out there. I can radio them from outside the building and have them look through a window, for cripe-sakes. Once they see me, they'll open the doors. They don't know what's happened to us. For all they know, we're dead! Ever think of that? Of course they won't open the doors for *you*."

"You know," growled Jahnsen through his teeth, "we spent years planning to get Lexi out of there and to safety. The least you could do is—."

"Hold on," said Madison, her voice fresh as if renewed with a sense of hope. "You already know I got out of the building through a covert entrance. I can get Justin back in the same way. We should be able to avoid any unwanted contact that way."

"If there's anyone there to come into contact with," Justin added.

"Madison…" Jahnsen softened his tone and relaxed his balled fists. "You can't go back out there. These episodes you're having, they could happen at any time." She could see that he was worried about more than her mysterious incidents—he worried about losing her altogether. After all, she was one of the four.

"Enough," said Zoey, calm yet confident. Her gentle demeanor startled the men standing firm, causing their human wall to split just enough for Jahnsen and Phil to lay eyes on her. "As long as Justin is with her, she'll be safe. You're right, though. We do need to sit down first. All of us. No more secrets. We need to lay all our cards on the table to figure out what to do next."

"Exactly—" Jahnsen breathed as Madison interrupted.

"Exactly why you need to start preparing a small unit to come with Justin and me to find Gavin and Maria. In the meantime, we'll clean up and rendezvous at noon in the war room."

Jahnsen opened his mouth, but the look on her face muted him. He might be older, more experienced, and the senior leader of LIMIT, but she currently held all the cards. And he knew it.

The sound of a mattress creaking behind them broke the silence. Zuri had sat up on her own and was scanning the room slowly from one face to the next. Pulling her legs to the edge of the bed, she carefully pushed her feet down to the floor. Aidan's eyes grew wide, shocked that she was moving.

"No," her airy voice stole their attention. "It's alright." She tilted her head back to look at the ceiling while taking in a deep breath. The entire room remained silent.

Carefully, she edged off the bed into a standing position, stiff like a mummy, complete with all the bandages covering her body; had it been a party or a typical hangout, the others might have chuckled watching her jerky movements.

"Only seven days after being struck by fourteen bullets and

she's walking on her own," whispered Aidan, surprisingly short on sarcasm. "And smiling too."

"We need a plan. I'll be ready in a few days, so we'll need a real plan to find the broken girl hurting Madison."

Lexi rose and gently placed her hand on Zuri's back, trying not to disclose her own shock at the immense power at work in her sister. "Tomorrow," she said, speaking first to Zuri and then to the entire room.

Zuri gave her sister a questioning look as if unaware of her own physical status.

"Tomorrow, Zuri. You need rest, and we… we need some time to digest the fact that you're up and moving right now."

Chapter 14
Thomas

"I've been over every inch for miles. There's nothing. No clues, no hints. Like I said, I've been over it." Joanna's zillionth question about the woods where her sister was taken, combined with the pain from his leg, had begun to do a number on him. She watched as he continuously wiped large beads of sweat from his forehead that had formed shortly after launching into their hike, worried that he would collapse at any moment. Still, he didn't complain.

His willingness to press on only temporarily eased her frustration that she'd had to wait another twenty-four hours before finally doing something productive.

"So what are we doing here then?" she snapped, stamping her feet, clearly reaching the end of her much smaller supply of patience. "You said you thought you had a lead. Why aren't we going there?"

"Joanna—"

"It's been a week! Anything could be happening to her!"

"Jo—"

"We should be—"

"Anna, stop! Look, Thomas may not know where they are, but he's heard stories. I haven't talked to him in months. Who knows? Maybe he's heard something new." Turning back toward her, he looked exhausted, not mad, as she'd expected. "Did I mention he also has supplies we'll need?"

"I…" she began to say before catching herself. The momentary look of desperation in his eyes took her breath away. Realizing there wasn't a hint of malicious intent in his actions, she took a deep breath then simply said, "Okay."

"We still have a ways to go. His place is on the other side of the creek." His unwavering stare caused an unfamiliar bubble of longing to well up in her chest. After a few exaggerated heartbeats, she broke the connection, shuffled forward, and waved him on. "And don't call me Anna."

"Got it," he said, chuckling.

Their trek took another three hours, done mostly in silence. She figured it probably didn't usually take him that long, but his leg hindered their progress. How he was still moving, she had no clue. Her own feet throbbed, though the pain helped her avoid the awful thoughts running through her mind until she saw the double-wide covered in vines and hidden behind overgrown brush just off the path. Nervously she pulled her hair out of its messy bun as if to cool down, only to throw it back up moments later willy-nilly. *Oh god… his friend Thomas has got to know something. Unless... what if it's him? What if he's in on it too?*

Sucking in a deep breath, she straightened her back, pursed her lips, and caught up with Brandon. She didn't want whoever was in that mobile home to look outside and see a weak little girl.

"Alright, let's do this," she said.

Joanna had concocted an entire life-or-death, guns-blazing, dramatic hostage-taking scenario on the short walk up to the shanty. To her surprise, they were met by a giant shaggy dog bounding out from the man's front door. It joyfully greeted her by knocking her to the ground and attacking her with slobbery licks. This was not how it played out in apocalyptic movies. The dog never *licked* a stranger to death.

"Luna, give 'em a break, would ya?" Thomas met them with a handshake and a beer. The beers looked like they had been sitting in a bunker for the last decade. Raised to be polite, she motioned to her water bottle. He obliged her by topping it off. Brandon flashed her a warning glance to let him navigate the conversation. She nodded in submission, quietly letting them catch up, listening intently for any red flag Thomas might reveal. Yet, every word showed him to be reliable.

Sitting on her hands to keep from fidgeting, Joanna waited while Brandon took his sweet time loving on Thomas's dog, Luna, to keep her from roughing up his bad leg.

"Sure you don't want anything for that leg of yours? I've got some painkillers in the back."

"Nah, I'm good. Need to stay clear-minded. This beer

should help some." His smile was forced and Thomas picked up on it.

"Well, you're not here to see how interesting my life has been," his gaze traveled over to Joanna. "So let's get to the meat of it. What're you fishing for?"

Brandon nodded toward Joanna. "Her sister," he said, with a subtle sadness that caught her attention.

"Taken?"

"Bout a week ago, out by the Harris Plant. Right after this happened," he said, pointing to his leg.

Thomas winced at the thought of the bear trap. "Honestly surprised you haven't stomped on more of those over the years. Lost a few dogs that way."

Joanna flinched at the image.

"Thought we'd see if you'd heard anything lately? Run into any new news?"

He shook his head from side to side slowly. "Haven't heard much, but..." he paused then glanced back over at Joanna, "somethin's been happenin' lately. Not sure if it'll help y'all, but might mean more to you than me."

Joanna leaned forward as his southern twang forced her to pay attention to every word, not wanting to miss a thing.

"Anything's better than nothing, brother. What's going on?"

Drumming on her knees, she continued leaning in, nearly falling out of her chair when Luna snuggled up, panting and pushing.

"I drove down to Sanford for supplies a month or so ago, and... well, hey, you remember that guy Joe we met a while back? Helped me with some tech stuff to keep strays off my property?" Brandon nodded. "I ran into him. He was stocking up. Said they were goin' on a trip. Zoey, the dark-haired girl he lives with, and the hyper one, Aidan, were both with him. She had a hoodie on zipped up to her neck. Which was weird cause it was hot as blazes. Anyway, when she turned, I saw something strange. Like purple lines zigzaggin' across her face. Weirdest thing I ever seen."

Joanna had no clue what this had to do with anything and her drumming grew faster and louder.

"Said they were headed to Pennsylvania. Had a job up there on the tenth but didn't share much else."

Seriously? What is this? Story hour with Uncle Redneck?

"And then the other day, there was this strange, uh..." he said, looking back and forth between Brandon and Joanna with a hushed voice, "You might think I'm crazy."

Might? Might! You're talking about running errands!

"Well, I don't even know what to call it, but there was a moment when everything seemed to go silent. No critter squawks, gruffs, or growls. Heck, even the breeze seemed to take a break. Luna picked up on it, so I don't think I was dreamin', you know?" He looked at Brandon, gauging his response.

Brandon scrunched his eyebrows, squinting, considering the strange story. "Well, what do you think it was?"

Shrugging his shoulders, Thomas shook his head, saying, "Not sure. Felt familiar. The last time I felt something like that was back when the power plant blew. Just before it happened, everythin' just stopped for a few seconds."

Brandon cocked his head to the side. "Yeah. I think I recall that. Never gave it much thought."

"Funny thing 'bout it though, that was the tenth." His brows came together, waiting for his old friend to laugh. When one didn't come, his forehead smoothed. "Just thought it a bit strange, is all."

Brandon gave a noncommittal *hmph* in response.

Thomas got to his feet somewhat slowly for a guy in his forties. Pain flashed over his face as he straightened his back. "Ya know," he stopped mid-motion and turned back. "I took Luna out fishin' the other day. Down around by the creek. Little White. Know the place?"

"Yeah, the old fire training area?"

"Yep, yep. I noticed the roads over that way had been driven on pretty heavily. Thought I heard some folks, so I got a little closer to check it out. Didn't see anyone, but it also didn't look the way a building does when the forest takes it back, you know?"

"Is Oakley still out that way?"

"Not sure. Been some time since I saw him."

Brandon's shoulders tensed, but he managed to hide it pretty well by taking his time to stand up. Nodding, he said, "Well, thanks, Tom. I'm not sure what any of it means, but can't hurt to check it out." He put out his hand to shake his old friend's.

"Yeah, yeah, every bit helps." Turning toward Joanna. "Sorry about your sister, young lady. If anyone can help, Brandon can."

His large hand enveloped her small one in a surprisingly gentle way. "Thank you, Thomas. I really appreciate that."

"Call me Tom, ma'am." He went to release her hand and stalled a half-beat too long when the light caught Joanna's eye and sparkled. The sight reminded him of the last time he saw Zoey.

She gave him a quick and awkward smile, unsure how to take the look on his face. Shaking his head, he let go of her hand and grinned back, looking slightly confused before stepping back.

She'd arrived expecting hostility and was now leaving, having met one of the nicest people she'd come across in years.

"Oh, I almost forgot." He turned the code on a lock and opened a cabinet that looked well secured to the wall. "Just in case you need 'em, I picked these up from Woody's the other day." He handed her a small pistol and a box of rounds, then another box of a different caliber to Brandon.

Joanna was shocked. Having had a gun years ago, it had long since run out of ammo. They weren't easy to find if you could find them at all.

"Serious? Woody from the rifle shop?" he said with a smirk. "How the heck did he come across these?"

"He has his ways, I guess." Then, shifting his eyes and waving them to lean in close, he whispered, "I think he's building them in his basement at his place over in Broadway."

"Our lucky day then." Brandon's nod of gratitude seemed to be more than enough payment for Thomas. She couldn't believe his kindness. She would've had to give someone a kidney to get this up in Ohio.

They gave Luna a final pat and headed out the door. Before Brandon could step away, Thomas touched his arm. When Brandon looked back, Thomas quietly said, "Did you notice her eyes? The brightness reminds me of the spark I saw in

Zoey's that day in town. I've never seen that before. You?"

Brandon shook his head then looked out the door at Joanna walking back to the woodline. "No. I haven't."

Neither man said another word about it.

A few minutes of silence back on the trail was all Joanna could muster. "So what do we do now? Where do we go? It sounds like that fire department place he was talking about, Little White, I think, could lead us somewhere. Who's Oakley?" Joanna wanted to take off at a sprint for wherever it was. If she had any idea at all which way to go, she'd have already left.

"It's not a fire department."

Joanna's head shook, confused. "What?"

"The FTA is where fire departments trained newbies to put out fires. They also had a shooting range out there."

Brandon turned his head and caught her annoyed eye.

Bringing the topic back to Oakley, he said, "Thomas met him in town after the grid failed. He was in the military at one point, just like Tom. Didn't know each other then, but common ground made all the difference when the world changed." Pausing to look east and then west as he spoke, slowly taking it all in. "Oakley took over the FTA early on with a few other guys." He stopped and looked up at the trees.

"Why are we stopped? Shouldn't we be going out there?"

At first, he didn't respond. Joanna's cheeks flushed as she clenched her teeth.

"We are. But I can't get there like this," he said, looking down at his leg. "We need to drive."

"Okay. Let's drive then. Where's your car?"

"That is what I'm trying to determine," he said slowly.

"I stashed one about a mile from here two years ago, just in case."

"Keys. Give me the keys! I'll go and bring it back so you don't have to walk." Anything to get him moving faster.

"I would if I had directions to give," he said, scanning the trees.

Her hands were up and her fingers bidding him to toss her the keys when she saw his eyes open wide, the way a child does when a birthday present lands in their lap.

"Got it. That way," he said, pointing nearby at a spot about ten feet up a tree at an oddly shaped arrow notched into the bark.

Chapter 15
Not Alone

Iron Prison | August 18, 2029 | 4:18 a.m.

Janice, along with several other women, huddled around Addie in a corner of the room. They instinctively felt the need to protect her. Whether it was because she was the newest capture or that her abuse surpassed theirs, it wasn't clear.

Addie's mind was foggy as the pressure in her head squeezed her temples like a vice grip. Her memories jumbled together. She had blacked out after the first hit to the head by her abductor. The few flashes of memory she had were inside a dark, dirt-lined tunnel with broken concrete. The more she tried to remember, the worse the pressure.

Every day the brutal monsters would pull her out of the cell, no longer by her hair as they'd long since shaved her head. Once they passed through the iron doorway, everything changed. The cave transformed into a regular building. They would push her down a dingy, white hallway to an empty, windowless room. In fact, there were no windows anywhere that she'd seen. Though she couldn't be sure, she guessed they were underground.

The monsters called it the "practice room." Across from where they tied her up was a one-way mirror. She felt them watching as they pushed her mentally and physically to the edge and beyond. She'd only seen this type of militarized torture in R-rated movies she was too young to watch but managed to finagle before the grid failed. Whatever game they were playing, they wouldn't explain the rules. In fact, they didn't explain anything.

One or two men would come in with her. They didn't hide their faces, which meant they never intended to release her. Except for one man, his face was always covered. He occasionally joined in only to stand in a corner, arms crossed, staring at her as the others alternated between physical and mental abuse. She might have risked creating a plan to call 911 if it hadn't long since been disbanded. Along with the police, the national guard, and every other public safety organization. She was alone, and she knew it.

They spent their time trying to get something from her, to draw it out of her in the most horrific ways. Had she known what they wanted, she might have given it to them. But she didn't. So, she just kept repeating that she wasn't anyone to them. That she was a nobody.

As she drifted to the edge of sleep, huddled in the corner and surrounded by women who meant well, the darkness behind her tightly-closed eyelids exploded with colors. Adeline had a passing, half-awake thought that this was what delirium felt like. The colors swirled around her, weaving their way from one woman to another as they huddled by her side. The image made her smile, causing a wave of warmth to ride up her spine and settle in her mind as deep comfort. Seeing them in this manner, with her eyes closed, she knew she must be dreaming.

Through the mist of colors, a vision of Joanna's pleading face appeared. Her sister was searching for her. Only she wasn't alone. Beside her were the faces of several others. Women she'd never met yet somehow knew. And they were determined.

Before the darkness of sleep fully consumed her, all of their faces, including Joanna's, melded together until they were one being, strong, full of color and life. Then their eyes opened.

Two beautiful, glowing eyes.

A prism of light emanated from them, hitting her in the chest. So bright. So fierce. She shuddered at the sight.

The eyes could see her. This person, this band of women, knew her.

I'm not alone, she thought, before succumbing to a deep sleep and wild dreams.

Dreams

No moonlight, just darkness, dirt, silence—except for the occasional bleat of a goat. They held onto one another. Muck and sweat covered their skin. The smell of male body odor nearby. They could feel something coming for them. Scared. Not of what was coming, but what they sensed followed behind.

Each of their memories sourced from a different perspective, yet all filled with adrenaline and fear.

Zoey and Madison had been injected with a fluid that made

them drowsy. Instead of lulling them to sleep, it simply left their bodies listless as their little minds spun in terror.

Lexi and Zuri weren't injected. There wasn't time. The woman that grabbed them simply snatched them from their patch of dirt, huddled against the cinder block wall, cold and shivering.

Joanna and Adeline, wide awake and struggling to hold one another tight, were pulled apart. Simultaneously, another girl curled up beside Addie was hoisted into the arms of a giant. A flickering light illuminated the dirt in another empty corner of the room as if someone was missing. One of them had been taken several nights before and never returned.

They floated through the dark in silence until they heard a cry from the shadows. Not the cry of a child but a man bellowing in the distance. Cracks and flashes of gunfire like thunder and lightning filled the air. Screams and shouts assaulted their ears. All the while, they floated along, curled up and carried by these strange adults.

A man ahead of Zuri and Lexi carried the girl with evergreen eyes and dirty blond hair under his arm like a football. He struggled to keep her small frame to his side, out of the way, while shielding each of their little bodies from the spray of bullets. Suddenly he fell backward, almost knocking them down. He was hurt. He fell with the girl in his arms and didn't get back up.

Still floating, it was pitch black. Silence returned except for heavy breathing and the thud of running feet. The woman carrying Lexi and Zuri kept running. Her arms were tired, and her grip was growing weak. They laid their heads on either side of her shoulders, tightening their hold. She seemed to run faster as a result, as though their touch gave her strength.

Swiftly, though gently, they dropped to the ground. The sand was gritty under their little fingers, sticking to their sweaty legs. Clouds of sand swirled around them and their hair whipped in the wind. The galloping thump of a helicopter in the distance pricked up their little ears and brought hope. They could feel one level of tension ease as a greater wave of panic took its place.

The sting of the blowing sand on open skin brought them together, holding one another tight, shielding each other from the sting the best they could.

Despite her quiet voice buried beneath the pounding of the helicopter, they heard the woman say, "This isn't good. The bird won't be able to fly into this!"

"They will, Doc. They're almost here!" *shouted the man next to her.*

"Addie!" Joanna gasped as a vision of her sister burst into her mind.

In a different location, Zoey, Zuri, Lexi, and Madison, each in their mind's eye, caught a vision of a grown woman: head shaved, face bloodied, body beaten. *Adeline.*

"No!" Zoey cried out. Her vision of crystalline onyx eyes penetrating her own, though quickly fading, startled her awake. A man's voice rang out in her ears as the vision faded. For the first time, she knew who it belonged to. *Jahnsen.* It was Jahnsen who was there when they were saved. *Doc.* He'd called the woman Doc. *Doc? It can't be.* The revelation made her weak, but the more those words circled through her mind, the clearer the woman's face became. *Younger, but the same.* Doc. *My Doc.* Dr. Sheila.

Through hazy eyes, she saw Justin asleep in the chair next to her bed. She found him hovering more and more by her side. It was odd. It was the place Joe usually occupied, but she felt comforted and at peace with Justin there. It wasn't the constant worry or anxiety that her surrogate brothers, Aidan and Joe, usually projected. This was different. And she welcomed it.

Touching his leg, his eyes opened. A smile spread across his face.

"Justin?"

"Yes, ma'am. Everything okay?"

Nodding, she asked, "Could you wake up Joe and Aidan? I need to talk to them."

He didn't ask her any questions. Didn't interrogate her concerned look. Just gingerly rose to his feet with a slight cringe from the lingering pain of the assault that brought them together.

As her eyes followed his rise from the chair, she caught the faces of the other women in the room. All sitting up. All fully in tune with one another.

When Zoey made eye contact, their hearts confirmed what their minds revealed.

It was a shared dream. They'd all felt it. Re-lived it.

And they knew without a doubt that there were others and that they needed to find them. Now.

They were in danger.

Chapter 16
The Round Table

"**O**h my gosh! I wished for this! On my tenth birthday, I one-hundred percent *dreamed* of this moment!" You could see the whites of Aidan's eyes as he slowly walked around the giant circular table.

Joe didn't miss a beat. "Knights of the round table."

It took a moment to process before laughter erupted.

"It's legit!" sputtered Madison with a snort. "That's exactly why it's round!"

Jahnsen smirked, slightly offended. "Hey, look, it was as true then as it is now. No one's fully in charge. We're all equally—what? Seriously!"

Just watching him trying to explain made them laugh harder. Shaking his head, he sat down, threw his hands up, and waited for them to get themselves together.

Half of them were hunched over, holding their ribs from the pain of their injuries. As one person regained composure, someone else lost theirs, and the cycle started again. It was hysterics level. No one had felt free to find levity since they had arrived at LIMIT. This was the moment they needed to relieve some stress before addressing their next move.

When they all calmed down, Madison was the first to speak. She took a deep breath and said, "We need to cover a lot of ground today, so let's start with our side." She nodded towards Jahnsen as a hiccup broke her composure.

Looking around the table the way an impatient father might size up his unruly children, he said, "As you know, we call ourselves LIMIT. Leading Innovative Measures In Technology. It's what our organization was called prior to the collapse of the grid. Essentially we were working on prototypes for different technologies that could be incorporated around the world during wartime events. That was our unclassified mission anyway. Within the inner circle—"

"Of the round table," Aidan said under his breath, snickering until Zoey snapped her gaze at him. "Right, sorry," he whispered.

"Our classified mission was reconnaissance of persons of interest," said Phil, stepping in. "The tech we built or modified was used in the effort. We'd explain away the tracking of individuals as test operations."

"It just so happened to coincide with the tracking of six girls we rescued in two thousand eleven." His eyes scanned the room, looking at each woman sitting there.

"Us," Zuri whispered.

"It's the dream." Zoey was looking down at her hands in her

lap. She took a deep breath and lifted her head to look at Jahnsen and Phil. "We know who you are."

"Or at least who you were," Lexi added.

Both men leaned back.

"We, uh, had a dream," Madison shared.

"Why didn't you just tell us who you were when you first came to our apartment building?" Zoey asked.

"We weren't positive it was you, and we didn't want the past to influence your decision to help us," Phil offered.

Aidan sat up in his seat. "Oh, that was a decision?"

"Sure, yes, we may have pushed for it, but ultimately you made the choice to go," Jahnsen said with a hint of guilt.

Phil cleared his throat, breaking the growing tension. "Uh, what do you mean you learned about us in a dream? As in, all of you had the same dream?"

Madison nodded. "We woke up around four this morning. It was some sort of conjoined dream with all of us in it." She was calm and professional as her eyes flickered between the other three women. "Connected, yet each of us experienced it from our individual perspectives. We stayed up afterward, kind of closing the loop on a few things."

Zoey stepped in. "And we remembered there being eight of us. Not six. From our memories, we think two girls were left behind, or...." She let her words trail off, not wanting to say it out loud.

Jahnsen and Phil glanced at one another, unsure what to make of that new information, then waited for the girls to finish.

"We know that the two of you were there," continued Lexi, seamlessly taking over as if the four of them had rehearsed what to say.

"And a woman," Zoey's voice cracked. "Doc. Our Doc. Doctor Sheila."

They expected the men to be shocked that they knew of her, but neither moved a muscle.

"Is she part of this?" Zoey asked. "Is she the reason you found me? Us?"

"In part, yes," Jahnsen offered. "She's not a member of LIMIT. We invited her years ago, but she said she wanted to live a normal life. Be a regular doctor. Help people where she could."

"You see, she was a part of your rescue mission from the very beginning. She's the one that pushed us to continue our efforts to find the lost children, especially once we'd given up hope." Phil took a breath. "Our Tier One commander didn't believe any of you would still be alive, but when intel came in that there was talk of a group of children hidden in the desert of Kandahar, she said she knew it had to be you.

"She was the reason we found you. She never gave up."

"Zoey, what do you mean there were eight of you in the dream? During the rescue, there were only seven. Unfortunately, one was lost during the mission along with the operator trying to rescue her."

Glancing at the others, Zoey replied, "We've only been able to put a few pieces together after our abduction. Somehow, Madison recalls it pretty vividly. She's filled in a lot of gaps. We were so young. Most of those memories are gone. Before we ended up out in that desert, we remember being held in some place with a lot of white walls." Her eyes squinted, straining to visualize it. "We were kept together in a room with beds. We'd huddle together on one, though, warm and safe.

"They initially would only take one of us at a time to do whatever they were doing, but—"

"I remember," cut in Lexi, turning toward Zoey and grabbing her hands. "We were on the bed shaking, cold. Zuri had fallen asleep and her head was on my leg. You were crying, so I put my arms around you. A man came in and pulled you from me. We tried to hold on, but we weren't strong enough." Zoey's breath caught in her throat as the memory began to form in her mind. "As he pulled you into the room, you screamed louder and louder. I remember I wanted to be with you so badly. I just wanted to protect you. I think I…." Lexi looked down. "I think I somehow tried to protect you. When I did, I could feel everything you were going through."

Zoey's eyes were wide and red and focused on Lexi.

"After that, they began bringing us into the room two at a time. More compliance, you know. I think it actually bonded us all the more to one another."

"And I was partnered with a different girl," said Zuri.

Lexi spun around to her sister. "That's right. Instead of pulling me in with you, they grabbed the other girl. She was so tiny. Both of you were."

"Maybe you were paired by age?" Justin offered.

Their story answered some questions but provoked even more. For a minute, the room was silent. Each one picking at the pieces in their own way.

"But there were eight of us at that time," said Madison, confident in her memory. "And there were eight of us in the desert. She wasn't there as long as the rest of us. Maybe that's why your intel only spoke of seven."

Jahnsen and Phil nodded in agreement. "Would make

sense," Phil answered.

Justin took his hand off Zoey's shoulder and placed it on the table. "Okay. So how did they end up in what sounds like a research facility, then whisked off to the desert? And what happened to the girls after you rescued them?"

Jahnsen hesitated, looked at Phil, then slowly shared, "The intel on that is not as clear. When we rotated into Afghanistan that year we were briefed on incomplete intelligence alluding to a group of abducted Western children. It wasn't clear whether they were Americans, Europeans, etc., and nothing specifying how they got there to begin with. The military had members embedded with the Afghani people. After a few months, we had enough evidence placing the children in a specific village in Kandahar. Once we had a 95 percent confirmation rate, the President approved the mission to rescue them… well, you."

"How did we get to Afghanistan, though?" Zoey's voice was barely audible and her red eyes were wide.

"We don't know. There was a Western doctor called Dr. H. We weren't able to get any good photos of him to determine his identity. He wasn't on-site when the operation went down. Our orders were to capture him, but somehow he escaped. We continued to monitor through our embedded military folks out there, but there was no chatter on him. He was a ghost."

"Alright," cut in Joe. "So what about VISP? How did they, or you, know where to send us?"

"Jones and Madison," answered Phil. "Jones was part of our team when we found you. He wasn't on the ground with us. He was an intel analyst feeding us information throughout the rescue operation. Over the years he gained rank, and when the grid failed, he was brought in as the Director of VISP. He knew what we had been doing at LIMIT, so he kept in touch. The board at VISP decided that if Lexi," his eyes skirted to Lexi and Zuri, "ever woke up, they would terminate you. Mainly due to fear of the unknown."

"I'm confused," said Madison, raising an eyebrow. "So, *did* you know Zuri was there? Why would Jones have kept me in the dark?"

"No, Madison. We only knew of Lexi." Jahnsen confirmed.

Phil added, "We knew of Lexi, but he gave us Zuri's location. He clearly had ulterior reasons for not sharing that there were two girls."

"It doesn't make sense," Justin said, shaking his head. "Not just that he didn't share information on both girls, but that everything could possibly come together like that on the same day."

Madison was slowly unraveling the answer as the words came to her, "Because Lexi was waking up. We knew we couldn't keep her subdued much longer. I fed Jones information on the side since I had no way to connect with LIMIT."

"Why only give us information to rescue Zuri in the first place? Why not both? We had the resources." Phil couldn't put the pieces together.

Madison shook her head as she processed. "I think—" she started before it struck her. When she looked up at the faces around the table, she was sure of her realization. "I think Jones believed one way or the other I'd get Lexi out. But Zuri was a different ballgame. She was so far underground, he knew it would be infinitely more difficult."

"It still doesn't explain why he wouldn't at least share the intel that both girls were in the building," Joe said.

"Maybe he thought he was protecting me? Or himself. He was already taking a risk by having me there with her. Knowing I was one of the abducted girls myself."

"Honestly, while this helps, we don't have enough insight to understand why Jones did what he did, but you're all here." Whether he intended to or not, Jahnsen's words came across as a bit of a pithy pat on the back despite the setbacks.

"Not all of us," said Lexi, staring him down.

"No. Not all of you. But that's why we're sitting here. To find the others."

Zoey nodded, though unsettled, with a tinge of suspicion growing. *What does he get out of all this?*

Their combined information was a lot to digest, and, once again, each of them sat silently, wrestling with their own thoughts.

Finally, Jahnsen broke the silence. In a low and gruff voice, he said, "Something happened out there the night we rescued you in Kandahar. There was a huge sandstorm coming in...." The women could all see that moment in their minds as he spoke. "When we got to our rally point, waiting to be picked up by the helicopter, the sandstorm was rapidly growing in strength and scale. They didn't think they'd be able to land. All of a sudden, we—" He stopped himself, not knowing how to proceed until he saw Lexi give him a nod to continue. "It looked like the sand was clearing up around us. Almost like there was a shield or a dome of clearance. Suddenly, the pilots could see us plain as day at the rally point. When we looked down at all of you, your eyes were..." He took a breath. "Well, they were glowing."

"Each of you had your glowing eyes on Zuri, and Zuri was looking up at the sky," Phil added.

"We had no way to explain it. The pilots themselves had a better visual, and what was happening could not be explained by any sort of low-pressure weather system moving in," said Jahnsen.

"So you witnessed our powers firsthand? How did we then not end up in some facility like lab rats being tested on?" blurted out Zoey, wincing as she recalled that two of them had. "I mean—"

"It's okay. We know what you meant." Lexi allayed Zoey's guilt with a subtle smile.

Jahnsen cleared his throat. "I think we just decided once we were on our way back that there was no way to logically explain what happened. We'd look crazy if we tried."

"We also realized that you had been through enough in your very short lives," said Phil. "No matter what we saw or didn't see, you all deserved a chance at a regular life."

Lexi and Zuri held hands. Their lives hadn't been normal. They hadn't experienced the love of a family. Not until Justin found them.

"Did anyone end up with their original families? Their birth parents?" Lexi's voice cracked. "Do you know where the others are now?"

The room felt warm and the air heavy as they all thought of their own families, each lost in so many different ways. "Yes. A few," said Phil, attempting to add an air of positivity. "Some of the girls' families, however, were killed during their abductions. Others, we simply couldn't find anyone they were legally tied to." His eyes settled on Zuri and Lexi.

"We tried as best we could to follow where the girls were placed. Without being too obvious, of course, since we had no way to reasonably explain why we would." Phil looked at Madison. "A guy in our unit, he and his wife adopted Madison here, which made it easy for us to watch her develop." Then to Zoey. "You had gone back to your grandmother, which was an incredible reunion."

Tears filled Zoey's eyes as her chest constricted. It was only her grandmother. Her parents were some of those killed during the abduction.

"Joanna and Adeline went back to their parents." A smile spread across Phil's face as if remembering that particular homecoming. "By some miracle, they were still alive. They had been out on a date the night the girls were taken. The babysitter was asleep in the living room as the girls were snatched right out of their beds."

Jahnsen looked at Zuri and Lexi. "They couldn't find your family. No one could. Eventually, you were medically cleared and put up for adoption. The best they could do was keep you together." He paused, thinking through the events, and just enough time for the girls to take in a deep breath in anticipation. "Doc Sheila tried to adopt both of you." Looking away, he remembered Sheila's pain when she was notified. "They denied her. She wasn't married and she was still on active duty at the time. They didn't think it was a good fit. We tried to keep up with your whereabouts, but you were no longer in our custody. They transferred you both so many times to so many different foster families...."

Everyone at the table felt it in their chest. Zuri was clenching Lexi's hand so hard neither of them had feeling left in their fingers.

"But *I* found you," said Justin, leaning toward them, his

voice wobbly with a frog in his throat. "Both of you. And we are a family." Moving in between them, he wrapped his arms around them both. Silent tears fell as he shifted back, keeping his hands on each of their shoulders. Looking around at the others in the room, he clarified, "I found them on my way home from work one day. They were hiding in some bushes. Wearing nothing but rags, dirty, and clearly hungry. As soon as I got them home, my mother called social services. She fell in love with them immediately."

Lexi and Zuri listened to him tell the story. Neither recalled how it all happened back then. They remembered living with brutal parents who weren't their own and who would, time and time again, get rid of them. They were unwanted, at least until Justin, their new brother, found them.

"Once social services determined who they were, we discovered how many homes had abandoned them." He locked eyes with Lexi. "Bobbie loved you with her whole heart the moment she laid eyes on you. There wasn't a child out there she wouldn't care for. Social services agreed to let them stay. They officially became my sisters."

Zuri furrowed her brow as a thought entered her mind. "How come you weren't scared of us like everyone else?"

"What's to be scared of? A little girl who could make mom's garden grow the sweetest, juiciest tomatoes in the county just by singing to them?" A big smile spread across his face, which triggered her own. Looking at Lexi, he said, "Or a girl who could shield her baby sister from bees trying to sting her while they sat in the grass playing with dandelions?"

Lexi gasped, remembering those moments long forgotten. "After watching Zuri get stung once while outside playing, I found a way to place an invisible bubble around us." *It's how I protected Zoey that day,* she thought. *Why we're bonded.*

"Wild, right?" he said with a laugh. "Can you imagine? Me and mom sitting on the porch watching you girls play only to notice bees bouncing backward about a foot away from the two of you. And you, without a care in the world."

"Justin finding you was how we were able to begin tracking you again. After the adoption went through, you became more discoverable in both public and government searches," said Phil.

"You two were the reason I went into neurology. The older you got, the stronger you became. Mom had to homeschool you." Justin pulled his eyes from his sisters, then spoke to everyone at the table. "They were both incredible to witness. Zuri seemed to have all this, this," he stuttered, searching for the words, "energy, or power, but with minimal control. Lexi was a natural parent to Zuri, even at a young age. Whenever she would see Zuri getting ahead of herself, Lexi's little face would scrunch up, like she's doing now, trying to determine the best way to diffuse the situation. Like a reflex. It was beautiful."

As Justin spoke, an image appeared in Phil's mind that now seemed to make sense. Clearing his throat, he said, "On the night of the rescue, I remember noticing Zuri's face as she looked up to the sky. Eyes so bright they didn't look real. Lexi sat there, arms wrapped around her, looking peaceful, almost as if she was giving Zuri approval to do what needed to be done."

"And the other girls focused on Zuri and Lexi from where they sat. Their crystalline eyes looking straight at them," inserted Jahnsen. He couldn't believe all the puzzle pieces coming together.

Madison turned to face Zuri and said, "Sitting in the dirt,

I could feel a sort of buzzing sensation in my body. Like I was getting stronger. First, I felt a vibration like the one we seem to feel when we touch one another, then almost rippling. I could feel my body lean, as if pulled, in your direction."

Zoey leaned forward, nodding in agreement.

Lexi sat up straighter in her chair and whispered, "I remember now. I told Zuri to make the dust go away."

Zoey put her hand on Lexi's. They both felt the subtle undercurrent of vibration in the touch. Their unique power resonated within each of them and all the more when together. Something they were becoming accustomed to. "We did that. Together. But Zuri," Lexi said, pausing to collect her next thought, "you are the catalyst."

Every eye in the room moved to the petite woman. Tiny despite her age. Wise despite her limited experience and education.

"So even then... even then we all had this capability, somehow we knew how to work together at our core. We would've been too young to have been trained to do that, right?"

"I knew it," Aidan said under his breath.

"Knew what?" scoffed Joe, rolling his eyes, waiting for something dumb to spew from Aidan's mouth.

Looking directly at Zoey, he said, "You *are* witches."

"Never one to disappoint," said Zoey before throwing a pen at him.

"Hey! I'm just saying. I called it, right? Am I right?" Proud of himself, he leaned back and began to throw his feet up on the table but paused, remembering the honor infused into the round table, before placing his feet back on the floor.

Joe hung his head in embarrassment while a few of the

women around the table chuckled.

Leaning forward, Lexi scanned the room as it quieted down and said, "I'm not sure about the whole witch part of it, Aidan, but we do have an idea of what each of us is capable of. To a degree, anyhow."

"We've been observing one another and sharing quite a bit over the past several days and here's what we know. I have the ability to create a sense of calm over an agitated person or group of people. When we were still at VISP, Lexi threw some sort of force at me, like an invisible wrecking ball. Instinctively, I raised my arms to brace for impact, and somehow I shielded it."

Lexi hardly remembered that moment. What she could recall came to mind in fuzzy snippets.

"Zoey has always had this ability to read a person," said Joe. "She seems to know if they're lying. Know if they're dangerous or not." Both Aidan and Justin nodded in agreement, having witnessed it themselves. "Came in handy out there on our own."

"Zuri can do quite a few things," Justin said, chiming in. "Move things with her mind, like sand in a storm. She could make things grow—"

"Which I think relates to her ability to heal," said Madison, her gaze traveling around the table to all the injured. "We've all been crammed into that one room for eight days now, and every wound is healing ten times faster than it should be."

"I'm not sure we've scratched the surface of what she can do," Justin said, merely stating what they were all thinking.

"I have always been able to reign in the things Zuri could do. Keep her from hurting herself or others." Lexi paused to look at Madison. "I'm so sorry I did that to you, Madison. I don't even know what I did."

"I promise you. It's okay." The love in her voice was earnest and eased Lexi's guilt.

Remembering the night Zoey woke up screaming, claiming that the woman she was dreaming about needed her help, Aidan said, "Don't forget, each of you is also connected in such a way that you can feel what the other is feeling. Not only that, but I think you can talk to each other at any distance. I know Zoey did."

"So, all of you have these abilities," said Joe, "yet, you're not related. Any idea how you may have gotten them?"

The ultimate question.

"You're right. It's not familial," said Lexi. "Do you think we had them from birth? Or maybe whatever was done to us when we were abducted caused it?"

No one could answer.

"What about the bonds each of you have?" Joe wondered, looking around the table.

Lexi took a deep breath and shared her earlier thoughts. "It sounds like whatever I did when we were being held captive in trying to protect Zoey, maybe I kicked off the mysterious bond we have now. The trauma of it was shared between two of us at a time. Zoey could feel what I was going through to the point she was physically affected when I was at VISP." Zoey's deep purple webbing was a mirror image of her own. It alone was the evidence of their connection. She didn't have to say that one out loud. "Madison is connected to someone not in this room, and Zuri…." Looking at her sister, she quietly said, "Zuri is different than when we were younger. You're so quiet now." Her eyes flicked to Justin. "Justin said that since you woke up, it's as if you've been in another place. Here, but not here." She held

Zuri's hands in her own. "Do you feel someone else? Are they why you're not fully here?"

Finally, Zuri, the youngest member at the round table, spoke up. "I think… that sounds right. I'm not sure. It just feels dark. Like a heaviness washing over me."

Aidan quietly made his way to Zuri as she spoke. Crouching down beside her, she turned toward him. The anxious lines around her eyes smoothed over as Aidan put his hand on hers and said, "Zuri's connection is trapped. Like she was. Wherever she is, she's unable to move, and like Lexi and Zoey, the physical part of it all is keeping her subdued. Unable to reach out, communicate, experience her true self." His eyes searched hers as if genuinely seeing answers the rest of them could not. "I think that you need to find a way to separate your connections from one another. Put them in a box in your mind so you can still feel them, or, maybe, acknowledge them, but not be hurt and consumed by them."

His suggestion shocked everyone. Not because it wasn't valid. In fact, it made complete sense. It was simply because the idea had come from *him*.

Zuri blinked, straightening her back as if infused with a small dose of confidence.

Everyone in the room was distracted by Aidan's revelation and it took moment before anyone noticed Madison sliding from her chair down onto the floor. Her arms shook as she tried to hold herself up. Joe's chair flipped back with a loud crash as he launched to his feet to get to her side.

Zuri, blindly reaching for Lexi, whispered, "Adeline needs us. She's lost. We have to find her."

Hearing the name *Adeline*, every woman in the room

envisioned her battered face.

"When do we leave?" said Aidan, still gripping Zuri's hand.

Chapter 17
To the Dungeon

"I'm going back down to try again." Gavin smacked his hands on the table a little louder than he should've as he stood up.

"It won't do us any good! You've tried everything you know of."

"Sitting around is getting us nowhere. It's like we're just waiting to die!"

Maria's eyes grew wide before closing tight. Her face fell. She was tired. Exhausted actually. The emotional rollercoaster was taking its toll.

"We could always leave." Grant's groggy voice was barely audible from his cot.

"And go where?" Gavin growled.

"Anywhere, really." Grant shrugged. "We know we can get out of the building. We could bring supp—"

"What about the guys that took Justin and the others?"

"We haven't heard from them in two days, right?" Grant said, shifting to his side.

"Yesterday." Maria sounded dejected.

He looked over at her. "I didn't hear any—"

"You've been asleep since Tuesday," Gavin said.

Grant blinked several times. "I mean… was that yesterday? Or like days ago?"

He was genuinely confused. The fact that every day was basically Groundhog Day stirred up an out-of-place swell of laughter in Maria. It really wasn't that funny, but she couldn't help herself. "I'm sorry. I have no idea why that's so hilarious!" Snorting, she laughed harder at their bewildered expressions.

Gavin's shoulders began to shake. "Solid point. I suppose Tuesday could be any day at this point." He tried not to give Maria the satisfaction of laughing, but before long, he gave in to a deep belly laugh.

Grant made his way over to their table as the laughter faded.

"He's right," Maria said after a minute of silence and deep breaths. "We could just leave. Check the surroundings and take any car out back with a full tank."

"Did they say anything new yesterday over the radio?" Grant asked.

"No. Same spiel." Maria looked at Gavin. "Maybe you were right."

"Come again?" His eyes popped open.

"Don't get all high and mighty." She waved off his expression. "Maybe we should just respond. I mean, if we left here, where would we even go? It's not like I have a condo in New York or an empty estate waiting for my return."

Both men had no worthwhile answer. Their own homes were likely uninhabitable as well.

"Not to mention, and don't take this the wrong way, but are any of us really capable of living off the grid?" Grant's words came off as flippant, but the truth was on point.

"I mean, there are still communities out there, right? What about where you were, Maria? It wasn't that long ago," asked Gavin, his hopes dashed by Maria's forlorn expression.

"If that was an option, I would've never left. The truth is that the hospital I lived in and continued my work in finally succumbed. There were just too many people and not enough resources. Unlike here," she said as her eyes dropped to her hands and her voice grew soft as if reliving the scene. "I'd gotten a message several years back that VISP was recruiting neurologists like me for a special study. I declined because my work at the hospital was important to me.

"Then the hospital was overrun. The group charged with protecting it and maintaining the resources rebelled. Back when VISP tried to recruit me, they'd given me a radio. There was a channel and codeword taped to the back of it. I dug it out of a drawer and decided to give it a try. And what do you know? After all that time, they answered my call."

"Jones," Gavin whispered.

Maria nodded. A moment later, she turned to face Grant with an inquisitive expression. "At D5, Gavin tried everything to get that door open yesterday. As brilliant as he is, he's a moron with electronics. Any chance you're handy with wiring?"

Gavin huffed, glaring at her from across the table.

"Double moron," mumbled Grant with a mouthful of prepackaged muffin. "I have no business touching electrical things."

"Crap! Thank the heavens we aren't stranded on a desert island. We'd all die on the first day."

Choking, Grant spit out bits of muffin, caught off guard by Maria's rant.

"She pulls no punches. You'll get used to it," said Gavin without missing a beat. "Besides, isn't that what you meant earlier with your *living off-the-grid* comment?"

Holding up a hand as though acknowledging defeat, Grant circled back to the door. "Are we sure we want to know what's behind it? The sealed door?"

They stared at one another, contemplating his question. "I feel like the answer is yes. The devil we know, right?"

Gavin took a deep breath and stood up in front of them. "I agree. Here's what I'm thinking. I'm going back down to D5. If anything happens, go into the security office and hide in the closet. I've already cleared out the space.

Maria rolled her eyes. "Seriously?"

"Dead serious."

"I think if anyone was going to come after us, they would've by now."

Clearing his throat, Grant said, "Any idea what's down there?"

"None. It definitely accesses something everyone but the three of us knew about. If Lexi, Zuri's…" he paused.

"*Sister*. Go ahead. Let it roll off your tongue, Gavin. She has a sister, and they're both exceptionally badass," said Maria, kindly offering him the word he was looking for.

"You miss one little day of work and all hell breaks loose," Gavin muttered under his breath.

Smacking his arm, she said, "Hopefully, Lexi isn't down there. I hope she somehow got out. We know if she's down there, then she went from a glass prison to a dungeon."

"But if Lexi did manage to go out that back door, whoever it is that found Justin and everyone else may have her as well."

"If she was with Madison, maybe not," said Grant, sounding hopeful.

"Do you think Madison knew something we didn't?" Gavin asked.

Grant let the question hang. There was always something about Madison that seemed different. Her connection to Lexi was stronger than his. She always offered more care and kindness than the average doctor. However, they only had one single patient for years, so it made sense that she would develop a bond. Looking back at his own actions, though, he admitted that he treated her the same way. "I'm not sure. But she was with me when everyone else in the building was gone. Yet she's nowhere to be found. So, yeah, I guess she might've."

Maria and Gavin immediately thought of Justin and his connection with Zuri.

"Alrighty!" Gavin clapped his hands and grabbed his backpack. "Third time's a charm, right?"

Chapter 18
The 7th

Addie's head was strapped tight against a metal chair. He told her the metal was good for conduction, but all she could think about was the unrelenting cold chilling her skin and the hard edges making her bones ache.

She spent hours in that windowless room. Unlike the prison's darkness, this room was absurdly bright. Across the room was a wall-size mirror, and she had no doubt that he was watching her from the other side.

She'd determined they thought she had superhuman capabilities, but their methods for evoking these so-called skills made no sense. The other girls had gone through the same thing. They must have failed at what these men wanted from them because the only time they were ever brought to the room was to be tortured *for* her. None of them ever sat in the chair she was in. Instead, always strapped to the wall in front of her as if she was supposed to miraculously protect them from harm. Or maybe cause it.

Addie stared into Janice's eyes. Janice had been the first friendly voice she'd heard when she arrived. Now she stood pinned to the wall in front of her. Eye to eye. Defeat covered every inch of her face. Blood, new and old, saturated her ragged clothing. The man in the corner didn't hide behind a mask, which meant he wasn't afraid of her knowing his face. He knew she was never leaving.

The rolling table next to him held an assortment of tools. Through blurry eyes, Adeline could see light glinting off knives and other objects. He'd used them all on Janice. Several on Adeline.

Janice's eyes lifted just enough for Adeline to see the fear welling up in them. Not the usual fear of being manhandled and beaten by the unforgiving torturous demon in the corner, but a fear Addie hadn't seen on the woman's face before. Even the man in the corner stood up a little straighter as Addie heard the soft click of a door closing behind her.

She could feel him before he spoke. His presence weighed down the heaviness already filling the room. Yet it was strangely familiar, like a passing scent that catches your nostrils and brings up forgotten memories.

"Good morning, Adeline." His voice sweet. Calm. "We know who you are, Adeline. We know you have a gift. Maybe several. This would be a lot easier if you would show us what you can do. We don't want to hurt you or Janice. In fact, it would relieve a lot of the suffering for her and the others out there."

There was no anger or intimidation floating through his words. Quite the opposite, he sounded polite, even concerned.

She was too exhausted to be defiant, but she wasn't going to beg either. "I don't understand what you want or what you think I have to offer."

"It's very simple. I watched you do it the first day you were here." His voice was cheerful as he came to her side. Finally, she could see his profile in her peripheral vision. Bending down, he whispered, "You remember, don't you? The way you protected yourself by pushing the guards away without ever even touching them? Did you think I wouldn't see that?"

Her eyes pinched shut as she struggled to think back. It was mostly a blur. She thought it was a dream or hallucination.

"I can see you're doubting my words, so here's what we'll do. I'm going to have this gentleman in the corner continue to work on Janice until you feel you're ready to do something about it."

Bucking up against her straps, Addie wanted to make him feel pain. More than pain, she wanted to kill him for what he was doing.

"Oh! You don't like my plan?" he chuckled from behind. The room went uncomfortably silent for several seconds, and then, without warning, his face was in hers. His hand gripped her jaw so hard that her teeth dug into her cheeks. She could taste copper filling her mouth. "DO SOMETHING ABOUT IT!"

I know that face!

Her body tensed and her fists clenched as her knuckles turned white.

I don't recognize him as he is now. No! He was a younger

man—maybe in his 20s.

No matter how hard she tried, she couldn't break from his grip.

Dear god! But he tried to save us. It makes no sense. How did he become so... so evil?

A fierce and deep fire made every inch of her skin burn before an invisible wave of energy radiated from her body. Like a plastic bag in the wind, she watched as he was violently thrown back from her and into the wall before crumbling to the floor.

Addie had hurt him.

She did it.

It wasn't a hallucination.

As quickly as she felt this sense of control, she was devastated by the repercussions. Janice, now unconscious, was hanging by the straps around her wrists. Whatever it was she just did, the horrible man crushed Janice between his body and the wall as he was repelled backward.

"No!" The scream left her lips though she was unable to hear over the ringing in her ears.

What have I done?

The man in the corner stood open-mouthed. For a brief moment he looked terrified but his fear was quickly replaced by rage. So caught off guard, she closed her eyes and braced for the impact. With fists still clenched and body tense, Adeline jolted with a shriek when he began undoing her restraints instead.

With her eyes still closed, a burst of colors began to shine. She could see him amidst the explosion of color. Swirling reds and blacks formed the contours of his body.

The shock of it confused her, and the colors dissipated when her eyes opened to find his face only inches from hers. Her false hope that he might release her was again replaced with terror.

His eyes were black. Soulless. He loomed over her like a human shadow and she knew he had no plans to save her.

Once unchained, he grabbed her by the neck and yanked her from the chair. Trying to pull his hand away, she saw pinpricks of light flutter through her vision. Once in the hall, he turned and slammed her up against the wall, feet off the ground. He spoke, but her ears continued thumping from a lack of oxygen. She didn't need to hear him to know he meant to hurt her.

Addie lifted her knees up and braced her feet on the wall. With all the strength she could find, she pushed against the wall. Her forehead collided with his cheekbone, and for a second, he lost his grip. That was all she needed to break free.

Adrenaline carried her down the hall. A pull tugged at her with every step. She wanted to believe she was moving toward an exit, some passageway to get her out of the cold iron prison, yet knew deep inside the pull wasn't bringing her to freedom.

Crashing through the door at the center of the hallway, her one good eye registered nothing but black. The room was dark, lit only by the yellow light of a bedside table lamp. It should've felt ominous, but instead felt... lonely. After closing the door behind her, Adeline painfully pulled a nearby dresser in front of it. She knew it wouldn't hold but thought it might buy her some time.

Falling to her knees, her lungs burned with the pain of exhaustion. The pulling continued, like gravity, only this time at her back. So strong her skin tingled. Sensing without seeing, she felt the woman behind her. The shades swirling around her were dark, and she didn't need to lay her eyes on the woman to know. It wasn't the inky black of that abusive demon in the torture chamber but the obscurity of evil having been done to her for so long that it was all she knew.

Addie, still catching her breath, moved as though underwater. Her arms sluggish and slow, as if suspended in liquid. Near the corner of the room, she made out the silhouette of the woman lying on a bed. Making her way to the bed, pain shot up her legs with each step as she realized several toes had broken during her escape.

The woman looked more like a girl. So small. So still. With her eyes closed.

Addie reached out to touch the girl's arm only to feel an electric current as her fingers inched closer. As soon as Addie's hand grazed her skin, the young woman's eyes flicked wide open. Suddenly, Addie could see her deep espresso irises glistening in the yellowed light.

Tense and once again clenching her fists, Adeline froze in place as the woman's life of pain streamed through her mind.

Instead of ripping her hand back, she grasped the girl's arm. Her chest was tight and her knees weak, causing her to drop to the cold, hard floor, barely catching herself.

Pitch black. Giant arms picking her small body up. Sharp pain piercing her back. Dirt in her eyes. Then nothingness.

Dirty rooms, one after another. Scrap foods, scarce water. Beatings by day. Nightmare by night.

Screaming. Her own. Then someone else's.

Forced to hurt others. No contact. No touching. Just creating and receiving agony.

The images coursed through Addie's mind relentlessly as she fell face down on the floor.

Awake, yet frozen. Her eyes shifted back and forth, rapidly moving, processing what just happened but with little to compare the horror to.

This is how this woman lives, she thought, trembling. *No way to move. Trapped in her own body. Hearing everyone and everything around her.*

"Help me." Addie heard the small voice echo in her mind.

Madison's back arched at an implausible angle.

Joe had been sitting next to her as she talked about her life since the fall of the grid. Her body contorted, throwing her elbow into his cheekbone. "What's happening?" he shouted, leaping to his feet.

Without warning, she collapsed, her limbs weak and unable to catch herself. It was like deja vu as he caught her head before it hit the ground.

Hovering while wiggling his fingers as if feeling out his next move, he grabbed her shoulder, gently rolling her onto her back. An incomprehensible crystalline glow emanated from only one of her eyes.

Madison's left eye was so dim the shimmer was nearly gone, and the color, instead of emerald green, had become dark as midnight in a forest as he watched.

"Madison?" he whispered, his voice shaking. "Can you hear me?"

Madison's breathing calmed and her body relaxed. Her eyes were already open, but now they began to focus.

"What just happened?"

She blinked several times as warm tears filled the laugh lines around her eyes and trickled down to her ears.

"Adeline found the seventh."

Chapter 19
Be Still

August 19, 2029 | 6:17 p.m.

Brandon was on the ground with Joanna's small frame wrapped in his big arms. She wasn't unconscious but she wasn't fully aware either. The secure embrace and the heat against her cheek from his chest made her want to nuzzle further into his protective arms.

"Can you hear me?" His concerned voice echoed into the subconscious of her mind. "Anna? Are you okay?"

Muddled images of her sister raced through her mind as if they were coming from some far-off place. But not just Adeline, there were other women too. And she'd seen them before.

Coming to her senses, she became aware enough to realize Brandon was gently pushing her damp hair back from her face. For just a moment she let him comfort her, his strength seeping into her bones.

Cracking open her eyes, Joanna slowly sat up and maneuvered out of his arms. "Thank you," she sincerely offered with a gentle smile, attempting to relieve his obvious anxiety despite her surprise and concern. It was the first time he'd shown her genuine kindness since Adeline disappeared.

"You're welcome," he whispered, clearing his throat. "Do you know what just happened to you?"

Her eyes glistened, and she could feel her body tremble, but this newfound strength he'd given her kept the tears at bay. "I'm about to tell you something you might find disconcerting, maybe even unbelievable," she said, followed by a deep sigh. "So I'm going to apologize for what may sound crazy in advance."

Brandon stared at her in silence.

"Addie and I have always been a little different. When we were very young, we were abducted. Neither of us remembers much about it, which we always thought was probably for the best. I remember our parents telling us early on that we were as close as sisters could be… probably something all parents say, right? But after we were rescued and brought home, we weren't just close…" she said, pausing to gauge his reaction, "we were, uh, able to communicate without actually speaking."

Brandon continued to stare, only somehow displaying more compassion.

She continued as if answering a question she assumed he'd ask. "Hard to explain, I guess. Little things, mostly. Like a whisper in my mind is the way I hear it. That is unless something significant is happening to one of us, then it's louder, clearer, almost like I can see her as she's experiencing something and vice versa."

Brandon shifted his position, listening intently.

"She always felt things stronger than I did, though." Joanna hung her head, knowing what she was about to say would sound even more ridiculous.

"It's okay, Anna. Whatever you need to say." Brandon's voice was soft. Despite her frustration with him over the past few days, his undeniable sympathy melted a piece of her heart.

"She could, somehow, just by looking at someone, tell if they were a good person. You know, if they truly had a deep sense of goodness in them. Or vice versa, darkness. The darkness, she would say, didn't always mean evil. Sometimes it was simply sadness. Or fear. Or that some trauma had occurred in their life and they were carrying it around, not allowing themselves to be happy."

Brandon looked away. Clearing his throat in a gruff yet shaky voice, he asked, "Did she, when we first met, did she notice anything about me?"

"Yes."

His question meant he believed her. So, with greater confidence, she explained those last few moments before they lost Addie. "Just before she went back to get her book, I asked if we were safe to go with you. She said you had that darkness around you but that it was from pain, not because you were a bad man."

Shaking his head, their eyes locked. A few moments ticked by before he asked in a playful yet serious tone, "What about you? Is there something you… see? Or feel beyond what us mere mortals can?"

"No. She's always been the stronger of us, I suppose."

He stared at her. It was just the two of them in a world that no longer required people to play to the crowd. She wasn't live streaming on Instagram or trying to get likes on FaceBook. She had no reason to exaggerate or lie. He knew she believed what she was saying, so he wasn't going to argue the point.

"She's strong, Joanna," he said, his chest tightening at the thought of her sister suffering. "When Adeline hurt her arm, I noticed she wasn't in tears. In fact, she hardly seemed to notice. Wherever she is, she's fighting. She'll keep fighting until we get there."

He pushed her hair back away from her face and offered her an encouraging smile. Her leg was beginning to cramp, so she adjusted her position on the floor. As she did, her knee brushed against his stretched-out leg.

Suddenly, a face washed over her mind causing vertigo. It was a girl she didn't know. Fuzzy but clear enough. Caught off guard and beginning to lean to the side, she realized the girl's face wasn't born from the depths of *her* mind. It was from *his*.

Brandon grasped her shoulder firmly before she could lean any further. His touch started a wave that quickly became a tsunami of memories. *His* memories.

"Chocolate eyes," she whispered, helplessly tumbling into his subconscious.

His grip tightened as she spoke, pulling her into his chest, enhancing the images through constant contact.

Laughing around a fire, his arm around her waist.

Pushing a wayward lock of wet hair out of her eyes in the rain.

Running through woods, cut by branches, finally fear in her eyes.

Then dark nothingness.

His face in anguish. Searching. Screaming. Fighting the air. Desperate.

Joanna's body convulsed out of his arms, sucking in air that didn't seem to fill her lungs.

"Joanna!" he shouted, scrambling to pull her back to him. "I'm here! I'm here—"

"No!" Her arm shot out, pushing his reaching one away.

Her breathing was labored. He noticed a pained expression awash on her face.

"I'm sorry," he whispered, not knowing what else to say.

That's when her tears fell. After several moments her head lifted and his eyes caught hers. Shining so brightly, he couldn't look away. He'd never seen anything like it. Golden flecks in a crystal prism.

"No, uh, I'm sorry," she managed to say, wrestling with the foreign, pain-filled memories now flooding her mind.

He wanted to reach back out to her, but the moment had passed.

Chapter 20
The Connection

Lexi walked into the Joint Operations Cell in awe. Every inch of three of the walls were covered in the biggest flat-screen monitors she'd ever seen. She had been there once before but had been so crazed at the image of her sister that she hadn't noticed the immensity of the space. The monitors displayed calm scenes of real life. One showed people walking around buildings, another simply showed smoke rising from chimneys atop bungalows, and yet another screen focused on images near bodies of water. One, in particular, seemed to be zoned in on a building right next to a lake, while another looked like it was just over some desolate woods.

And none of it made sense to Lexi.

Madison placed her hand on her friend's shoulder. Lexi felt

the now familiar tingle of her touch and pulled her eyes away from the screens.

As if Madison could read her mind, she said, "It's a lot to take in, isn't it?" Lexi gently nodded. "Jahnsen and Phil spent quite a few years since it all happened pulling this together. We have drones in many places around the country and even overseas. They help us keep tabs on what's going on out there."

Looking back at the digital windows into the rest of the world, she said, "It's just… wouldn't all of this take a lot of people out there to be working with you on this?"

"Not too many. We only need one or two people for each drone. Some work for us specifically. Others allow us to use their drones as long as we're also monitoring things they want to keep track of."

"This is incredible." So fascinated by the scenes in front of her, she didn't notice that all other conversations had gone silent. A feeling of wonder sent goosebumps up her back, causing her to pull her eyes from the screens. Looking around the room, she noticed that most of the staff had risen to their feet, headsets covering one ear, and all with their attention on her.

With a subtle gasp, she took a small step back toward the door.

"It's alright, Lexi," Madison said, putting her hand out to steady her.

"Why are they looking at me like that?" Feeling exposed under their scrutiny, she glanced down to make sure she wasn't.

Madison chuckled. "They just can't believe you're here."

"Why?"

"Because they've been watching and waiting for you for a very long time, and to have you standing in this room with us is a miracle. With Zuri and Zoey here, it's beyond what anyone believed possible." The sparkle in Madison's emerald eyes caught everyone's attention.

Both felt it at the same moment, a shift in the atmosphere as Zoey and Zuri entered behind them. Zuri, pushing herself in a wheelchair, navigated to her sister's side and leaned her head against Lexi's hip. Lexi squatted and faced her sister. "How are you feeling? You shouldn't be out of bed."

"I'm doing better, Lex."

Lexi looked up at Zoey in question.

"I think she's going to be fine. Just give it a few more days," Zoey said.

It was incomprehensible that Zuri was even sitting upright. She'd somehow managed to take fourteen bullets. Some had just grazed her, but several were full-body hits. As small as she was, it was a miracle she survived at all. Just as important, the last ten days had given them time to discover how it happened in the first place. Zuri had made a choice, or maybe it was just a reflex. At that moment, out in the field, she decided she didn't want anyone else to get hurt. Somehow, the real mystery of it all, that decision transpired into her becoming a magnet for the bullets.

Lexi pulled her eyes away from her sister and back to the stunned faces around the room. She was about to speak when Zoey asked, "Madison, how did you end up being Lexi's doctor and yet secretly remain a part of all this?" She gestured to the room itself.

"Short version? I was kind of raised into it. My dad," she began, with a sigh and a gentle smile, "was one of the operators that saved us. After he and Mom adopted me, I was raised in military life. I went into medicine, and after the grid failed, Director Jones asked me to be part of his team. It made sense, really. I was already working for LIMIT, and the opportunity put me right where I wanted to be. I guess you could say I became a mole."

Zoey's lips began to move with a dozen more questions ready to fire, but Madison's eyes told her it wasn't the time.

Instead, Madison raised her hand to get Jilly's attention. She was Jahnsen's top intelligence analyst. "Jilly? Would you help me out with something?"

"Of course, ma'am."

"I told you, you can call me Madison."

"Yes, ma'am."

Madison huffed, rolled her eyes, and said, "Would you please give these ladies a quick overview of what we do in here? In layman's-terms, please."

"Sure thing, ma'am. Right this way, ladies." Jilly maneuvered to where a few monitors had live feeds. She shooed the individuals sitting there out of the way so Lexi and Zoey could sit. Zuri rolled up behind them to get a good view between their shoulders.

"See these six boxes? Each shows a live feed from an unmanned aerial vehicle flying overhead at different locations."

"Live?" Zoey was shocked, thinking, *Joe needs to see this.*

As if on cue, all three men walked into the room. Spotting the girls, they came up behind them to watch what was going on.

Jilly continued without missing a beat. "Each of them shows a location we believe one of the girls might be, or in your case, had been."

"That's our apartment building!" Aidan's arm stretched between the girls' heads and pointed at the screen.

Doc Sheila was on the rooftop tending to her plants. Zoey felt a slight pang in her chest, watching her up there doing what she'd done every day for years. It suddenly struck her how much she missed going up to assist or chat. She'd always felt a kinship with the woman, believing it was because Doc was just the kindest person she knew.

She felt Joe's hand settle on her shoulder and knew he could tell what she was thinking.

Was this a betrayal? Did Doc know the whole time who I was and was just spying on me?

Blinking away the sting in her eyes, Zoey pointed to another square on the screen. "This looks familiar. Where is this one?"

"This is not too far from your apartment, actually. It's near the Harris Plant. An old training area for the local firehouses to practice putting out blazes. It was also used for weapons training, like a shooting range." Jilly was a wealth of knowledge.

"And you think one of the girls might be there?" Justin asked.

"It has potential. We only recently started tracking that area. During one of the night flights over top of your apartment building last week, an odd signature showed up at the edge of the feed. We sent the bird to investigate and caught additional irregular data.

"Immediately we sent a scout to the area and learned that several girls had gone missing from the vicinity over the years."

"Is that unusual considering the state of the world?" Lexi asked.

"Not particularly, but the strange heat signatures and

excessive electrical pulses registered by our bird is what's so intriguing. It's what kept us watching. After all, you're no longer there to cause the disturbances, right?"

Joe caught Zoey's eye. "That's Oakley's place."

With a deep breath, her back straightened. "Do you think he could do something like that? Keep someone against their will?"

A barely perceptible shake of his head told her he wasn't sure.

Justin caught their exchange. "Do you know who's out there?"

"I know who *was* out there. Couldn't say if he still is," said Joe. "He's prior military, so if he is, maybe he's working on something causing the signatures you're seeing." Despite his attempted explanation, the hairs on the back of his neck raised, uncomfortable with where his thoughts were leading him.

Needing more time to process the possibilities, he tabled it and instead brought the conversation back to the big picture. "Based on what I'm seeing and what Justin and the others shared yesterday, are we saying that most of these girls are from North Carolina? Or may even be there now?"

Jilly gave a curt nod. "Not just North Carolina, specifically Sanford and the surrounding area."

"But why? Why there?"

"After they were rescued, Ft. Bragg—"

"Liberty," Joe corrected.

She gave him a side-eye but continue on, "*Liberty* was their initial recovery location. Once cleared, they were either reunited with family or fostered out to locals."

"But they weren't all from that area to begin with, were

they?" asked Justin.

"My family was already there," Zoey said, her eyes shifting in thought. "I was born and raised in Sanford."

Madison's eyes now glowed, having removed the contacts. "So did I, down by Cameron," she stated, becoming aware of the connection.

Justin's heart raced. "That's where I found Zuri and Lexi, although that was after the abduction. I lived in Broadway. My father was military and retired there. I was going to school at Campbell University." He looked down at Lexi. "It's where I found you two."

The women looked at one another then back at the feeds on the screen.

"Where was everyone born?" asked Justin, turning toward Jilly. She looked at the women, then back at him. "Where were they born?"

"I was born at Central Carolina Hospital," said Madison, turning toward the others.

"Central Carolina," Zoey said, with a deep exhale.

"Adeline and Joanna were also born there. After they were rescued, their family moved to Ohio," Jilly added.

"So four of you were born in the same place, around the same time," said Joe, thinking aloud as he looked down at Lexi and Zuri. "We can't say the two of you were definitively born there, but it's possible. Which means—"

"Which means we need to get to that hospital and find those records," Zoey said, confident they were on the right path to finding answers. Staring at Joe, she declared, "We need to go home."

"We need to get Gavin and Maria first," Justin interjected.

Jahnsen stared at them, considering the scope of information having been revealed. "I'll assemble the team. Let's get kitted up."

Chapter 21
Where Are They?

Standing up, Gavin grabbed his bag, handed Maria her radio, then pushed her to the stairwell. She wanted to be on the main floor by the security desk as Gavin explored D5.

"Here, I'll help," Grant said as he picked up Maria's bag and followed. He was still feeling plenty of pain, but by some miracle, it was manageable pain. Not excruciating. Not crippling. He was able to compartmentalize it and continue on.

Gavin had spent the better part of the previous day trying to disassemble the D5 door. He felt he was close, but Maria was at her wits' end with the tedious process.

"Listen, I've got most of the panels off. I pulled some electrical schematics from the security office and think I know which wires keep the door sealed. Once I cut them, the door should open," he said, pleading his case, but he knew that look—hand on hip with lips pursed in a sarcastic *sure you do* kind of way.

Grant stood by the railing of the hidden stairwell eating a granola bar. Their pithy arguments were the highlight of his day.

"If this doesn't work, we'll leave, make our way to the coast, and start life over on a boat."

"That sounds like a terrible plan! *You* go float on your little boat. Just remember to bring me back dinner," Maria sniped back.

"Hey guys, can we just agree that after this round, if nothing comes of it, we get out of here regardless? Your bickering is wildly entertaining, but it's starting to feel like a tomb in here."

"Word," Maria agreed, giving him a fist bump.

Gavin looked back and forth between them. "Seriously? Did you just say *word*?"

Her stare in response let him know just how far he could push her buttons at the moment.

"God help me. Are we all clear on the plan?"

"Yes, yes. You get kidnapped, we hide in a closet or run out the back door, steal a car, and *Fast and Furious* our way out of here," Maria quipped, shooing him away.

Rolling his eyes, he reminded her for the tenth time. "Security closet. It's cleaned out for you already if you run out of time. Or, the black sedan just out the back door to the right."

"Sounds like a plan." Grant was pretty laid back. So much so that Maria had even asked him if he'd been a hippy in another life, despite Gavin's scoffing at the absurdity of her question.

After she and Grant were all set up, Gavin picked up his gear and squeezed her tight.

Squeezing back, she said, "Just be careful, and I want to hear from you consistently, every few minutes so I know what's going on."

"Look at that. The thicker the sarcasm, the more you care, is that it?"

"I *will* come down after you if I have to!" she declared loudly as she pulled away.

"Sure, Miss Hop-a-long. I know you would, but you won't need to." He was still smiling as he turned and headed out.

"Hey!" Grant called out, striding toward Gavin, putting several feet between them and Maria. He stuck out his hand for a shake, but when Gavin reached out, Grant pulled him in close.

"We don't know anything about why they left us, but if you're as close as you think you are to getting that door open, don't let them take you."

Leaning back and locking eyes, Gavin whispered, "Is there something you're not telling us, man?"

"Deductive reasoning. It's been ten days since they left and they're not back yet. If you manage to get in there, they may not let you out."

Gavin studied Grant's eyes and saw only genuine concern. With a nod, they released their grip.

Looking back at Maria, he repeated, "You know the plan. The keys are in that car, so take it and get out of here if you have to."

Until that moment, she hadn't actually felt fear. Gavin could see it wash over her face. Jogging back for a firm hug, he said, "I'll be right back."

Smiling, he disappeared into the stairwell.

Maria rolled to the opening, stood up, and hopped over to

the railing to watch as Gavin descended. Grant was right behind her. "Anything new?" she yelled, her voice crisp and clear several floors down

"Nothing different from before. Still doesn't look like the cameras are monitoring, but they may have just disconnected the power LED."

Waiting patiently was not her strong suit. Only a few minutes had passed, but she was itching to reach him again. As she raised the radio to call down to him, the sound of static came through, followed by silence.

"Gavin?"

There was no response.

"Hey, not funny. Did you make it to D5?"

More static. She waited a few more beats, but before she could press the button again, she heard a loud banging echoing through the stairwell from down below.

"Gavin, I need you to respond. Right now!"

As she released the button his voice broke through the static.

"Maria! Maria, get out! Get out of the building!" cried Gavin, fighting to get the words out in a mad panic.

Maria temporarily froze at the sound of his voice cutting through the speaker and, at the same time, echoing throughout the stairwell. She had never heard any voice as terrified as his in that moment.

"Gavin, run!" she shouted, shaking off the paralytic fear. "Get out of there!" she screamed even louder, partly into the radio and partly down the stairs.

More static came through, then, after a moment, his voice.

"Maria! Maria, ru—"

Gavin's words broke free from the radio, reverberating up

through the dark stairwell. It was a booming voice, definitely his, but a tone she barely recognized.

"Oh my god, this isn't happening," Maria whispered under her breath, barely audible with eyes wide open. Grabbing hold of the railing, she scanned the steps bracing for impact, but it was pitch black without a sound, a scuffle, or even a hint of the man shouting just seconds before. Taking the first few steps down the stairs, she was jerked backward when Grant grabbed the tail of her shirt.

"Stop! We need to go. Now!" Pushing, pulling, and half-carrying her, Grant shoved Maria into her rolling chair. He dragged her halfway to the security office before sprinting off to snatch her bag and finally racing back.

She squeezed the radio talk button so hard her knuckles turned white. "Gavin! Gavin, can you hear me?" Releasing it, she waited for any sort of response. Nothing but static came through. Again and again, she tried without success.

"I've got your bag. Let's go. We need to get outside." Grant started to pull her, but she shoved at his arm.

"Gavin!" She shouted once again.

His silence was overwhelming, almost disorienting.

Not willing to give in, Grant wrapped his arms around her and began to drag her across the lobby when the sound of footsteps echoed through the stairwell in front of them. Maria barely noticed the noise as her heartbeat pounded in her ears.

There's no way it could be Gavin, she thought. He would've responded to my calls.

"We won't make it out. There's no time!" growled Grant under his breath.

Abandoning his plan to evacuate the building, Grant pushed

Maria, still calling for Gavin, into the security office instead. Angry but submissive, she limped into the closet as fast as she could. Grant leaped in behind her and pulled the door closed, though leaving it ajar just enough to see through. The sound of their erratic breathing was all either of them could hear until footsteps loudly scuffled across the lobby.

Sitting at just the right angle, Grant froze in place, hoping to see the movements, weapons, or faces of anyone that crossed into the office. Unfortunately, the person that crossed his line of sight moved so quickly he only caught a glimpse, as if the intruder knew precisely where they were.

Maria, having seen the shadow pass by, held her breath.

Suddenly and silently, the closet door flew open and the silhouette of a man shouted with surprise and relief.

"Maria!" Justin said as he reached for her.

"No!" Grant yelled as he grabbed Justin's arm, ready to pounce.

"Wait!" Maria jumped up between them. "No, Grant, it's okay! He's one of us." They locked eyes until he understood. Then, looking back and forth between the two of them, he nodded at her before slowly releasing Justin's forearm. As he did, Justin pulled her in, squeezing her tight.

"Oh my god, where did you come from?" she asked.

Without introduction, Madison stepped into view behind him, causing Maria to jerk backward.

Justin put his hand on her back. "Hey. No. Maria, this is Madison. She's here to help."

"Madison?" said Grant, his voice gruff and confused.

"Grant?" Madison, shocked at the sound of her friend's voice, pushed past Justin and Maria to embrace him. "I thought…

I thought you'd died!"

"And I prayed you'd made it out of here," he said with a deep sigh. "Lexi?"

"She's fine, she's alive—"

"What about the others?" Maria cut in.

"Alive. Everyone is alive," Justin interjected.

Tears welled up in the corners of Maria's eyes, but with a deep breath, she shifted gears to the more immediate and terrifying mystery. "We need to find Gavin."

Justin took a cursory look around before saying, "Where is he?"

Not waiting for her response, Justin picked up Maria, maneuvering her back into the chair she'd left moments before.

"There's a hidden—"

"—stairwell. Yes, that's how we got in here," Justin finished.

"Well damn, you just know all the things now." Her sarcasm came out in full force, having been frustrated, frightened, and shocked all in a matter of seconds.

By the look on her face, Justin knew better than to respond.

"Okay, there's a D5 level."

That was something he *didn't* know. "As in a floor below ours?"

"Yes. Literally, only minutes ago Gavin went down the stairwell to check it out. I heard him yell, but then nothing. We were ready to make a run for it until we heard steps in the stairwell. We never would have guessed it would be you. Are you alone?"

"No, two of us in here, but there's a team outside waiting. We didn't want to scare you with a whole troop, you know, gear and guns and all."

Maria and Grant nodded.

Looking at Grant, Justin ordered, "Get her out the back door, now. I'm going down to find him."

"No! Wait! We don't know what happened to him," Maria yelled, grabbing at his sleeve.

"The sooner we check it out, the less likely we'll lose him." His stare into her eyes assured her he was most likely right. She released her fingers but couldn't bear the thought of losing Justin, too, only moments after seeing him again. Alive.

Justin nodded toward the door, indicating they needed to move. "Get outside, Maria. I'll bring him back." His eyes made her a promise she knew he couldn't keep. Calling for backup from the team outside, he and Madison made their way down the stairs.

Maria watched Madison, taking note of her quick actions and clear-minded demeanor, reminding her of a few others she knew.

Grant had already jumped into action, grabbing their bags and tossing them on Maria's lap, when Justin's voice startled them. "Maria? Did Gavin say anything? Was he able to get through this door down here?" She snatched her radio from her lap so quickly it slipped through her fingers and hit the floor.

"Hey, can you hear me? Does the signal reach?"

Without hesitation, Grant grabbed it and tossed it into her eager hands. "I'm here, sorry. No. Whoever was down there must've been waiting for him. He only told us to run."

"The door down here is similar to the one on our floor, but it's definitely sealed shut," he said, frustrated that Joe hadn't been with them, sure that he would've been able to open it.

Madison, positioned on the stairs behind Justin, was waiting to intercept their backup team as they descended the steps.

Just as Justin was deciding the best approach to getting through the door, it hissed in front of his face. Looking back and forth, he waved at Madison to retreat. Trained and experienced, Madison rounded the platform up to D4, staying out of sight, though ready to react.

As the door hissed, Maria's voice rang out from Justin's hand-held. "Gavin was messing with the wiring, hoping to hot-wire the door or something."

There was no reply from below.

"Justin?" yelled Maria. Her voice reverberated across the lobby and into the stairwell as much as it went into the radio.

Again nothing. Thoughts of Gavin flooded her mind. *Not again! Please, not again.* Her thoughts were spiraling out of control, in the dark on what was going on down there when her radio crackled.

"Justin? Justin, can you hear me?"

Grant froze, no longer racing to exit the building, instead torn between helping Madison below and getting Maria outside. Only broken, distant voices cut through the static over the hand-held.

"Not again."

Chapter 22
Time to Move

"**G**et your hands off me!" Maria fought hard against the eight or so men that had descended on her and Grant. Kicking and screaming, she tried to break free as the two of them were restrained and dragged back toward the stairs.

The guards had overcome Madison in a flash. Her lip was swollen and legs bruised from trying to fight them off in the stairwell, hoping to hold them off long enough for her backup team to arrive, but there were just too many. They suppressed her and found their way to Maria and Grant with little defense.

"You might want to put the lady down," came a familiar man's voice from around the corner of the hidden stairwell. All Maria could see was the barrel end of a gun, but she'd recognize Aidan's voice anywhere.

For a brief moment, the guards accosting Maria and Grant looked like they would fight back, but the ten others behind Aidan seemed to change their minds.

A smile spread across Maria's face as they were carefully lowered to the ground. Aidan's crew, which included Joe, Jahnsen, and Phil, spread out, surrounding the entire band of unknown guards.

"Thank you kindly," Aidan said with a polite nod as he walked the men back towards the far wall in the lobby.

As the guards lined up, Phil made his way around, pulling weapons out of their hands and holsters and passing them off to the others as he went along. "Just keeping it real fellas. Wouldn't want anyone to get feisty." With the final weapon confiscated, he walked up to Madison and touched her face. "You okay?"

"Yeah. Could use some ice and a Motrin, but I'm good."

He put his hand on her shoulder and gave it a little squeeze before moving on.

"So now you're going to tell us what you did with our friends," snapped Maria, piping up from the center of the suddenly crowded lobby.

Not waiting for an answer, Joe snagged an ID from the closest guard, thanked him, and headed back to the stairs. Two of Joe's men stayed behind to keep eyes on the sentries while the rest followed him and Aidan down to D5.

Once there, he waved the ID over the reader and the door hissed open. On the other side, he saw Justin and Gavin sitting on the ground about ten feet in, faces bloodied. "Looks like we missed the fun," Joe said and walked in, pointing his weapon at the few guards surrounding the men. A long hallway stretched out beyond them and he immediately realized that the floor wasn't laid out the same as D4.

"I take it this is where the throng of people that work on this compound are hiding out, huh? How about you move away from my friends," said Joe, as the men put their weapons down and hands up in the air, slowly stepping away from Gavin and Justin. Unwilling to give up easily, the guard furthest away took off in a full sprint.

"Hey!" Aidan yelled, taking off in pursuit as Joe caught the back of his shirt.

"Why don't we ask these guys a few questions so we know what we're up against before we blindly race off to our doom."

Justin and Gavin stood up and turned around so the zip ties could be cut from their wrists.

"What do you think?" Joe asked them.

"Based on what we've heard so far, there's a stretch of hall that leads into the bunker to the west side of the compound," Justin replied, rubbing the red, indented lines on his wrists. "My guess is that's where everyone's at."

"So the question is… do we really want to go deal with that, or do we just want to leave? After all, they don't have Zuri," Gavin offered.

"Or Lexi."

"It's unlikely there were any others like them here, so I vote we go," Gavin finished.

"Doesn't mean they won't try and track us down later to get them back." Joe knew people like this didn't just give up after all the years put into their research. They all knew that.

Aidan's eyes flickered from one man to the other before taking the badge out of Joe's hand. He opened the door they'd just come through then turned and used the butt end of his weapon to knock the ID reader off the wall. After that, he kicked the panel across the threshold and outside the door before shrugging his shoulders and saying, "I mean, we can at least slow them down."

Leaving the two remaining guards in the hall tied back-to-back in a sitting position, they stepped across the threshold. Aidan swiped the badge on the reader. As it closed, a big smile spread across his face while waving goodbye and snickering like a child. When the doory fully closed, he finished by knocking the remaining reader off the wall and making sure to tear as many wires as possible in the process.

"I think that'll hold 'em!" His excitement palpable.

"For about five minutes," added Joe, whose monotone response didn't diminish Aidan's fun.

"Nah, at least ten," Aidan shot back with a literal sparkle in his eye, which Joe noticed. For a brief second, he considered acknowledging the odd shine but decided it must have been how the light above hit him at just the right angle.

Gavin bounded up the stairs two at a time, shouting back to Aidan, "There could be another stairwell on the other side of the building. If there is, see if you can disable the other one too."

"On it!"

When they returned to the lobby, Madison was standing over the VISP guards who were now sitting quietly on the ground. Maria, on the other hand, sat in her rolling office chair, slowly moving up and down the line, giving the guards a piece of her mind.

She had just finished an impassioned monologue when she heard someone yell her name. "Maria," Gavin said, beelining toward her. As she turned, he pulled her into his chest, then held her out, checking to ensure she wasn't hurt as she did the same to him.

Justin knew from their intimate embrace that much more had happened since he last saw them. Maria caught his eye and he smiled. Grinning back, she mouthed *thank you* before burying her face in Gavin's neck.

"Time to go!" Jahnsen called out after ensuring all the VISP guards were now face-down on the ground and tightly secured. He led the way to the front door, no longer concerned with being covert.

Gavin, Justin, Maria, Madison, and Grant all stood inside the door, acknowledging that they were walking out of the building by choice for the first time since they became a part of VISP.

Justin swiped his ID on the pad and the doors opened. As the sun washed over them, they all felt a sense of freedom. So much had transpired it was as if they were finally breaking out of a prison they'd been withering in for years.

Stepping out onto the dirt, they heard footsteps running toward them from behind. Gavin grabbed Maria and pulled her off to the side of the doorway. The others jerked their weapons up and turned to face the attacker.

Red hair glimmered as the sunlight hit Aidan's bouncing head emerging from the door. Noticing that Maria was holding onto Gavin's arm, he stopped with a jolt. "Wait. You two happened? But… but I thought you were the love of my life?" he gasped, feigning sorrow and motioning as if he were stabbed in the heart.

Maria shook her head and chuckled at the sight.

"Guess I'm still on the market."

Chapter 23
Fire Training

Sanford, NC | August 21, 2029 | 7:17 a.m.

Joanna and Brandon could see the imposing smokestack from the power plant a few miles away from their position. No exhaust had poured from its gaping mouth in years.

After finding Brandon's hidden vehicle and watching him wrestle, plead, and curse while resurrecting it, they returned to his place to make a plan and pack supplies. Something had changed between them after Joanna's episode. She'd shared a secret that no one else in her life knew, and he hadn't scoffed or told her she was crazy. He actually seemed to believe her.

The drive to the FTA was fairly short, though it would've taken hours if they'd hiked. She was grateful to avoid walking through any more wooded terrain.

Having arrived less than twenty-four hours prior, they'd

already created a pretty solid time log of the men patrolling the grounds. The guards were armed, but their patrols stayed primarily inside the tree line of the property. Brandon and Joanna, not without some close calls, managed to stay outside of their route. They'd also taken note of several cameras on trees. A red LED on the side of each camera informed them which cameras were powered up and operable and which ones weren't and presumed to be off. Those that glowed red, they made absolutely sure to stay behind their line of sight.

"Here," he said, handing her a thermos full of water.

"Well, this is new," she said, disregarding his offer. "There's a truck coming." Five hundred yards out, Joanna could see a large truck through her binoculars making its way over a minefield of potholes into the fire training area.

Putting down the thermos, he reached for her binoculars, to which she handed them off as if it was a practiced move. They'd gotten comfortable enough with each other in the past week that their movements were becoming more naturally in sync.

"Yeah. That's an awful big truck."

"Seems a little overkill for just a few people, right?"

"Depends on what it's holding." Squinting, he could see the truck through the trees without the binos.

They watched as it parked next to an entrance with an oversized garage door. The door lifted, but it was hard to see inside the dark space from where they were perched. As it backed in, Joanna returned the binoculars to her eyes, hoping to get a better look.

"Interesting," she mumbled.

"What is it?" he asked, watching her eyebrows rise and fall as her mind churned up a series of thoughts.

"There are about five people in there unloading the truck. I can't tell what the boxes are, but my guess would be supplies. Maybe food—wait—yup. There are open flats of fruits and vegetables."

"Well, it's definitely not being delivered to sell at the local farmer's market. And this isn't a place anyone would come to barter for it."

"Do you think she could be here?" The hope in her voice made him internally wince. He wanted it to be true, but he also knew if it was, and she had been this close the whole time, he would feel like a colossal idiot. He let the question wash through him as guilt and anger took a seat in the pit of his stomach. It couldn't have been this easy.

Watching his face wrestle with the possibility, she placed her hand on his arm not having to say a word. She knew he was beating himself up. Not only regarding Adeline but should it turn out Kristine had been there too.

Changing the subject, she said, "So what do we do from here? How do we get in?"

"Great question," he muttered, swallowing the lump in his throat. "I think I have an idea. For now? We watch. I wanna see what they're doing with all of those edibles."

Addie felt dirt grinding into her cheek as she opened her eyes. She was back in the iron prison with all the other girls. Blinking the grit from her eyes, she slowly pushed herself up to a sitting position. The vertigo had hit her hard and it took some time to get her bearings. As the dizziness relented, her eyes sought out Janice, but instead of the young woman who had been consistently nearby, she now saw that the women had intentionally left a wide berth around her. Despite the confined space, the others stayed as far away from her as possible. She yearned for reassurance and the friendly touch of someone who cared about her, but the faces around the room were wracked with fear. All of them had dark shadows hovering over their shoulders, weighing them down with unease. Of course, Addie knew it was from the combination of torture and trauma they'd suffered. Huddling together, comforting one another. But it was also something else.

None of that comfort was for her any longer and she knew why.

She was the key target of the brutal monsters. She was the one being put through the gauntlet. Tested daily. And being tested meant the rest of them were guaranteed more suffering.

Because of her.

By her.

She knew what the man in the mask wanted. Even if she wanted to give it to him just to stop the abuse, she couldn't. Addie had no idea how to repeat what she'd done before. Truth be told, she barely remembered those moments happening in the first place.

And in the midst of all the suffering, she could feel the pull of the woman caught in perpetual sleep. It was endless. She knew the mysterious woman wasn't actually sleeping but trapped in her own body. Addie could sense that she'd completely withdrawn from life when she touched her. Her mind so disconnected from reality that she was incapable of moving any single muscle or joint. Unable to focus her mind. Unaware of her own being. The horror of it all made her sick to her stomach. Sick enough to throw up—not that there was much of anything to come up if her body did heave.

"All right, sugar!" The gravelly male voice rang out from the doorway. "We have a treat for you today," he said in a disgustingly sing-song way. "Food truck arrived! See?" he put his hands up in a *you doubted me?* kind of way.

His shadow fell over her. "Oakley knows that eating healthy helps your kind stay active and attentive. Sooo he went out of his way just to help you out."

Oakley?

His revolting face was angled down at her and carried a smile not meant for joy. "But only if you keep up the good work you're doing and don't give us any *trouble*." The last part was said while wrenching her arm upward, yanking her from the cold, hard safety of the ground.

His laid-back southern drawl seemed misplaced for the person he was. Images of a good ole southern boy with that sort of drawl flipped through her mind. Kind. Chivalrous. Respectful.

He was none of those things.

"Let's make Daddy proud, shall we?" Jerking her through the prison-barred doorway, she could hear the girls sniffling behind her. She felt their shadows grow darker, heavier. Each one praying it wasn't their turn that day.

With a last-ditch effort and a burst of energy from deep in her gut, she pulled her arm back as far as she could and screamed, "NO!" Her small fist connected squarely with the side of his face. To her surprise, she packed enough power to create a crunching sound beneath his skin and within his cheekbone. Unfortunately, her own brittle body took a beating as well. Holding out her mangled and throbbing hand, she could tell that at least one knuckle had broken in the process.

Barely breaking stride, he growled in pain. A growl that echoed throughout the dark and dirt-walled hall, sending shivers down the spines of all the women now cowering in abject fear. Grabbing Addie by the back of the neck, his foul breath stung her nostrils with no escape as he whispered, "Oh my dear, that was a mistake."

Chapter 24
Forgiveness

Grant woke up nauseous, his hands trembling. They arrived at LIMIT late the night before. Stepping out of the vehicle, they weren't immediately impressed by the minuscule building sitting in the middle of a field.

Seeing Grant's dismissive sigh, Madison said, "Hey, you know the old saying, right? Don't judge a secret ops facility by its facade. Wait 'til you see what's underground."

Tired, he thought, *just once, it would be nice to experience a secret base on a mountaintop with a great view and a heated infinity pool.*

Madison had brought everyone up to speed on each of the women during the drive. Grant felt some relief at the news but the knots in his stomach had grown tighter the closer they got. Witnessing Lexi's abilities firsthand on that final day was undeniably terrifying. However, he'd also seen her at her weakest and most vulnerable. Watching as the winding vines made their way up her body every time his team fought to keep her from moving, from living. He wasn't just an accessory to her abuse—he was her abuser. Convinced he was protecting her in the most humane environment possible. Now? He wanted to throw up.

She was asleep when they'd arrived, but now, with a full day ahead, his hands shook uncontrollably knowing he'd be face-to-face with her within the next few minutes. He'd been the recipient of her worst, which he deserved. But also her best. She'd saved him. He'd saved her.

Rolling over, he pushed himself up and decided that no matter what came of their reunion, he deserved whatever wrath she wanted to inflict.

"Grant?" Madison's soft voice came through the door.

He stood and opened it for her.

"I didn't want to wake you, but we need to go over the plan," she said, hesitating at the sight of his pasty complexion. "Is everything okay?"

"Yeah, no. I mean, I'm fine," he muttered, turning in circles, looking for his hoodie.

She could sense that he was nervous about seeing Lexi and wanted to tell him that she wouldn't be upset, that she was thankful to be free, or any number of things to calm his fears, but she also knew her words wouldn't stop him from beating himself up. "I'll be right out here when you're ready."

It took him a few minutes to put himself together before building up the courage to step out of the room. Madison was the only one waiting outside his door. With a nod, he dutifully followed as they stopped to pick up Maria and Gavin along the way to what she called the JOC, Joint Operations Cell. As they casually entered into the open room, he was distracted by the monitors on the wall. He'd never seen anything like it.

Maria and Gavin were met with smiles, hugs, and joy that everyone was alive and well. Receiving the same welcome, his trembling had begun to subside when the group parted. Lexi was just standing there in the open.

Holding his breath, he immediately noticed the spiderweb veins still winding their way from her hairline down below her shirt collar, stopping dead center on the bridge of her nose. He was shocked at how healthy and at ease she seemed to be. His feet froze in place along with his lips.

Lexi took several slow steps toward him until they were only a few feet apart.

Her eyes were glossed over with moisture, making the ocean blue bounce off the crystal sparkles even more vibrantly.

"I thought... I thought you died," she whispered, staring him directly in the eyes.

"I think maybe I did," he quietly replied, swallowing the lump in his throat. "But I believe you may have brought me back. That you saved my life."

"You were so still. I should have stayed, but... I was scared."

"It's okay, Lexi. It wasn't your job to save me. In fact, it would be understandable if you wanted me dead."

She shook her head back and forth without breaking eye contact. "No, you saved me."

"But I hurt you. All those years, I—"

"You did," she cut in, looking down at the floor between

them, her words stabbing at his heart and twisting his stomach. "But I suppose I hurt you too."

"It's not the same," he corrected her, his voice beginning to crack.

"I know," she tilted her head toward her sisters. "But I think… maybe if all this hadn't happened, we wouldn't have found each other." Zuri stepped forward and took her sister's hand.

Grant pulled his gaze over to Zuri, then the other women. Their eyes were all bright and shining. The room had an electric hum, and he could feel goosebumps form as the hair on his arms stood up.

Lexi released Zuri's hand and took another small step forward. "You saved me, Grant. And by doing that, we were all brought back together. I could never hate you for that." She wrapped her arms around him as tears fell down his cheeks and his chest began to heave. Hugging her back, it was then that he recalled the vibrations. Taking several deep breaths, the memory rushed to the forefront of his mind. Squeezing her tight, he whispered, "I remember this. I remember this feeling, lying on the floor."

He could feel her begin to smile. Pulling back just far enough to look into her eyes, he asked, "Is this how you saved me? How did you know?"

"I didn't. Not at the time. I was upset that I couldn't save you. Until you were rescued, I thought you were gone. That I'd never see you again."

The room remained silent, though as more people entered, the hustle of the day began to build. From off to the side, Aidan, giddy with the turn of events, chimed in, "Ladies and gentlemen, he felt the tingle. This is how a great love story is made right here, folks!"

Zoey, without missing a beat, hip-checked him, knocking him into a nearby desk. Sticking his tongue out and making a cry-baby face, he rubbed his hip then moved further into the room as laughter broke out in short bursts.

"Okay, everyone! Great job yesterday. Back to work. We'll do a back brief from the mission in one hour and start planning our next step to determine if there's a reciprocating threat from VISP after all this." Jahnsen turned toward the three new people they'd just rescued and held his hand to Maria. "We're really glad to see you're okay and have you with us. We'll take good care of you."

Maria cocked her head and looked him square in the eye before putting her hand in his. Her grip was firmer than most men, and her expression lethal. "Mhmm. And what took you so long? We were in there rotting. Starving. Terrified for our lives in hiding."

"But I... we..." he stammered, eyes wide at the accusation.

Gavin, reaching past Maria, took Jahnsen's hand while looking at her with a firm stare. "We *were* not, and we *did* not."

"Don't tell Mr. Jahnsen that! We could've been here this whole time recuperating if they'd kicked in the unlocked door a little sooner!"

"We're the ones that didn't respond to their calls, Maria," Gavin said, still shaking Jahnsens' hand while sparring with the woman he'd come to love.

Turning his attention back to Jahnsen, he clarified, "We appreciate the rescue, Sir. I'm a little turned around. Would you mind pointing me toward the infirmary? I have a feeling I'm going to need it when I let go of your hand."

Justin watched the unprofessional trainwreck of an interaction unfold, laughing with embarrassment.

As Jahnsen walked away, Gavin turned to catch Justin's expression. "What?"

"Who are you?" he blurted out.

"Listen," said Gavin, shaking his head, his cheeks turning red. "I think I was locked up with the Queen of Sass too long, my friend." With a burst of laughter, they embraced in a solid man-hug. "Missed you, Justin."

"Missed you too. Glad to have you back."

"We thought you didn't make it," said Gavin, choking up. "I watched through the window. It was… it was…."

"Terrifying? Yeah, it was. And a miracle any of us survived."

"How?"

"Zuri. Like an electro-magnet, she somehow pulled almost all the bullets toward her and away from us."

"Toward her, huh?" Gavin repeated, the wheels in his mind rapidly spinning.

Justin nodded.

"She was too inexperienced to push the bullets away from the group, which means she did the only thing she could think of at the moment." He wasn't really looking at Justin but instead scrolling through the images of the assault in his mind.

"We think so too. Now all the girls are working on figuring out what they're capable of. It's quite the sight to see," Justin said, smiling at the sight of his longtime friend.

"I bet," he said, squeezing Justin's shoulder before asking what he really wanted to know, "When's breakfast?"

Chapter 25
Home

"Home?" said the only girl in the room who dared get close to Addie. Addie had to turn her head to the left in order to see the girl out of her good eye.

"Yeah," Addie said, clearing her throat. "Where do you call home?"

Looking upward, her eyes seemed to scour the ceiling for an answer, all the while wrinkling her nose like a child might. Finally, she said, "I guess, once upon a time, I would've said Mississippi."

"But not anymore?"

The girl inched closer. She might have been older than Addie but was short, scrawny, and her hair was only beginning to grow out again into tight little ringlets. She supposed their abusers were too busy working her over to deal with anyone or anything else, like continuing to shave the other girls' heads.

"It's been a long time. A really long time. Sometimes I forget I've ever been anywhere else but here, wherever here is."

"What about your family?"

"I don't know." Her eyes caught Addie's before skirting over to a small group of women huddling together in the corner. "I guess they're my family now."

Addie looked around the cage at the girl's unexpected family trying to imagine any of them out in the real world. "How long have you been here?" she wondered out loud, suddenly afraid to breathe, knowing that her response wasn't going to be the answer she wanted to hear.

Turning back to face Adeline, she said, "I really don't know. Several winters. Maybe four or five."

Addie's one good eye opened wide. Nearly choking on her deep breath and parched throat, she exclaimed, "Years? You've been here for years!" Drawing out that last word, Addie's mind began to race.

The girl's hands started shaking. Nerve damage and exposure had robbed her of control of her limbs, particularly when anxiety crept in. Like a reflex, her hands lifted up from her lap in a rehearsed series of movements as she worked to settle the trembling down.

Addie reached up, taking hold of both of the girl's hands. "I'm so sorry. I'm sorry this happened to you." She took a deep breath, looked back at the main door, then quietly asked, "Have any of you ever tried to escape?"

The girl's knuckles turned white as she clasped Addie's hands. "A few times. New girls will try something. Most of us have," she said in a hushed voice, releasing Addie's hands. "But there's no way out. There never is. Some of them still have threads of hope in this… this hopeless place."

With nothing left to say, the young woman made her way back to huddle with the others. Turning around, her sunken eyes and sagging cheeks appeared even more exaggerated. "Adeline. It's not that we don't want to help you," she said, flicking her eyes to the heavy iron-barred door. "You see, you're the one they've been looking for this whole time. And they'll kill all of us to get you to do what they want."

Her half-hearted smile only made Addie feel worse, and her final statement stripped away any morsel of hope that they might help her or themselves if the opportunity arose.

Hope.

She's right. This is a place hope goes to die.

"Madison is getting worse, guys," said Lexi, her voice carrying her fear from the backseat of Joe's car. Madison wasn't seizing or contorting her body. It was worse than that. She was listless and pale.

Having rescued Gavin and Maria three days prior, they decided to leave Ohio and head to Sanford, NC. Their first stop would be Central Carolina Hospital on the hunt for birth records. There was a connection there they needed to tease out, and ultimately, without question, they needed to find Adeline and Joanna.

Though their ability to heal rapidly was one of the many bonuses since they'd found one another, they were still recovering. Most significantly, Zuri remained tender inside and out. Joe knew that even if they had all been in top shape, there was no way he could have avoided all of the infamous Midwest potholes. Between Madison's gift of serenity, and Zuri's ability to foster growth, which, as it turned out, also meant healing, their recovery was beyond the realm of the average human.

With Lexi was nearby, their individual abilities were stronger, more controlled, and more focused. Early on, Lexi didn't consider herself unique in comparison to Zuri. Yet, among this band of sisters, she no longer doubted what she had to offer was important.

It was like watching a miracle unfold as each one explored and engaged in depth their own gifts. As if suddenly and yet organically fully aware of how to use them like never before. When they were together, everything about the group was stronger. Only now, in the backseat on an open stretch of road, whatever was happening to Madison was something they couldn't diagnose, let alone combat.

There were a total of five vehicles in the convoy back to North Carolina. Zuri was in the cab with Madison, riding shotgun alongside Joe, while Justin and the others were in a different vehicle. Phil insisted on joining in person, while Jahnsen stayed back to manage the operation from LIMIT. From the home base, he could watch the *eyes in the sky* and prepare a full combat unit if necessary. Just to be safe, he sent a small contingent of operators on the road with them not only for protection but also for the impending rescue of Adeline.

Jahnsen wasn't too happy with their plan but knew he couldn't control what the women decided. They wouldn't be ready for, or even willing to consider, anything else until they'd recovered the rest of their sisters.

As it stood, they were in a race against time, helplessly watching Madison's eyes change for the worse. Where they once illuminated a crystalline green, only one remained a bright emerald, while the other now turned an unsettling midnight black. The crystalline in her dark iris diminished by the day. Lexi tried to protect her the same way she protected Zuri when they were little, but whatever was happening to her seemed to be coming from within.

Joe sat quietly in the driver's seat. He didn't understand it, but he could feel the electric vibration in the air and had come to recognize it as a side effect of the girls trying to do something the rest of humanity was incapable of. What he did understand, however, was that his new role among this expanding group of women was fairly similar to his old one with Zoey.

Be nearby.

Make the plan.

Drive the car.

So that's what he did. With his eyes forward on the car ahead in the convoy, he watched as arms flailed and heads shook, assuming some sort of intense conversation was unfolding.

Probably discussing the best way to infiltrate the fire training area and avoid detection, he thought. Joe was beginning to appreciate the professionalism of the well-trained, well-funded team expansion.

"See! You guys get it. Natural is the way!" Aidan shouted, bouncing in the back seat. Nearly ten minutes from his apartment building, his childlike excitement wasn't *just* about their current topic.

"That's crazy Joe would even argue the point. I mean, milk comes from a cow. How much more natural can you get?" said Justin, feeding into the argument while trying to hold in a laugh.

"*And* Zoey uses bananas, which somehow makes it perfect. See? Bananas? Hello, duh!"

Grant was seated up front in the passenger seat, struggling to keep a straight face. He pretended to nod in agreement with Aidan just to keep the entertainment going. For the first time in years, he felt like a real, ordinary man.

Zoey rolled her eyes and held up her hands in defense, trying to avoid Aidan's flying elbows. Catching Justin's eyes in the rearview mirror, he winked, which made her chuckle.

Aidan stopped mid-sentence, glanced at Zoey, then up at Justin. "Aw, man," he whined. "I knew it was too good to be true." Pursing his lips, he crossed his arms then turned to look out the window.

Flashing him a sarcastic *what's wrong?* look in unison, Zoey and Justin burst out in laughter. Aidan wasn't having it.

"We're here," said Zoey, sobering up as they pulled up to her building. Reaching over and grabbing Aidan's shoulder, a smile of gratitude washed over her face.

"Thank god," said Aidan, his pouting quickly forgotten. "I didn't realize how much I'd missed my bed."

Four other vehicles parked around them as they came to a stop. "We're probably terrifying everyone in the building with this entourage," said Zoey. She stepped out of the vehicle quickly, hoping to reassure anyone watching with her presence.

Everyone followed suit, stretching and pulling bags and supplies out of cars. Joe, Aidan, and one of Phil's men went inside to do a quick check of the place.

"This is where you live?" Lexi asked Zoey.

"It is. It's not perfect, but it's home." She smiled wide at seeing the old building again.

"It's out *here*. It's real life," said Lexi, turning in circles and taking in the neighborhood. "I think it's perfect."

Zoey wrapped her arms around Lexi, which created the now recognizable pulse between them—something that had become a welcome, familial feeling. "From now on, wherever we're together is home. This is just as much your place now, you and Zuri, Madison, all of us. Or we can find somewhere new. Either way, we're not going to lose each other again."

"Never," Lexi whispered, her cheeks blushing.

Joe emerged from the doorway. "All clear! Let's head in. I've got the keys for each of the apartments you guys can— AGH!" he shouted, jerking his shoulders up and nearly dropping the keys.

The hand on his shoulder offered a gentle squeeze.

"Sheila?" he said, turning to see her familiar grin, filled with an emotion he didn't know he felt until that moment.

"Joe? Are you okay? And Zoey?" Joe smiled then nodded out toward the vehicles. Sheila's eyes followed. Seeing Zoey in the crowd, she took a deep breath before letting out a heavy sigh.

"They're a sight to see, huh?" he said quietly.

Zoey, catching sight of Sheila, dropped her bags on the pavement with a thud. Her feet moved forward without any command from her brain. Memories like emotions swept in: working together in her garden, scrapes being patched up, a hug when she needed one. She recognized a feeling she didn't know was there until that moment. Sheila was like a mother to her.

She truly did feel at home.

"Hi, Doc," said Zoey, her voice now quiet and crackling with emotion didn't quite carry over to Sheila's ears. Regardless, any fear Sheila had about Zoey being angry with her for not sharing who she really was melted away with the look in Zoey's eyes. However, the shock of Zoey's face, now half-covered with a purple and black webbing woven through, turned her melting heart hard. Gritting her teeth and sharpening her focus, she placed her palm on Zoey's cheek and, with a slight growl, asked, "What happened? Who did this to you?"

Before Zoey could answer, Lexi's face appeared in Sheila's peripheral vision. Stumbling back, she gasped as the full impact of their similarities hit her. "Lexi? What on earth…."

Zoey placed her arm around Lexi's shoulders, dramatically revealing the mirror image of their shared trauma.

"How?" Sheila put a hand to her mouth then reached out to touch Lexi's face as well.

"Kind of a long story, but honestly, we aren't exactly sure," said Zoey, looking back toward Zuri and Madison. "We seem to be connected. All of us. In different ways. We can explain more later, but what we really need is—"

Sheila pulled them both into an embrace. "I'm so sorry this has happened to you, but I'm so grateful you've found each other."

Silently and without invitation, Aidan leaned in from behind Sheila and whispered, "It's because they're witches."

Zoey reached back to smack him but Sheila beat her to it.

"What? Just came to say hi to Sheila," he groaned, rubbing his arm before bounding past them back to the car.

Pulling back from the two women in her arms, a determined

look came over Sheila's face. "Let's get you girls inside and have a look at you."

"Hold on, Doc, we're fine. We just need you to take a look at—"

Turning, Sheila watched in shock as Aidan scooped Madison's weak body into his arms. "Aidan? Who's this?"

"Madison... and she's not doing so well, Doc."

"Why didn't anyone say anything? I'll meet you in apartment eight. I need to grab my med kit." Apartment eight had been turned into a clinic for Doc Sheila years ago. Zoey was all the more grateful they had as she looked around at their ragged group.

One shock led to another as Sheila caught Zuri maneuvering out of a vehicle with a cane. "Zuri?"

Zuri smiled, unafraid, looking at Sheila as if they already knew one another.

The bruises and bandages on the girl's body told a different story of trauma than her sister's. Sheila reached toward her, gently brushing a lock of strawberry blond hair away from her eye. Her heart broke, believing she might have spared Zuri and Lexi some of the pain they'd endured if she could have only kept them safe with her. Raise them as her own.

"Leave the bags for the others. Girls, come with me."

Chapter 26
The Plan

"This is insane," Joanna mumbled. She and Brandon were back at his cabin. Her body was covered in bug bites. Thankfully, he had an entire bottle of calamine lotion he'd never needed.

"It's not that bad. You look like, uh, you know…."

"I look like what?"

Gesturing toward her in a circular motion indicating her entire body, he said, "Fine, I lied. You look like a pink elephant." Walking over, he took the bottle and now pink rag she'd been using to apply the lotion. "Turn around. I'll get your neck."

She would've felt embarrassed, but the itching voided anything beyond her desire to scratch.

"Just know that deep inside my heart, I'm mad at you for the pink elephant comment." With a long sigh, she relaxed as the cool lotion hit her hot, itchy neck.

Looking at her splotchy, though delicate, neck, he was mildly annoyed that she was so severely not an outdoorsy person. And yet, at the same time, he wanted to squish every bug that placed so much as a scrawny leg on her flesh.

"There. Done," he said, clearing his throat. Quickly stepping back, he needed to put some space between her and this out-of-nowhere desire to protect her, even from the flying and crawling sort.

"Thank you," she said, shifting on the floor to face him. Her arms and legs remained spread apart, pant legs pulled up to mid-thigh, sleeves pushed up over her shoulders, and her neckline stretched so far out that it hung low on her chest.

He blinked several times at the live magazine ad for calamine lotion in front of him. "Were you out there naked? How does one person attract so many bugs? In pants. And long sleeves."

He would've given anything for a camera at that moment to relive the image anytime he needed a good laugh. And laugh he did. In fact, once he started, he couldn't stop.

"Oh, haha. Yeah, this is super funny right now. How come you don't have any bug bites?" she whined, struck with the infuriating urge to scratch her neck again.

Surprisingly, her whine sounded so pleasing to his ears that all he wanted to do was pull her to his side and hold all the critters at bay. Instead, between laughs, he replied, "Cause I'm too bitter for 'em. They know me. You, Anna, are fresh meat."

Ducking away from the pillow tossed at his head, he followed up with, "Hungry? We need to eat something while we go over our next move."

"The next move is easy," Joanna said off the cuff, though it hit Brandon like a slap in the face. "I let them take me."

Joe had provided keys so that almost everyone had their own apartment. However, just about everyone except the operators ended up in Zoey's apartment anyway.

Sheila had Zuri and Madison in apartment eight, assessing their injuries or, in Maddy's case, determining if there was a way to help her fight back the inner onslaught she was experiencing. Back in her apartment, Zoey prepped the sleeping areas while waiting for Jahnsen's last few guys to arrive. She wasn't good at sitting still.

"You know, I was really looking forward to sleeping in my own bed when we got back," Aidan grumbled, watching Zoey change his sheets.

"You could help me, ya know."

"If I did, it would be a betrayal to my bed."

"Aidan," she said, dropping the sheet, "you never sleep in this bed anyway! The couch is your usual go-to. You'll be fine."

"Fine. But if I catch one person drinking from my coffee mug, oh boy!"

Zoey knew that despite his joking, Aidan wouldn't have had it any other way. He understood that no matter what, these four women weren't going to be apart. He also knew that he had no plans of letting them out of his sight. A plan that Joe, Justin, and Grant equally shared.

Maria and Gavin, on the other hand, were more than happy to snag a key for the apartment next door but came right back to join the group after dropping off their bags.

Joe spent the brief time waiting for everyone to settle in by putting together optional rescue plans. He wasn't one to waste time, and watching Maddy get carried into apartment eight by Aidan solidified what they were all feeling—that their window of opportunity was waning.

Everyone gathered around the coffee table in their living room. The moment the apartment door clicked shut, Justin dove right in. "Alright, so what are we doing?"

Everyone's eyes gravitated toward Joe.

With his cheeks turning red, Joe took a deep breath and said, "So we know at least a few pieces of the puzzle. One, based on what Jahnsen's crew has and the visions you girls have had, we're fairly sure this woman, Adeline, is at the Fire Training Area. I know where it is. I've been out there before."

"You did the security out there for Oakley, right?" Zoey clarified.

"Yes," he said, clearing his throat and wiping small beads of sweat forming on the back of his neck. "The guy that was out there a few years back, Oakley, is supposedly prior military. From what I know of him and that place, it was essentially a bunker he and some buddies turned into their safe house. Like we did here with the apartment building. I'm not sure if he's still out there, though."

"After all this time, you couldn't find a source, a satellite image, not a peep on his present happenings over there?" said Justin, slightly annoyed.

"First, that's a Jahnsen question. I don't have the equipment for that, *nor* would I have ever thought there was a need to look. Second, he isn't the kind of guy to leave accidental traces of his whereabouts, if you know what I mean."

"Joe, it's okay," Zoey cut in. Putting her hand on his, she assured him, saying, "I know you had no idea what was going on at the training field and no one's blaming you. There's no way you could have known. After all, I didn't either. Overall, anything you have to offer is a good thing."

"Yes. It is," agreed Lexi. "That means you know much more about how to avoid their surveillance than any of us."

Zuri entered as Lexi finished speaking. Aidan jumped from the couch to let her sit. Maddy came in behind her looking much better than she had only a few hours prior. Sheila was known for her naturalistic healing and Zoey was again reminded how much she cared for the woman.

With a quick nod of thanks to Lexi and Zoey, he continued, "The second thing is we may be able to get confirmation she is, in fact, there based on Madison's… uh, connection."

Madison curled up on the couch, less pale but not 100 percent either. "I feel like, being here, I can sense her better."

"It's easier for me to feel her now, too," Zuri quietly piped in.

Aidan asked quietly, "Kind of like when we were at VISP and you were walking around the lobby area trying to reach out to Lexi?"

"Yes," mouthed Zuri, smiling at Aidan in confirmation.

"I can't believe how much I've missed," Grant whispered to himself.

"It's a lot to process." Lexi placed her warm hand on his forearm. "We can talk more later if you have questions." Her smile was infectious, even after all she'd been through. He couldn't believe how significantly the tables had turned, that she was now comforting him. She was right. It was a lot to process.

"Yes, so," Joe continued, "there are a couple guys that live pretty close to that location that I know. I want to chat with them both to find out if they've heard or seen anything recently that's out of the norm. The one, Thomas, tends to be pretty social. He might've heard if anything interesting or odd has been going on. The other, Brandon, lost his girlfriend out there in the woods several years back. He doesn't get out much unless he's getting supplies. Spends most of his time in those woods, though, so he may know if anyone has gone missing recently.

"I think that's where we start," he finished.

"Why don't I take a couple operators and head to the hospital, see if we can find any records?" Zoey knew Joe wouldn't like that idea, but someone had to go.

"I don't kn—" Joe started.

"I'll go with her," Justin quickly added.

Joe fixed his eyes on Justin for a moment before nodding in concession. Justin's closeness with Zoey grated on him, but he kept his thoughts and emotions in check.

"How about I follow up with Thomas and Brandon instead while you and one of the operators scout the FTA?" offered Aidan. "You'd be able to point out any changes made to your surveillance since you installed it. I think that would make good use of our time, ya know? And to be honest, I don't think we have much of it left."

Lexi squinted her eyes, honing in on Aidan. "Why do you say that?"

He hadn't realized the weight of his words until she'd acknowledged them. "I... I just mean, looking at Madison, she's getting weaker. All of you have been having nightmares at night, similar to what Zoey had with Lexi before we found her. Just, logically, I mean… I think whatever's happening to Adeline is only getting worse. Not better."

Everyone broke eye contact, uncomfortably shifting in their seats. Everyone but Zuri. A slight smile formed across her thin lips despite the heaviness of the moment.

"Hey, Aidan?" Zoey said. Standing up, she grabbed his arm and pulled him to his feet, asking, "Can I talk to you? Outside?"

As they exited into the hall, the rest of the group began to talk logistics. Zuri, however, was only half paying attention as her eyes followed Aidan and Zoey out the door.

Once inside the stairwell, Zoey closed the hall door, immediately unleashing a sharp interrogation. "What is going on with you lately?"

"What do you mean?"

"I mean, you seem to know things, or, I don't know, feel things lately that…."

"Don't make sense coming from me?"

"Yes!" she said, smacking him in the arm. "Where is it coming from? What was that in there?"

He looked down at the ground trying to collect his thoughts before speaking.

"See what I mean? You're thinking before speaking! What's that all about?"

"It's hard to explain. I mean. Seeing all of you together, watching what's happening to you, watching these gifts and powers come to light more and more as the days pass…." His arms moved as he spoke, as if they were trying to help him get his point across. "It's just… it's just very similar to some things I remember my mother doing."

Zoey's eyes grew wide in disbelief. "Wait. What?"

"I don't know how to explain it. Growing up, things were second nature to her. She seemed to always know what I was thinking, which by the way was *not* awesome as a teenage kid. She could feel things. Like when my aunt injured her foot, my mom felt it and called her. When my aunt answered the phone, she was sitting at the bottom of her staircase waiting for my uncle to race home from work and take her to the ER." Looking straight into Zoey's eyes, he said, "My aunt lived over three hundred miles away."

Zoey was speechless. They'd lived together, witnessed her own odd powers develop, and experienced crazy events as of late, and yet this was the first time she'd heard anything on the subject. Trying to process what he was saying, and with a few false starts, she asked, "Did your mother grow up here?"

"She was a teenager when her folks moved her down here."

Pacing in tight circles and breathing deep, she said, "Okay… so… I don't know what any of that means." Stopping right in front of him, she put her hands on his shoulders. "So maybe," she continued, her mind racing on overdrive, "I don't know, do you think *you* can sense things?"

He wasn't sure what to say. Finally, shrugging his shoulders, he said, "I mean, can't we all sometimes? My mother always said I had great intuition for a boy." He smiled wide, watching as his self-praise dismissed her all-too-serious curiosity.

"Ugh, you're a pain," she said, pushing him back and shaking her head.

"What! So now I'm suddenly not so special anymore?"

She stared at him, knowning there was more to all of this that he wasn't saying, but she also knew Aidan would only share when he was willing to. "Let's get back. We need to find out when we're leaving."

Aidan's faux smile faded as he took an extra long breath before following her in. There was a lot more he probably should've told her but the timing didn't feel right. Shaking off the memories, he left those thoughts out in the stairwell.

Chapter 27
The Reprieve

Addie snuggled into the warmth as if rolled up in a blanket. Comfortable and cozy, she soaked in the softness surrounding her.

It had been a dream. A nightmare. A horrible nightmare.

Settling in with a deep sigh, she tried to pull the heavy comforter over her nose, but her fingers wouldn't cooperate. Pain shot up her arm with each tug at the blanket. The shock opened her right eye wide, and her failed attempts at opening her left eye sent tidal waves of pain through her skull and down each limb. Pain that overshadowed that of her fingers.

Breathless, she slowly rolled over on the mattress, wincing in shock with every inch of rotation.

As her eye caught the brownish ceiling and drooping fan

overhead, she knew she wasn't at home. Wasn't safe.

The nightmare was real.

Sitting up, the room began to spin. The last thing she recalled was lying on the dirt floor with the other girls behind prison bars. Freezing. Alone. While she wasn't freezing any longer, the alone part hadn't changed.

The room was familiar. She'd seen it, or one like it, some time ago. The room with the woman in the bed. Alive but not moving.

Addie was torn. On the one hand, she hadn't been this warm and comfortable in so long that all she wanted to do was slink back under the covers and hide for as long as they'd let her. On the other, she knew she should be looking around for a weapon or a way to escape.

Sliding her legs across to the edge of the bed, she gently pushed herself forward until her feet touched the cold floor.

Instantly she regretted her decision.

Pain shot up her legs from her broken toes.

She collapsed back onto the warm mattress and focused on breathing. *In and out. Out and in.* She'd always been good at compartmentalizing and this was no different. Usually, she would separate her thoughts, hiding unnecessary ones in a corner in the back of her mind until she was ready for them. This time she separated her physical pain the same way.

Lying there, she could feel a vibration along the surface of her skin. She had felt it before over the years. It was always an odd but welcome surprise. Feeling pain in her foot and in her eye and in too many other places in between, she pushed the aches and burns away. Pushed them all into that dark space. Picturing each one in her mind as she honed in on the source, she imagined herself tucking them away in order to feel some relief.

Breathing slowly, one by one, the agonies spread throughout her body eased. Not completely gone, but no longer front of mind, defeating her. She had no clue how long she'd been there or how she got there, but her mind was clearer than it had been since she arrived. For the first time, she felt rested.

Exploring the room, she maneuvered to a desk in the corner that held some paper and a pencil in a drawer. *I know what I'd like to use this for,* she thought with a small burst of laughter, envisioning the pencil being jammed in one of those horrible men's eyes. There was a chair by the bed and a door next to that. Thinking it was a closet, she opened it to find a bathroom.

"Oh!"

Fumbling through the doorway, her hands landed on the cold, smooth edge of the porcelain sink. The dim light revealed a face in the mirror that was unrecognizable.

She turned on the hot water, internally celebrating as it ran cool and clear before turning warm. Putting her face under the stream, she simultaneously drank as the water washed over her face. *I never thought I'd be so grateful for running water.* When it became too hot to bear, she pulled her face away and thrust her hands under it.

A shower.

Her good eye noticed it in the mirror, and before she had time to think, she flung open the curtain.

Addie started laughing.

This isn't really happening. I must be dreaming.

She turned the nozzle and it rained.

Turning quickly to undress, vertigo hit, causing her to fall to her knees. The cool tile beneath her helped steady the shakes until the world stopped spinning. Grasping the porcelain sink, she cautiously stood back up. With the water running, she hoped anyone paying attention would think she was busy cleaning up.

Slowly, she moved out of the bathroom and into the bedroom. Looking at the ceiling, the corners, and the minimal furniture in the room, she searched for cameras and other devices that would tell her she was being monitored.

Not seeing anything, she grabbed a piece of paper and the worn-down pencil and began to write:

Joanna,

I love you. Those are the first words I want you to read if you ever get your hands on this letter. I'll love you forever, no matter what happens.

I don't know where I am, but I think I know what they want. What he wants. Remember, as girls, we pretended we were witches? That we had power? I guess we were pretty spot on. Turns out there are things I can do. Things you can probably do. And they want it.

The man in charge here is named Oakley, though I couldn't say if that's a first or a last.

I've been having dreams or visions where I see more women. More than just you and me in the place we were taken to as little girls. I see us all together, but not as we were then. We're all grown up. It's pretty surreal. Sometimes I can't tell when I'm awake or dreaming. Whoever these women are, I think they're looking for us. You need to find these women. I don't know why, but I'm convinced they'll help you. Protect you. I think they'll love you like I do.

If you ever find this note and I'm not with it, just know how much I love you and how thankful I am to be your best friend.

There's one more thing I need you to do. There's a woman here. I think she's like us, but she's been hurt so badly. She needs them to save her. She needs you.

Don't give up. Don't ever give up. I'll always be with you.

Love, Addie

Addie read the letter over several times before folding it into a little triangle. It's something she and Joanna used to do when they were little to pass notes. She tucked it into the desk drawer before looking back at the bathroom. *Why not?* It had been quite some time since she felt hot water on her body. It didn't matter if it was too good to be true. She was getting in it.

Taking her dirty cotton pants off but leaving everything else on, she noticed the kaleidoscope of black and green, blue and purple bruises now covering her legs alone. Old cuts and gouges in her skin left dried blood smeared around them. Stepping into the steam of the shower anchored her back to reality in a way she didn't realize how much she needed. As the hot water hit her scalp, pain from the contusions caused her to flinch. Gritting her teeth, she remained, letting it wash away the dirt, blood, and old tears.

That's when she felt the shift.

The atmosphere felt heavier.

Her good eye opened just in time to see the shadow on the other side of the curtain.

"Glad to see you're awake." Addie knew that voice. *Oakley.* "You've taken an awfully long shower. I assume you're pleased with the accommodations we've given you?" It was less of a question and more of a threat.

Leaning against the back of the shower, her eye searched for anything she could use to defend herself. There was nothing.

Soap.

Grabbing it, she rubbed as fast as she could on her hands, arms, and over as much of her body as she was able.

"Time's up, sweetheart." Ripping the curtain back, he snatched her wrist, but her arm slipped right out of his grasp.

Grunting, she threw her full weight at him, causing him to slip back on the floor and land hard on his tailbone. She knew she'd hurt him, just not enough to stop him.

Addie ran for the door and flung it open only to see two men standing on the other side.

"Oh, look at this. Is it my birthday?" One of the men said as he elbowed the other.

"Looks like Christmas came early!" His yellowed teeth were more pronounced in the soft glow of the hallway light.

They each gripped an arm and lifted her off the ground, dragging her back into the room as Oakley stormed out of the bathroom. His men had grown unnaturally cruel over the years, taking pleasure in causing pain.

"Hey! I didn't give her a chance to recover so you two could destroy it."

Growling, they dropped her on the floor next to the bed. Oakley held clean hospital scrubs out to her. "Put these on. Now." It was obvious he also wanted to cause her pain, only a specific kind of pain, and managed to keep his bloodlust reigned in. "I went to all this trouble to give you a good night's rest and a chance to clean up. This is how you repay me?"

Addie grit her teeth, not so much from pain but struggling

to keep silent, knowing that no matter what she said, this was going to end badly.

"That's alright. You can repay my kindness in the practice room." The torturous place where was supposed to practice her abilities for them. Just hearing the words made her light-headed. As of yet, she'd practiced nothing other than her pain tolerance.

"Today, my dear Adeline, I have a true test for you. It's going to be fun. With you being rejuvenated, you'll be able to see what you're capable of. We all will!" There was a flash of excitement in his eye. "Then we'll start having some real fun, if you know what I mean?"

He didn't wait for an answer, just shut the door behind him and told his men to bring her down the hall in five minutes.

Chapter 28
Getting Caught

"**R**ed, you read me? Over," Joe said into his radio. He was at the FTA doing surveillance and wanted to see how Aidan and Lexi were making out gathering information from Thomas and Brandon.

The operator that came with him was about a hundred yards away. He signaled to Joe he was going to move further around the back of the building. They were maneuvering counter-clockwise around the compound, annotating surveillance, guards, movement, and anything else of interest.

"Red, can you hear me? Over."

"Yeah, I hear you, Gray. We're coming up on Brandon's. Thomas wasn't there, so we'll retry his place when we're done here. Anything on your end?"

Joe smirked at the sound of Aidan's rather formal demeanor, assuming that he must have been trying to play it cool in front of Lexi since he wasn't being his typical annoying self over the radio.

"Quiet. We're doing a full recon. Looks like the cameras I installed haven't been touched. Whoever's using it hasn't changed anything I did so far as I can see. Good news for us."

"Whoa, brother! Hold down your excitement over there, would ya!"

Okay. There it is. "See anything out of place over at Brandon's?"

"Not yet. I'll keep you posted."

"Roger."

Using his binoculars, Joe trained them on his recon guy to see how far he'd gotten. Once he spotted him, Joe moved his binos in a slow arc back to the building. It was quiet. The windows were dark. He couldn't tell if the lights were off or if the windows were darkened from the inside.

The surveillance cameras were all still functioning, so they were definitely being maintained. If the rest of the equipment he emplaced on the property hadn't been moved, then his job just got a lot easier.

He briefly considered walking up and knocking on the door. After all, he knew the guy, he just hadn't seen him in a while. And it's not like he could pick up a phone and let the guy know he was coming, considering there were no public phone services since the blackout.

"Blue, what's your position? Over."

A few seconds later, the operator whispered back, "Half click back from target on North side. Over."

Joe scrunched his forehead, squinting in thought. "Why so far? Over."

"Foot traffic on the perimeter. Check your nine."

Just as he said it, Joe heard leaves rustling far to his left. He whispered into his mic, "I'm made. Stand-down. If I'm not out in ten, head back and inform the others." Without another sound, he turned to see a guy in fatigues slowly walking in his direction. The man hadn't seen him yet, so as silently as he could, Joe pulled off his pack, tucked away anything that would look suspicious, then gently laid it down behind a tree.

Crouching down, he maneuvered to a tree several feet away before making a show of kicking some leaves and pretending to zip up his pants. Casually walking toward the building, he braced for impact and listened to the guy trying to sneak up on him.

"Stop right there," the man commanded. Joe, pretending to be surprised, turned around.

"Hey. What's going on? Whoa, what's with the hardware?"

The man walked up, stopping a few feet away with his weapon pointed at Joe's face. He didn't say a word, though his body language said all Joe needed to know.

"I was just coming to see Oakley. Seems he's beefed up his security a bit since I was here last."

"Seems like it. Now it's time for you to leave," the man said in a low, gruff voice as he took the safety off his weapon.

"Whoa, man, that's not necessary. Oakley knows me. I did some work out here for him."

The man slowly lifted his finger and placed it on the trigger.

"Here's the deal, I came to see Oakley. You should probably let me do that. He might not be too pleased with you if you turn an old friend away… we both know how he can get."

"Don't care who you are, man. Turn around. Go home."

Joe gauged how far this guy might take it if he refused to leave. He knew he could physically handle the guy, but would it do more harm than good. "Look, just radio him and tell him I'm here. With this kind of security, I'm guessing he might need my help further. It's what I do, man. I'm the one that put these cameras up." He pointed to the far tree where he knew a camera was attached.

The guy's eyes flicked over to it. After a moment's consideration, he said, "We'll see about that." The man kept his weapon trained on Joe as he reached behind his back for his radio. "Home base, I got a townie on the property. Says he's a friend of the Commander."

The Commander? Joe thought, mulling over this new piece of information. *Now Oakley is known as the Commander?* That alone upped the ante for the entire operation.

Several seconds ticked by before a response came. "Bring him in."

"Roger." Keeping his weapon trained on Joe, he said, "Put your piece on the ground."

Joe knew common sense would tell anyone that he was carrying. Not too many people ventured out without at least some form of weapon. Pulling his gun out from the holster at his back, he put it on the ground.

The guard flicked his own weapon toward the main building. "Let's go."

"Yeah. Got it. I'm going."

As he walked away from his gun on the ground, the guard picked it up and put it in the back of his pants. *Damn, that was my favorite one too. I'm not leaving without it.*

Knowing that Jahnsen's man was out there watching, Joe signaled him to let him know he was alright and to stand fast. Joe didn't want him leaving just yet, but he also didn't want him to make a rash move.

"You out here alone?"

"Yeah, man. We've had some weird things happening in town. Thought I'd come out to see if Oakley was having any issues."

"Uh-huh."

They made their way to the entrance of the building without exchanging another word. The sound of the forest floor crunching beneath their feet suddenly seemed particularly loud.

"Go in," the man said, nudging Joe with the tip of his weapon.

Joe turned the knob and entered the brightly lit room. He was right. They had blacked out the windows on the inside. *Another red flag probably worth paying attention to.*

"Wait here." Walking to a stairway door, he disappeared as another guard, already in the room when he entered, took over holding him at gunpoint. Joe tried giving him a friendly nod but only received an indifferent stare. He noticed the guy had broken his nose recently, and his cheekbones showed greenish-gray signs of bruising. *Something rotten's happening around here, that's for sure.*

A few minutes later that same door burst open and Oakley came walking in with a slightly too-dramatic smile at the sight of him.

"Holy crap, Joe! It's been too long!" Oakley said as he walked up, holding his hand out for a hearty shake. "Put that down!" he barked at the guard, smacking the end of the gun.

Joe put out his hand with a fake smile of his own. "Hey, Oak. Looks like you've increased your security around the place since I saw you last." He said it without any accusation, just observation.

"Yessir. We've had several break-ins. Luckily, I found a few more guys to help out with security—until we catch them anyhow."

"Nice. And sorry about that. I didn't mean to scare your boys," said Joe, cutting his eye to the guard that found him, now standing behind Oakley. The guy forced a blast of air through his nostrils and offered a subtle growl of disagreement but didn't say anything.

"Nah, these guys don't get scared," Oakley said with a laugh, "but they do have itchy trigger fingers. Glad he held his at bay or that could've gone all sorts of wrong." He chuckled again at his own joke. "Course, you have skills of your own, so you'd've probably given him a run for his money." His smile widened even more.

Joe made a show of looking around the room. "I see my surveillance is holding up. Any issues?"

"Nah. So far, so good."

"Have you had to add any others?" he asked casually. "You know, unwanted guests."

Oakley didn't answer, keeping his smile in place a little too long before shaking his head and diverting. "So what are you doing all the way out here, man?"

Joe acted as if he didn't realize Oakley deflected. "We've, uh, had some enhanced crime out by our place. More than the average cat burglar, if you know what I mean? I wanted to see if anyone else was having issues." He paused before adding, "We also recently had a friend go missing." As Joe spoke, he watched Oakley's facial features and body language for any measure of change. "Zoey met her a few years ago. The girl was traveling and stopped to stay with us for a while. Then a few weeks ago, she said she was going out to find some weird plants for Doc over there."

Oakley's eye twitched at the mention of Doc. His jaw muscles began to bulge and his lips pursed as if in anger, but only a flash before he brushed it off. "Sheila still over there with you guys?"

"Oh yeah. Yeah, she's still there."

"Must be nice having a doc on hand when you need one," he chuckled, but the sound wasn't exactly humorous as the two other men in the room subtly shifted their stance.

"Yeah, real nice. Have you gotten up with her yet? It's been a while, but I seem to remember the last time you mentioned wanting to meet her."

"Unfortunately, no. Not yet. Guess we've been lucky enough not to have needed one. After all, you know what they say, if you don't have your health…."

"I don't know about that," Joe shot back, nodding toward the guard at Oakley's back with the broken nose.

"Long? Nah," he said, laughing a little too hard, the way you might at an inside joke. "He's always getting into scrapes. Too tough for a doctor, though."

Long. Long. I wonder if Jahnsen knows a Long? he said to himself, sensing that Oakley was losing patience with their conversation and decided to circle back and dig a little deeper. "I just thought I'd come by, see how you were and if you'd seen a girl wandering your woods. I wasn't sure if your cameras were still working out here. Thought maybe they might've caught something. Zoey's pretty worried."

Oakley shook his head slowly, side to side. "Nah, I don't think so." He looked at his guys standing in the room and they shook their heads in unison. "The only folks we've seen were those few guys trying to break in a while back, at least not until today," he said with a wink, his false smile beginning to wane.

"That's too bad. You were my last ditch effort."

"You think she came out toward us?"

"Honestly, we're not sure. This direction makes the most sense with the woods and her search for wild edibles, ya know? We already checked north by Jordan Lake but couldn't find any signs."

"What about west?"

"Maybe. We did a cursory look that way, but getting to on foot is more difficult. Going through town is more dangerous, you know?"

Oakley pretended to ponder other options while Joe intently set to memorizing everything he could about the room he was in.

"Well, if anyone pops up, I'll sure let you know," Oakley said, clapping his hands and slowly moving Joe toward the exit.

"So, what's going on with you these days? How are you holding up?" asked Joe, pretending not to notice the advance.

Oakley paused with a look of mild frustration and said, "Uh, good. Yeah. No issues, really. Well, of course, added security. But you've already heard all about that, haven't you? Can't be too careful these days, right? You know how it goes."

Joe looked him dead in the eye. "Yeah. I sure do."

Neither spoke for a moment.

"Well, I suppose you'll be wanting to get back. Hate to get stuck out in the woods after dark. It can get sketchy out there. You hike over?" Joe knew the man was gauging how much of a threat he was to him. If he had a vehicle, it would raise flags.

"Yep. Since she left on foot, I've been trying to follow the most likely paths she could've taken. But you're right. It's time I head out. I appreciate—"

Oakley's eyes widened as the lights suddenly started flickering, relieving the tension that had been building between the two.

He turned to Long and flicked his eyes toward the stairwell. Without a word, the man hurried out of sight.

"Everything okay?" Joe asked, slowly moving toward the stairwell.

"Yeah. Course. It happens sometimes when the generator gets low. Long will take care of it. Weren't you on your way out?"

"Odd. When our gennie goes out, the lights don't flicker like that. Want me to take a look at it? Could be a—"

"Yeah, we're good, Joe," said Oakley, putting his arm around Joe's shoulders and walking him toward the door. "Just add a little more fuel and it'll be all good. But hey, I appreciate you checking in on us. If we see anyone around the area, though, I'll definitely send one of my guys to let you know. What did you say she looked like? What's her name? In case she pops up."

"She's pretty small. Dark hair. Name's Addie." He hoped he wouldn't regret revealing so much but wanted to see if the name triggered a response.

He wasn't let down as Oakley's eyes hastily glanced at one of the guards.

"That's unfortunate. Yeah, we'll keep an eye out. Be safe heading back," he said in a hurry, releasing Joe's shoulders as he opened the door. "Monroe here can walk you out to the perimeter."

"Nah, don't bother. I should be fine."

"Sure? It's no problem."

"I'm good."

Like a dog impatiently waiting to go for a walk, Oakley looked ready to jump out of his skin.

"If you don't mind though, I'd like my gun back." He pointedly looked at the guard.

"You took his weapon?" said Oakley, tilting his head toward his man. "Sorry about that Joe. Just doing their job."

Taking the weapon, Joe shoved it back in his belt.

"All squared away? Great. Safe travels, Joe."

With a nod and a quick wave, Joe purposefully walked in the opposite direction from where he dropped his pack. He needed Oakley to believe he was heading back to his apartment building.

After clearing Oakley's final surveillance camera, he circled back to his pack, quietly gathered his gear, and, grabbing his radio, whispered, "Blue, this is Gray. You read me? Over."

"Here, Gray. You good?"

"What's your position?"

"Heading toward 421. Meet you at the rally point?"

"Roger." Feeling unsettled, Joe began to clip the radio to his belt but decided to hold onto it as he made his way to the road.

The flickering lights kept cycling through his mind. It seemed important. Something was happening. He decided to reach out to Aidan feeling that none of this was coincidental.

Switching channels, he keyed his mic, "Red, this is Gray. You read me? Over."

Ten seconds went by with no response. "Red, Gray. You there? Over."

After another pause, Joe keyed his mic. "Red, report."

Just before he pushed to talk again, Aidan's out-of-breath voice came over the line. "It's Lexi. She's down. Not sure what happened, but it's like a repeat of Zoey."

Joe swore under his breath. Aidan knew better than to use names. Picking up his binoculars, he trained them on the building he'd just left. The lights were still flickering.

"What do you mean she's down?" Joe turned and picked up his pace.

"I mean, whatever's going on, even though it's Madison that's connected, it was strong enough to bring Lexi down too."

"Where are you?"

"Brandon's driveway."

"Heading there now."

"No! Go back. I'll get her home. We need to move on this. Tonight." Any hint of Aidan's usual jovial sarcasm was gone. He was scared. He was also ready to fight.

"Roger," said Joe, choosing to trust Aidan's discernment. "Brandon should be able to patch her up if needed. See if he'll come with."

"Got it."

Joe didn't waste any more time. Picking up speed, he met up with the operator where they'd left their vehicle. Jumping in, they raced back toward his apartment complex.

"What happened back there?" The operator asked.

"A lot. Looks like we're doing this sooner than later."

Chapter 29
Bait

"**I**'m not using you as bait." Brandon's tone was unwavering.

Joanna had suggested it multiple times and Brandon wasn't having it. "Drop it. You know that's not happening."

"But it makes the most sense! Let me be the rabbit. I can walk through the woods close to the FTA. We saw the security cameras. We know they'll see me. When they take me, you can follow."

"Do you even hear yourself? They will hurt you. *Hurt* you, Anna."

"If Addie can survive it, so can I."

"If!" he said, motioning with his hands.

Joanna sank back at the thought of Addie not coming back

from this. Shifting her eyes back to Brandon, she pushed the idea deep down inside. "If they try to abduct me, we'll know they're most likely the ones who took Addie. You'll know where I'll be, and you can get reinforcements if you have to. What about Thomas?"

"Thomas would not agree to put you in harm's way."

"Well, Thomas isn't here. We are. Besides, don't you know anyone else that could help?"

Brandon thought about it. He was kicking himself for being such a hermit all these years. He knew a few people that might be willing, but he hadn't seen them in so long. It was a big ask for an acquaintance. "No."

"Ugh! You're exasperating," she cried out, squeezing her head with her hands and turning away.

"Crying won't make me change my mind about putting you in a position that could kill you," his voice was intentionally cold and his words sharp. He wanted the idea dead and gone. Even more, he wished he had an undeniably brilliant alternative.

She looked up slowly. No tears were evident, only more determination. "Tears?" she said, almost too quietly. Standing up slowly, her cinnamon-gold eyes burned a hole right through him. "I'm out of tears, Brandon. And we're out of options. I'm going in there. You aren't my father or my boss, and this isn't a prison." He winced at the *father* comment. Especially considering the dreams he'd been having about her lately, not to mention the emotional rollercoaster she'd put him on. He wasn't old enough to be her father. Not even close.

"You're right about that," he replied, matter-of-fact, suddenly aware of an alternative. "However, there's always another way. Listen," he said, motioning for her to sit back down. "What we need to do is go out there during daylight hours to take down the cameras. We'll go right before sunset so that if they're using infrared in the dark, the cameras won't be switched over yet. Joe, a guy I know, is a tech wizard, and he's taught me a few things over the years during the few times we'd have a drink with Thomas."

"So there is another guy we could ask for help!"

Brandon narrowed his eyes. "Maybe. I haven't seen him in quite a long time. Regardless, we'll take out one camera, then see how long it takes for someone to come out and fix it. One of us will monitor the camera while the other will keep an eye on the building. One way or another, we'll be able to get an idea of how many people, guards, etc., are connected to that building.

"Once we have that information, we'll be able to make a better plan. We know from our surveillance that there isn't a lot of foot traffic. And power seems to flicker at certain times of the day and night. I wrote down some… hold on." Flipping through the pages in his notebook, he paused at one set of notes and said, "For three days the power flickered at ten a.m., seven p.m., eleven p.m., and three a.m. And it would happen anywhere from an hour to three hours at a time."

"Also," Joanna added, "during those times I always felt drained, sometimes having weird thoughts or visions. Something terrible is happening to my sister in there. We don't have time to sit around watching the guards walk the property."

"I know," Brandon replied quietly. "But it wasn't all four times every day. So whatever they're doing at that time is impacting their power supply. We know that every time it happens and finally comes to a stop, there are hours before it happens again. It looks like there are at least ten to twelve hours before those lights flicker from the time it ends."

"Okay, what makes more sense then? Do we attempt to infiltrate during the time the lights are flickering? Or in-between?"

Brandon smirked at her use of *infiltrate*.

"What?"

"Nothing." He shook his head and checked his smile. "I think it's better when the lights are flickering—that way when we're knocking out cameras on our way in, it may be less conspicuous to anyone watching."

Her head nodded as he spoke.

"Have you ever been inside the place?"

"Yes, but it was years ago. The best I can do is get us around the main floor. I know a stairwell leads underground, but I couldn't tell you what's down there."

"Okay. Anyone else you might know? Thomas? Jay, John—"

"Joe," Brandon corrected, rubbing his chin. "Actually, you may be on to something. I know he does jobs for folks with security. He set up something for Thomas and asked if I wanted anything out here but I said no since I'm way off the beaten path."

Joanna took a deep breath, smiled, and rubbed her hands together. They were finally on to something and it felt good. Just as she turned to sit down, a severe pain struck at the top of her neck, causing her to violently arch backward.

"Anna!" Brandon jumped from his seat to catch her. Her back was at an impossible angle and her face twisted in pain.

He turned quickly, wrestling to get a better hold of her. As he did, he caught movement in his periphery. *Who on earth?*

he thought, swiveling his head back toward the window. Just outside his front door, Aidan was there kneeling on the rocky drive and trying to contain the contortions of another woman lying on the ground.

"What the…."

Chapter 30
In Awe

Aidan hoisted Lexi's limp body over his shoulder and began to pound on Brandon's door. Unwilling to wait for an invitation, he kicked it open, shocked by what he saw. Brandon was leaning over a small, blond woman. His eyes darted frantically around the room at the sudden intrusion, eventually landing on Aidan. Aidan's gaze locked onto the woman, and for a moment, he swore it was Zuri lying there. The woman's chest rose and fell rapidly as sweat beaded on her forehead. Eyes wide and hearts racing, both men were in full panic mode.

Brandon gestured toward the couch, where Aidan quickly laid Lexi down, checked her pulse, and wiped her forehead. As their rigid bodies relaxed and waves of pain appeared to subside, the women lay still. The air between them felt heavy and charged, like a brewing storm.

The hair on the men's arms stood up. Aidan flashed a look at Brandon, knowing full well what it meant. Brandon, however, looked around the room in confusion, silently taking in the feeling and watching Aidan to gauge his response.

Lexi was the first to rise from the strange power that had possessed her. Slipping off the couch, she whispered, "Joanna?"

At her name, Joanna's gold-burst eyes opened and her head turned toward the familiar voice.

"Lexi?"

Lexi nodded and did a double take at the golden sparks glinting from Joanna. Reaching out, she pulled Joanna into a tearful embrace. The electrical charge in the air hummed. Aidan knew the healing that was taking place between them, both in body and mind. Brandon sat back, staring in disbelief and quietly rubbing the goosebumps on his arms. He watched in awe as Lexi's eyes glittered with an otherworldly intensity, the likes of which he'd never seen. And her skin, it was like a living, breathing work of art—like an intricate tapestry done without the use of thread, ink, or a skilled artist's hand.

Joanna's breath caught in her throat as she stared disbelieving into Lexi's face. The woman before her was a dream made flesh. A vision that materialized countless times in her mind's eye. Cautiously, Joanna traced the intricate patterns etched into Lexi's skin.

"I can't believe it's really you… that you're really real," she murmured. "I've seen your face in my dreams, but.…"

Lexi smiled. "I know," Her voice barely audible. "Me too."

Joanna's mind raced with questions but only one pushed its way to her tongue. The one that had been weighing on her heart and mind since she first saw Lexi's face. "Did someone do this to you?"

Brandon leaned forward, straining to listen in on their whispered interaction.

"Yes. It's a long story, but I'm okay. I just can't believe you're here," Lexi replied, shaking her head as if suddenly waking from a dream. "Here… Oh my god, Aidan, we've found her!" she stammered, gripping tightly onto Joanna's shoulders. "Joanna, do you know where your sister is?"

The question knocked the wind out of her. Tears immediately welled up in her eyes as words refused to form on her lips. Looking at Brandon, his eyes echoed the sad defeat of her own countenance.

"We think we know where she is," he offered, looking directly at Lexi, attempting to muster up a bit of confidence. "But we haven't been able to confirm it." He turned to Aidan. "If you're both here, clearly there's much more to the story? Adeline's disappearance isn't a fluke, is it?"

"Oh, man. So much more than you could imagine," Aidan said as he rose up, stretched his legs from the crouched position he'd been in, and plopped down on the couch. "Like she said, it's a long story. But since you're here, and they've been reunited, seems we can knock off a few of the missing chapters."

Giving them a brief rundown of events, he paused from time to time, raising and lowering his voice for dramatic effect. Brandon and Joanna's eyes were wide as saucers at several intense points as they worked to comprehend his insane story. Lexi, however, simply shook her head at the pageantry.

"And Zoey?" was all Brandon could muster as his mind raced.

"She's okay. It seems that within the connected group of girls, each one has a special bond with another." He glanced over to Lexi. "Zoey and Lexi are like mirror images. Those lines on Lexi's face are identical but opposite on Zoey's. We believe Madison is connected to your sister," he said to Joanna. "She's been experiencing a lot of similar symptoms, or communications, whatever they are, they're like what Zoey experienced when Lexi was in trouble."

Joanna gasped, thinking out loud in a hoarse whisper, "So Addie feels the same pain that caused what happened to you?"

Lexi shook her head. "No, no, Joanna. This is something different. We're not sure what Adeline's going through exactly—"

"It's bad. It's horrible. I've seen visions of her and...." she said, trailing off as the blood rushed to her head, rapidly inhaling shallow breaths and grabbing her heart.

"I know. We know. We're all connected," said Lexi in a soothing voice while rubbing her back. "That's why you've seen me and the others in your thoughts. There are seven of us. Maybe eight. The stronger we get, the more we can feel what the others are going through. It's just that the one that's bonded feels it as if it's happening to them."

"Is that why I keep getting glimpses of what Addie is going through?"

"Yes, and at times it's stronger. We can all feel Addie to a certain degree. But Madison is somehow… she's essentially bonded with her. So what she feels seems to be the strongest."

"So… so this happened to you?" she said, beginning to breathe fast and shallow once again.

"Yes, but I'm good, Joanna. You'll be alright too," Lexi

said with a smile that eased the budding anxiety. "The most incredible thing is that we found you. We had no idea you'd be here, but we found you."

"How *did* you find her?" asked Brandon.

"Well, like Aidan said, at LIMIT, we were concentrating on the Fire Training Area as a possible location for Adeline." Laughing, she added, "You," looking at Joanna, "were a happy accident. Aidan and I came to talk with Brandon to see if he had any information about recently missing girls. Who knew he'd be harboring one of them!" she said, squeezing Joanna's hands with a smile. "The others will be so glad to see you and know you're okay."

"I am okay. And I am excited to see them," she said as her face fell. "But Adeline isn't. She's not okay yet. She isn't here to reunite with everyone." Flashing a look back at Brandon, she closed her eyes and gently began to cry.

"We know. And we're going to find her. We have some people out there now scouting the area."

"She's not doing well. She's hurt. They're hurting her more and more every day." Joanna stood up and moved to the side of the room.

"We're going to find her, Joanna. Before the worst happens, we'll find her."

"Is it Oakley?" asked Brandon, knowing they were already pressed for time.

"Joe radioed just as we got here. I didn't catch any details because Lexi had just collapsed, but when we get back to the apartment we'll be making a plan to go in."

Brandon's face hardened. "We've been scouting it as well." He told Aidan about the patrols, the lights flickering, and the cameras.

"Dude, that sounds like a lot more people to deal with than Joe imagined. He's the one that put up the surveillance out there—which will make breaking in a whole lot easier, you know, so long as they haven't moved any of the equipment."

"I thought about that. Figured he might be the one to have installed them. That's good. Real good."

Joanna stepped toward Lexi and said, "So let's go. Let's go right now!"

"We need a better plan," said Brandon, placing his hand on her shoulder. "We need to link up with Aidan's friends and these other women. We—"

"We have a plan! Lexi, we—" she blurted out as her eyes literally flashed with excitement.

"No." Brandon's voice was hard. "That's not a plan. That's suicide."

Joanna shrugged his arm off her shoulder. "It's the only plan. If they take me, you guys can follow."

"Wait. What? Take… you want them to take you?" sputtered Lexi, shaking her head in disbelief.

"She wants to use herself as bait and have me follow."

"Yes." Joanna's voice was just as firm. "It makes the most sense. Then he'll be able to see exactly where they take me."

"It makes *no* sense. There's no guarantee that I'll be able to track you once you're taken, and with all the guards they have, we'll need more people on our side."

"Whoa!" yelled Aidan, holding his hands up to hush the crowd. "Hey, I see what you're saying, Joanna. I really do. But that is a really dumb idea."

"Aidan!" Lexi cut her eyes to him. "Joanna, I completely

underst—"

"No! You don't! None of you do. She's *dying* in there. She's my sister! I'm not waiting any longer. You can either come with me or not. But I'm going!"

Lexi quickly but gently put her hands on either side of Joanna's face. "I understand. I understand, Joanna. More than you know."

"Then you know I have to do this," declared Joanna as their eyes locked. "I would rather die in there with her than live out here without her."

Lexi didn't have to speak. She knew exactly how she felt. Wrapping Joanna up in her arms and squeezing tightly, she said, "I know."

"Listen. This isn't our first rodeo. Zoey, Joe, and I rescued Lexi's sister from that corporate sci-fi torture chamber with a cafeteria. It did *not* go well. The short version, we saved them. But not without a buttload of bullet holes, blood, and bruises."

Brandon and Joanna froze in place.

"We don't need a repeat," Lexi said under her breath. "Joanna, if we do this together, we'll have a fighting chance. We're *stronger* together."

Breathing deep, Joanna looked down at her hands. "I think I can feel that actually. It's like, there was this humming or something when you hugged me. I could feel a tingling on the surface of my skin down through my bones."

"That's it. That's how you know," Aidan said, kindly but firmly, happy to play the role of the mentor for a moment. "Just like Lexi said, you're all connected. And it gets stronger when you're together or doing something with your gifts side by side."

"What do you mean?"

"Turns out," said Lexi, stealing Aidan's thunder, "each of us has something special we can do. When we're together, those gifts are enhanced."

"How many of us are there again?" she asked, only to answer her own question. "Eight, right?"

"As far as we know. As far as we can remember, anyhow. With you, there are five of us now. Going in alone could get you hurt or killed. Our best chance is together."

Joanna looked back at Brandon, who nodded in agreement.

"She's right. I've seen it with my own eyes nearly every day since they've been together. You need to stay with us," Aidan pleaded. "You need to trust us."

Joanna's hand rested on Lexi's forearm and, with a sigh, she gave it a squeeze. Suddenly a vision violently rocked her, dropping her to her knees. Lexi felt immense pressure well up from within Joanna's body and rapidly spread throughout every fiber of her being. Broken images of Adeline flickered through her mind.

"Joanna? Hey. I'm right here," Lexi cried, kneeling down and holding fast to Joanna's arms. "Can you hear me?"

The wave of images passed just as quickly as they came. "I saw her. Tied to a metal chair. I saw her broken and beaten. Twisted and evil faces floating in and out of sight. She can't wait. I have to go *now*."

The images were brief but permanently etched in Lexi's mind the moment she touched Joanna. She knew there was nothing to stop her from chasing after her sister.

Brandon's face flushed with anger. "No! I'm sorry, but this doesn't change anything. We need them, Joanna. They already know ten times more than we do, and we don't know if Joe has learned anything new." His angry tone quickly dissolved into pleading. "I could just force you, but...."

"You could. But you won't." She turned toward Lexi. "I don't think she'll make it 'til morning."

"We're going tonight, Joanna. The plan's already in motion. Please don't do this," Lexi joined in the pleading, though sensing she'd already lost the argument.

"I'll wait until dark before I do anything. I'll drive to Highway 1, veering off north of the FTA and hiking in. If you make it there before I hit the forest, we'll go in together. Either way, I'm going. I can't let them—" she swallowed hard. "I can't let them kill her."

Brandon's jaw tightened. "*We* will go." Turning to Aidan, he said, "Hurry."

Chapter 31
Anti-Savior

"**I** picked her up. Green eyes, blond hair—carried her under my arm. I was fully involved. Neck deep in the rescue mission. I even took bullets trying to save the girl *and* our medic who held two of your little friends." Oakley sniffed. Not the sniff of emotion, but a bowel-shaking build-up of rage sort of inhale.

"I was there. And they left me." He took a step closer to Adeline. "Did you hear what I said?" Two more steps and he stuck his face right in her own. After dealing with Joe, he'd returned to find her unconscious in the practice room. After several hours of waiting for her to wake up, his rage peaked. "Did you hear me?" he bellowed. "They *left* me!" His eyes bore into hers. "Whatever happened to *leave no man behind*? I mean,

I gave my life for you! For *you*!" As his last word rolled from his lips, he swung around and hit her across the face with such force the veins in her left eye broke, causing any remaining white in her eye to turn blood-red.

Pacing circles around her, breathing in and out in a calculated manner as if it were a practiced technique, Oakley inhaled long and slow before stepping back into her line of sight. He grabbed her face, cinching tight around her jaw, then jerked upward, forcing her to look at him.

"Turns out the bullets didn't kill me." A deviant smile spread across his face. Adeline couldn't help but overlay the classic animated Grinch's sly-smiling face over top of Oakley's. "Just got the wind knocked out of me. I grabbed the girl and ran. Did exactly what I was supposed to do. Ran to the rally point," he growled, releasing her face with a shove before stepping away to pace again.

Addie's head was swimming from the initial blow, but his words began seeping in. *I was there... I gave my life for you...* she repeated over and over in her mind. His words sounded all wrong. She knew she and her sister had been abducted as little girls, though memories of that season in her past rarely came to mind. But his claim triggered something, snapshots of images about one of the men who had been lost when they were rescued. *Could this really be him?*

"My headset was damaged either in the fall or by the graze of a bullet. No one could see me as I ran. Sweat poured into my eyes and sand whipped my face, but I could still see what was happening. The closer I got I could see this… this half circle around them. A clear space with them safely within and sand just holding still in the air all around." He laughed a little too loud before saying, "It made no sense. No sense! So I stopped where I was. Not sure if I should keep running or hold back. The girl in my arms was awake. She shouldn't have been considering the meds I dosed her with. And she was staring straight ahead. Even in the pitch of night with the sand battering us, I saw this light coming from her eyes. I felt a vibration against my side that grew stronger every second." Oakley put his hand on her shoulder. "Kind of like the rapid pulsation I can feel coming from you right now," he said with his Grinch-like smile before turning away.

"The next thing I saw was the helo landing, so I started running again, but no one saw me through the sandstorm or over the noise of the chop." He shook his head back and forth. "I mean, I was standing *right* beneath the helo seconds after it took off, but did it come back for me? Nope." Turning, he looked into her eyes and whispered, "They just left."

Though she was still reeling from the hit, she considered responding to his story. A sarcastic *poor baby* echoed in her mind as he spoke, but in her current position, she knew that keeping her mouth shut was the better way to go.

"So, I got to thinking. What did I just see? What just happened? Are these girls more special than the rest of us? More special than other little girls in need of rescue? What was our real mission here? Did *you* do that thing with the sand? I mean, I knew as I was running to the rally point that the helos likely wouldn't have been able to land in the storm. But for some reason, the sand cleared in that one little space. Just enough," he chuckled, holding up his thumb and forefinger, demonstrating how narrow the clearing was.

Doing her best to hold her sharp tongue, Addie politely

asked, "The girl in the other room, is she the one you saved?"

"Yes! See, you're getting it. I *saved* her. *I* did. No one ever came back for me. For her. *I* had to save us. And I did." His face lit up at her acknowledgment. "I raised her as my own. Loved her. She's my daughter. I cared for her. I still do, in fact," he boasted, standing a little taller, feeling vindicated by her words, by her acknowledgment that he was the one that kept her alive.

"You mean—" Addie started to say, wincing at the pain resonating from the left side of her face, "you mean the woman in there that has no bodily function? Can't speak? Can't move? That's you *saving her*? Loving her as a *daughter*?"

His Dr. Jekyll and Mr. Hyde routine had her head spinning. Two long strides carried him back to her. Face to face, he put his hands on either side of her head and squeezed like a vice. She feared her cheekbones were going to shatter any moment beneath his meaty grip.

"*SHE* gave up! We had a good thing going until the power grid failed. She could see things before they happened. That girl made us a lot of money when she was young." He softened his grip but didn't push away from her. "Things got even more interesting after she hit puberty. Moving things around with her mind. Helping people…" he said, pausing for effect. "She could… let's just say she could be very persuasive." His eyes drifted and his grip softened as dark memories grabbed his attention, twisting his face. "Until she thought she could use it against me. As if I hadn't given her the best life. As if she didn't owe me for *saving* her!"

Oakley's hand pulled back as if to strike Addie again. Instead, he paused, let out a deep sigh, and dropped his arm to his side.

Once again, he looked at her with sadness. A deep-rooted sadness that seemed to wash over him and entirely out of his control. "But you're here now. I knew I'd find another one of you. It was only a matter of time before you came looking for her. People like you don't exist. I knew that eventually someone would come looking, maybe even be pulled toward her."

Addie began to chuckle, which slowly grew into laughter until she was almost in hysterics. Watching like a curious dog, Oakley backed up several steps.

Suddenly her laughter died on her lips, and with a quick snort, she spit what little moisture was in her mouth directly at him. "Are you kidding?" she yelled, again catching him off guard. "Is this a joke? She didn't *pull* me here. I was just out hiking. Your goon found me. End of story! You are disgusting. You think beating me will do what? *Make* me do something extra *special* for you? Or beating the others in front of me to have my magical powers pop out so you can use them?"

She erupted with laughter again. A deep belly laugh as he picked a knife up from the table.

"We'll see," said the Grinch. "I'll be honest with you. I mean, I feel like I can talk to you openly at this point. After all, you're a rare, fearless kinda girl, aren't you? So let's just be real with each other. What do ya say?

"Macie, her gifts grew as time went on. I eventually realized that if I could get her blood pumping, she would grow even stronger. What's the fastest way to get someone's heart pumping, you ask? Well, obviously fear. And once she no longer feared for her own life, she had to fear for others. Catch my drift?" he said, motioning toward the women in the iron prison down the hall.

"But then, one day, she just stopped. Gave up. She was still alive, I suppose, but an absolutely useless waste of superhuman power."

Tears mixed with blood ran down Addie's face like a river, slowly turning her shirt a dark and dirty magenta.

"Tsk, tsk, tsk… Does that make you sad?" he mocked, strutting towards her while staring into her eye. "I mean, hey, I didn't throw her out with the trash, right? She's here. She's safe."

Adeline scoffed, "Safe. Yes. This place is what I think of when I think of safe."

"Feel free to mock me. It's fine. The reality is, I've only kept her here as long as I have because I was waiting for one of you to show up. So, really, it's your fault her lot in life might be subject to change." His eyes bore into hers. "Cause see, if you can't rouse her from whatever dead-brained state she's in, well then… I suppose that I will be throwing her out with the trash after all."

Addie blew out a snotty cry at the thought. "No, no, no! You can't do that! I'm not special like her. I can't do what you think I can."

His hand gripped her cheeks so hard her teeth drew blood cutting into them. "Oh, but you can. I've watched and rewatched the video from your first night here. I told you before, I saw what you did, throwing those men around like rag dolls…" he said, pausing to wait for her eyes to focus on his, "and you never even touched them."

Chapter 32
Separate the Pain

"**M**addy, I found a connection! We scoured the archives at the hospital. You won't believe what we found." Zoey dropped the armload full of files onto the kitchen table.

"Ma'am?" said Rich, the operator. He had assisted Zoey at the archives and was standing with his arms twice as full as hers had been.

"Oh, sorry. Yeah, put them on the table. Thanks, Rich."

The operator nodded and left the room just as Justin entered with another pile of files. "This is going to take us forever to sift through, Zoey."

"I know, but it's here! Somewhere in here is the reason for all this. I can feel it," she said, her eyes shining brightly. The adrenaline pumping in her veins made the crystals in her eyes reflect the kitchen light into a kaleidoscope of colors.

Justin froze in place. She caught his stare and suddenly the archived files vanished from her mind. The way he was looking at her. The pull she felt. It was as if they were the only two people in the world.

He took a step closer. Instantly her chest felt heavy and throat dry. At first, it was slight and she attributed it to the pull between them. Then it became heavier. Thicker.

Her breathing quickly became restricted, and the struggle to breathe burst the budding intimate bubble that had formed around them. "Justin?" she uttered, barely getting his name out before her knees buckled.

"Zoey!" He grabbed her arm before she collapsed and helped her to the living room.

"Maddy…" Zoey whispered, her voice thin and rough from the pressure constricting her chest. Maddy was on the couch, caught up in the throes of another connection with Adeline.

Twisting and turning in a panicky attempt to reach her, Zoey pushed the weakness down as hard as she could and scrambled to her side. Zoey interlocked her fingers with Maddy's and instantly terrifying images swirled through her mind.

A crooked smile.

Eyes raging.

"…do it now…"

Pain.

"…pin her arms!"

Blackness.

Zoey's grip released with a long exhale. Maria, Gavin, and Grant rushed into the room having felt the hair on their arms rise.

"Maddy! Oh my god." Maria dropped by Zoey's side and placed a hand on Maddy's knee. "What happened?"

"Another episode," said Justin, having only partially released his hold on Zoey. "It seems that whatever Madison is experiencing has spilled over onto or into Zoey."

"Her pulse is too high," said Gavin with his fingers on Madison's neck. "She could have a heart attack at this rate. Zoey, what happened?"

"It's Adeline. It's terrible," she choked out, still gasping for air. "She's not going to survive what's happening to her, and she's taking Madison with her."

Maria jumped up. "I have sleeping and heart meds in my bag."

"Grant, go get Sheila," Zoey said, slowly regaining some of her strength. "Please!"

Grant, holding Maddy's free hand, recalled the feeling of laying in Lexi's lap in the medical bay at VISP. The same vibration he felt back then was seeping into his fingers now. But Zoey's plea snapped his attention back to the present, and, not wasting another second, bolted out the door.

Justin wasn't sure how to help, but he was committed to staying close enough to hold them down if either one began to seize.

Zoey looked at Maddy's free hand, wanting to hold it, to offer some comfort, but knowing the cost of doing so. Out of nowhere, Aidan's advice popped into her mind. *Separate your connections with one another... enough that you can still feel them or maybe acknowledge them. But not be hurt by them.*

He was right. They needed to separate themselves. Her

eyes traveled to Maddy's wincing face. Steadying herself, she reached over and interlocked their fingers.

Gritting her teeth from a jolt up her spine, the initial darkness and pain took over. Aidan's words played on repeat in her mind. The edges of the consuming blackness started to disintegrate while the throbbing in her temples eased from the vise-like pressure. Slowly, she managed to subdue the vibration felt throughout her body until it was minimally pulsating in her hand and arm.

Cautiously leaning over, Zoey whispered in her ear, "Maddy, it's Zoey. I'm right here. Can you feel my hand? I need you to hear my words. Focus on my voice. What you're feeling isn't happening to you." The muscles in Zoey's legs burned as she propped herself up to lean over Madison. "This is happening to Adeline. You aren't being tortured. You're safe. I'm right here with you."

She felt a soft touch on her shoulder and knew Sheila had arrived. "Madison, I need you to push yourself away from it. The darkness. Envision a box in your mind. Open the box and push all the darkness into it. Press it down into the box where you can see it, like watching a movie, but where you can no longer feel the weight of it."

Trembling, Zoey's legs gave out and she fell back.

Sheila crouched down and put her arm around her. "How can we help?"

Zoey saw Phil kneeling down at her side as well. Gavin was back behind the couch next to Grant, while Justin was sitting within arms reach of the both of them. *All of these people cared about her. Cared about them. All of these people are ready and willing to sacrifice so much for me... for every last one of us.*

"I don't know what to do. I don't know what I'm doing or how to help." Sheila touched the sides of Zoey's face, using her thumbs to clear the tears under her eyes.

"Yes, honey. Yes, you do. The same way you know when someone is lying to you. It's like breathing. You already know what needs to be done. Now it's time to do it." Zoey nodded. She trusted Sheila. Leaned on her instincts.

Turning toward her newfound sister lying on the couch, she had an idea.

"She needs to see me," Zoey mumbled. When no one moved a muscle, she repeated herself with more conviction. "She needs to see me!"

Bracing her hand on the coffee table behind her, she stood and looked at the others. "I need you to hold her down. Keep her from moving as much as you can."

No questions asked, they rearranged their positions to put their hands on Madison to keep her body from contorting as much as they could. Zoey put one leg over Madison, straddling her so she could look directly into her face.

She shook her hands and slowly grasped Maddy's right with her left. With her right hand, she placed her thumb and first finger onto Maddy's left eyelid. "Madison, I'm right here. I need you to see me. Once you see me, you'll know you're not the one living the nightmare. We're going to separate you from the torment, and we're going to do it together."

As she whispered, she began to open Madison's left eye.

Her eye was rapidly moving back and forth until it focused on Zoey. As if jolted by an electrical current, Maddy sat up, frantically drawing air into her lungs like she'd been drowning. With arms fighting to flail and legs struggling to break free, she gasped and groaned until Zoey wrapped her up in a firm embrace.

Stern faces eased and smiles slowly reappeared as gratefulness filled the room. For the first time in days, everyone seemed to feel a sense of relief as the terror eased from Madison's body.

After regaining some composure, Maddy asked, "How? How did you get me out of there?"

Zoey leaned back, relieved to be reunited with her friend. "I knew if I—" she began, but her words halted in her throat as Maddy's eyes connected with her own.

"Oh! Madison!" cried Sheila, the shock in her voice drew everyone else in the room one step closer. They stopped cold when Madison's gaze finally looked their way. Justin sat frozen, having seen it the moment she opened her eyes.

Zoey waved her hand over Maddy's eyes, "Maddy? Can you see?"

"Of course I can. Why? What's wrong?"

"Zoey? Do you think you can move over for a minute?" Switching places, Sheila gently placed her hands upon Madison's face, feeling bones, temples, and behind her ears.

"What are you doing?" said Maddy, weak and confused.

"I'm just making sure there isn't any damage to your face or head. Does this hurt here?" She pushed on a space behind Madison's ear.

Madison shook her head back and forth.

"Here?"

Again nothing.

"Do me a favor, honey. Close your right eye."

Madison did as she was told.

"Anything different?"

"No," Maddy whispered.

Shela smiled. "Alright, close both eyes for a moment." She waited about five seconds before saying, "Now open your right eye."

As soon as she did, Madison jerked backward. "Oh!" she gasped.

"It's okay. It's okay," Sheila said softly, keeping her hands steady on Madison's head. "Can you tell me what you see, Madison?"

Her jaw moved a few times as she tried to work out a description. "I, well… it's black or just dark?" Her eyebrows scrunched together as she struggled to understand what she was seeing. "I mean," she mumbled, pulling gently away from Sheila and looking around the room as if for the first time. Pausing as she passed each person in the room, she said, "It's odd. I mean, I can see. Just not in the way I normally can. I'm not blind, though." Taking a deep breath and drawing strength from her medical experience, she continued, "It's like I can see heat signatures. I'm looking at Zoey. I know I'm looking at her, but it's almost like… infrared? I—" she inhaled a choppy breath, like you might after a long cry, frustrated that even her educated vocabulary wasn't offering her the correct verbiage.

"Hey, honey. It's alright. Look here, look at me," said Sheila, her bedside manners were legendary. Her voice so soothing it left whoever she was treating relaxed and focused on whatever she needed from them.

"Okay. Close both eyes again for me. That's it. Perfect." She placed her hands back on either side of Madison's head. "I'm going to lift your eyelids. Don't fight it. I'm not going to hurt you." Opening one eye, then the other, she compared them based on size of the iris, color of the whites, and so on. Taking a penlight from her pocket, she flashed it over each eye and watched them dilate.

After completing the exam, Sheila sat back with her hands in her lap. "Alright, close your eyes one last time. Before you open both eyes together, I want you to actively pay attention to the first thing you see. Not just the what of it, but how. Go ahead and open your eyes."

Maddy did as she was told and slowly lifted her lids. "I see… normal. I just see you in front of me. Nothing different."

"That's not a bad thing. It's actually common in people that have had head injuries. I used to see it when I was on active duty. I'd have soldiers come back from war with a one-sided eye or brain injury. With both eyes open, their good eye was working extra hard for the not-so-good eye. With both eyes open, they could see normally. However, when it was just the bad eye that was open, their vision was distorted, or even completely blind in some cases."

"She's right," Maria said, startling the women who seemed to be in their own world. Maria, along with all of the men, had been nodding as Sheila spoke, familiar with how the brain works. After all, they were the ones responsible for Lexi and Zuri at VISP. It was astounding how much knowledge was in the room. Maria looked around, "I think we should get together and review the neurological pathways all of the women are using. It might help us to help them. On that final day at VISP with Calla Lily, we learned more than we could've imagined. We brought all the data with us too. We just haven't had a chance to dissect it."

"Zuri," Gavin said quietly to Maria.

"Sorry, yes. Zuri. It's just when I think of that place now, I feel like Zuri and Calla were two different people."

Madison sat up a little straighter and said, "The difference here is, I never had a head injury, and what I see out of my *bad* eye isn't necessarily bad."

"You're absolutely right," Grant added, kneeling beside his co-worker and friend. "It's incredible, though, isn't it? I mean, not that it was by choice or without pain, but it is a gift. Maybe when you're feeling up for it, we can do some tests to see what else that eye of yours can do?" he said with a smirk, which caused her to chuckle.

"FYI, I'm not going to live in a glass box."

Maria and Gavin laughed, both at her adamant tone as well as out of a sense of guilt.

"You sure?" said Gavin with an awkward smile. "I mean, there might still be one intact back at—"

He was cut off by the sting on the back of his arm from Maria's slap.

"I was kidding!" he groaned, rubbing his arm.

The look she gave him convinced him to mouth *sorry* to Madison.

"It's fine. Really." She smiled. "Remember, I was outside that box too."

With so many doctors in the room, their brains were buzzing with the desire to analyze Madison. To their credit, though, they all stayed on task.

"Thank you," Maddy told Zoey, gripping her hand.

"For what?"

"For waking me up… And for the box."

"Box?"

"You told me to put the pain inside a box right before you opened my eyes. To view it from the outside, like a movie. It worked."

Zoey leaned forward until their foreheads touched. Thankful that Maddy had been cognizant enough to hear and understand.

"I think that's the way. I think it's a good way to separate the painful, real-time connections between each of you. At least for now," Sheila said, her gentle voice reaffirming.

"I'm going to steal Sheila for a few minutes, okay ladies?" said Phil, clearing his throat. Looking at Sheila for approval, he helped her up. "Outside?"

Sheila smiled and followed him out the door.

Chapter 33
It's in the Past

Phil steadied his racing mind, adjusted his shirt, and pulled the door shut behind him, separating them from the challenges on the other side. Turning toward Sheila and carrying the weight of what they'd just experienced, he felt like everything hung in the balance. So many wants without an obvious path, either forward or back—back to the feelings they once shared so many years ago.

Their eyes locked in a wordless exchange. Sheila searched for something in Phil's expression and, without warning, walked straight into his arms.

The warmth of her body pressed against his, Phil felt a wave of peace wash over him. It was a fleeting respite between two people with shared histories and one that they both desperately needed.

As they pulled apart, tears welled up in her eyes. Phil lifted his thick hand and used his thumb to carefully wipe away the drops.

"Hey, old friend." His hushed voice was gritty with emotion.

A small laugh escaped her lips with a smile. "Hey, old friend."

"Who are you calling old?" he snickered back. Their shoulders shook with laughter as the improbability of them being together again hit home.

"It's been a while since we got to do crazy together." Phil stepped back, slowly releasing her, and leaned against the wall.

"Sure has," she said, sitting on the stairs behind her. "I'm grateful you've kept me in the loop, though. When Zoey and the boys left, I knew in my heart that they would all find each other."

"It's because you never gave up on them."

Her eyes fell to her hands. "When you called me, it felt like we traveled back in time. To the day we found them, you know?"

He flashed a gentle smile, nodding slowly.

"Just hearing you say you thought she was awake, I couldn't believe it. I—" she paused, scared to admit her thoughts out loud, "I guess I'd started to believe it wasn't true. That Zuri was never there in the first place. I think maybe it was easier to believe she'd died along with her sister than it was to envision her trapped like that all these years."

"But they're both alive," said Phil, stepping closer, stopping himself from going all the way. "I've missed you."

A smile crept into the corners of her mouth. "Me too."

"You look well."

"So do you, just a little older. And maybe a little more plump." Her smile was infectious.

"Oh really? So that's how we're playing this?" he said with a laugh, unable to hide the serious feelings just below the surface.

"I'm sorry," Sheila said, this time keeping her eyes locked onto his.

"For what?"

"Leaving," she whispered. It was one word, but there was a lot behind it.

"You did what you had to do. No need to apologize. You've been by Zoey this whole time."

"It's not that. I mean, it is. But…" she stammered. "I just, I needed the space. To figure out who I was. What I wanted. And then all this happened," she said, waving her hand in the air.

Phil let her settle in for a moment. "You know, we've been keeping track of Zoey all this time on the belief she was one of the seven."

"I assumed so."

"I actually… I would sometimes when the drone was overhead… well, I would see you sometimes. Tending to your plants on the roof."

She cocked her head at his confession but didn't speak.

"It was nice. Like I still had a way to spend time with you."

"So… you were stalking me?"

His eyes flicked to hers, wide as ever. "What? No, I was just checking in! Oh, I see what you did there."

"If we're being honest here, occasionally, on a clear, calm day, when I could hear the buzz of it high in the sky… well, sometimes I would catch a glimpse of it up there hovering, secretly hoping it might be you on the other end of the feed."

Phil narrowed the gap between them, crouching down next to her. His knees popped as he did, and she watched as pain flashed across his face. His hands on hers, he explained, "There is nothing for you to be sorry for, Sheila. Back then, when we came back with the girls, I knew they were your sole focus. Their well-being consumed your heart. You did everything you could to adopt them. *Everything.*"

Sheila managed to restrain her tears as he spoke, but the knot in her throat kept her from replying. Instead, she leaned forward and put her head on his shoulder. When she could finally speak again, she said, "I shouldn't have left you though."

He ran his fingers through her hair and softly said, "It wasn't the right time. For you. For me. I was never mad at you for leaving."

He pushed her back so he could look into her eyes. "We're together now, aren't we?" The rare, wide smile he revealed, something no one else had witnessed, was meant only for her. "Are you up for this again?"

She took a deep breath, then released it slowly and said, "I don't know if anyone is. But it has to be done. At this point, I'm as ready as I'll ever be."

"This time will be different. They're grown women and fully capable." They both knew *capable* was playing it safe. "I'm right by your side. Whatever you need."

Her love for him had never wavered, and from the tone of his voice, she knew his hadn't either—that he wasn't going anywhere as long as she didn't push him away.

Leaning forward, she kissed him. It was a welcome warmth she hadn't felt in so long she'd almost forgotten it.

"Well, I think I missed that the most."

She smiled.

Nodding in unison, they intuitively knew the quiet bubble they'd created for themselves was about to pop.

"We need to check on the girls. Start preparing to leave when the others get back," Sheila said, the wheels in her mind already turning.

Phil gently touched her shoulders and said, "I'm thinking we give it five more minutes."

Smiling, she leaned in for one more kiss.

Chapter 34
Get Ready

"**B**randon said what?" Joe asked, incredulous at Aidan's update when he and Lexi walked into the apartment alone.

"They decided to get a head start," he shot back. Exasperated, he rubbed his hand over his face, working to keep his anger in check.

"They?" Maria repeated.

"It wasn't just Brandon. There was a woman there—"

"Joanna," Lexi interjected, watching Zoey, Zuri, and Maddy's eyes open wide in unison.

"I know. The fifth. She was there."

"How could she have met you and not returned with you?" asked Justin, shocked.

"That's crazy," joined Gavin, surprised at the news. "Didn't you tell her who you are? That you're connected?"

"She didn't have to," Aidan mumbled, plopping onto the couch and elbowing the cushion.

Lexi held up her hand, motioning for a pause on all the questions. "Yes. She knew the moment she laid eyes on me. But something happened as we walked up the driveway to Brandon's house. She and I both felt it."

"We felt it here too," Zuri said quietly as if still reflecting on the event.

Lexi watched as all the girls nodded. Her eyes bounced from one to the next. But when she saw Maddy's face, her breath caught in her throat. "Your eye!" she cried, rushing to look at her straight on.

"I know. Hideous, right?" she said with a light chuckle.

"Have you seen me lately?" said Lexi, pointing to her face, a slight chuckle leaving her lips. "What happened?"

"I'm not sure. Whatever Adeline's going through socked me and left my eye this way."

"Can you see?"

"Yeah. Just... a little bit differently, I suppose," she said. Another powerful change meant another trauma.

Lexi took a deep breath and stood up. "Look. Joanna wanted to come back with us, and Brandon did push for that. However, we both... well actually," her eyes flicked from one woman to the next, finally landing on Zoey before saying the words she knew they all dreaded, "all of us know that Adeline is out of time."

"She's hanging on though. Waiting for us," Zuri confidently protested from the recliner in the corner. Everyone in the room hushed.

"What's that, Zuri?" Aidan asked.

"She's not out of time. I can still feel her." As a general rule, no one argued with Zuri.

With a sigh of only partial relief, Lexi said, "We need to go tonight."

"Yes. We do," agreed Joe. "But I haven't even told you what happened out there yet."

After describing his experience at the FTA, there was no question—they had to put their plan into motion and only had a few hours until dark.

"What's their plan?" asked Phil. "What exactly are Brandon and Joanna going to do when they get there?"

"Surveillance," Aidan chimed in. "At first, anyhow. Find the right timing, I guess. I gave Brandon our radio channel so we can link up when we get close. They said they'd try and wait for us til dark before they move in—"

"Joanna wants to use herself as bait," Lexi cut in.

"No!" Sheila felt gutted. Phil, shaking his head in disapproval, pulled her against him.

"We need to get out there before they do," Joe said matter-of-factly. It was the first plan of action everyone could agree with.

"Alright. Let's pack it up. Phil, will you pull the operators into apartment five so we can review the plan. Everyone else, once you're set, meet us there as well. We're leaving at eighteen-fifteen. Questions?" Joe scanned the room, making eye contact with each and every one of them. Despite having been strangers little more than a week before, an unbreakable bond had been forged between them and they all felt it.

Zuri's small hand raised from the back. "What time is eighteen-fifteen?"

Chapter 35
Burning

S he could taste copper in her mouth. The flavor spread with the liquid oozing between the crease in her lips as her head hung low.

Adeline was tired. She wanted to keep fighting, to push through the agony, but her body had reached its limit.

Somewhere, in a distant part of her mind, she heard Joanna's voice saying, *Don't stop fighting. I'm coming. Don't let them kill you.*

Adeline's heart skipped a beat. She knew Joanna would never stop looking. Which meant they would eventually get her too. *He* would get her. But her resolve was slipping. She could feel her body shutting down, failing. *She* was failing.

Janice, her only friend in that prison, never returned after that day in the practice room. In her place, chained to the wall, was the only other girl who dared to connect with her. The guards had seen them talking and now used her as emotional bait. The room was quiet, no whimpering, no heavy breathing, nothing. She was torn between hoping the woman was still alive and hoping the sweet release of death had taken her.

A shadow fell over Adeline as a soft, damp cloth unexpectedly wiped the blood from her mouth. It was a strange feeling. The gentle touch of another human. Her left eye was sealed shut from the swelling and what she assumed to be permanent damage. Her right eye was swollen too, except she still managed to see through a thin slit when she focused. The man standing there wasn't new. She'd seen him around. Shuttling them like cattle to the showers and bringing them food when they were allowed to eat. Just never in there. In *that* room.

Memories were scrambled, but she didn't think she'd ever witnessed him abusing any of them. Even still, her stomach turned at the sight of some semblance of kindness. Although it was hard for her to see, she sensed the shades around him weren't malevolent like the others. On the contrary, they were surprisingly bright. Her heart beat a little faster as she realized that this individual actually possessed a dose of goodness.

The ringing in her head was constant. Now, with her heart beating faster and her mind swimming, she struggled to listen behind the shadow, catching only fragments of his words.

"*...sorry this is happening...*"

"*My...is Keeps...*"

"*...going to get help...*"

"*...he's coming...*"

He jerked away from her as quickly as he arrived when the

latch on the door clicked.

"What are you doing in here? You're not cleared to be in this room," Long's voice boomed like a cannon, reverberating through her brain and causing her to lose all connection with the man.

Regardless, she could tell that Long had the other guard up against a wall.

"I know. Look, I'm sorry," he said, straining to hold his own. "I'm just itching to get my chance, man! I've been here almost a year. When's he going to give me a shot?"

"When he decides!" growled Long, his words followed by a grunt and the door slamming shut.

Please, god. Please don't let him still be in here. I can't... I can't do it.

The whisper of the previous kind voice was now replaced with the assault of rancid breath in her nostrils and cracked lips that grazed her own. "He's not ready. Still too soft. Someone like you needs someone like me to handle you." His greasy hand grabbed her shirt and pulled her to him as far as the straps on the chair would allow.

Adeline's good eye could make out little more than the wounded nose of the man.

There was nowhere to run. No one to help. She couldn't keep letting them do this to her. To the others. *What can I do? How can I possibly stop any of this?*

With a shiver, she felt heat rising from her abdomen. It continued to spread through each of her limbs and up her neck. As it spread slowly, the intensity of the heat grew. A burning in her brain began at her temples, up through the top of her head, on down through her spine. It was as if hot coals were being stoked from the inside out. She'd felt something like this before, but not to this degree. The burning sensation became excruciating. She could hardly bear it. Addie needed a way to release it but had no idea how to control it. Trying to recall how it worked that first day in the prison, her mind chaotically turned the event over and over, but there was no rhyme or reason, nothing she could find to manage it.

The monster watched as she writhed in pain, glancing side to side, searching for where the vibration was coming from. When the hum of electricity pierced his ears, he recognized the source.

"I know what you're doing." Long's momentary pause was his missed opportunity of escape.

The pulse she released from her core emanated from every inch of her body and spread out in concentric circles around her like an invisible nuclear blast. The impact directly hit Long, who had nowhere to run. She watched the event unfold as if able to see clearly beyond her physical sight. She stared as the skin on his face rippled the way flat water does when a rock is lobbed into it. When his body hit the wall, she heard various bones cracking and the air in his lungs getting pushed outward with a loud, slow groan.

The cool cement under her cheek was a welcome feeling. Without realizing it, the blast had released the bindings around her wrists, allowing her body to crumple to the floor. She imagined steam rising from the heat of her skin. Somehow she could suddenly feel everything around her without having to open her eyes. She knew where his body lay, where the table with his tools sat motionless, and that the door was only three paces away from the bottom of her foot. She imagined herself now able to move in any direction, around any object, in the dark, and without the need for sight. The possibilities offered hope. Hope where the helpless, broken woman hanging on the wall said there was none.

With her eyes closed, she began to focus. Clearing every unnecessary thought out of the way, casting off all notions of fear, she centered her focus on hope until she could see in her mind's eye shadows and shades of gray. Only now, they made up the contours of the bodies in the room and the hard edges of objects surrounding them. As every shape became clearer, the grays shifted and separated, some into reds. A deep onyx swirled around the grays with red woven throughout. This blend of colors defined the contours of the body on the ground nearby. Long was hurt and afraid, but mostly he was angry. The red that blanketed most of his body continued to thicken as he reoriented himself and began to move.

I know that didn't just happen so I could end up in chains again. She pleaded with her body to move. *Legs, it's now or never. Come on! If I can see without my eyes, I can make my broken body move. I hear you, Joanna. I hear you!*

Chapter 36
Ain't No Moment Like This

"A in't no moment like this moment."

"What?" Maria cocked her head to the side. "Did you become a cowboy in the last five minutes?"

"Nah," said Gavin, laughing. "I just remember my dad saying that when I was a kid."

She took an extra moment to respond. "He probably had a one-liner on hand for anything. That the best you got?"

"Well…" he said, looking her in the eyes before taking in the beautiful horizon as the sun set, "we're here. The sun's going down. God only knows what's going to happen as the night unfolds. I can't help but think this moment, with you in this light, is a moment I should remember."

Blushing, she turned toward the gorgeous orange and red

skyline. "I guess you're not wrong," she said, her sass turning into a smile. Leaning her head on his shoulder, she breathed in the cool evening air, appreciating the scene in front of her before turning and giving him a gentle kiss. "We should probably head over there."

He burned her smile into his mind. No matter what happened, he would remember that moment.

Maria's hand felt cold as he helped her to her feet. Wearing the boot Sheila had given her allowed her to walk while providing support for her ankle, though not enough to make her of any use on the mission. Needing someone to keep watch anyway, Maria planned to hang back at their rally point. She may not have been fit to join, but she wasn't going to sit on the sidelines. Grant planned on remaining with her, along with one of the operators assigned to be on the receiving end of potential injuries.

Sheila, carrying her med-bag, was suiting up with Kevlar. Looking at Phil, she smiled and said, "Reminds me of the good ole' days."

Phil glanced over at Gavin and Maria, then back to his own long-lost love. "You don't have to do this, you know. I mean, I wouldn't be upset if you hung back with Maria." He said it nonchalantly, but his eyes burned in earnest.

"I'm sure you wouldn't," she said, playfully bumping into his shoulder. "But you know as well as I do who always managed to win in combatives."

"What? Come on now. I let you win."

"In your dreams," she shot back with a subtle laugh that dissipated on her lips. "I need to do this. For the girls. For myself." Resting her hand on his, she said, "I feel like there's a lot more I should've done all these years. I shouldn't have walked away. Maybe if I'd kept trying—"

"Stop."

The harsh, rapid sound of his voice startled her.

"You did everything you could back then. Even after, you stayed close. No one's judging you. You were and have always been there."

"But—"

"No. Sheila. If it wasn't for you, these girls would no longer even exist. You pushed to go in and get them. You believed. You've always believed. There's nothing to prove." He held her hand tightly. Insistently.

"Maybe not, but right now, there's one thing I *can* do. I can be there to help Adeline and anyone else in there that's suffering. That's something I can do."

Phil leaned in and kissed her forehead. "Yes, ma'am. You can. Let's go do this."

Joe's voice rang out and everyone came to attention. "Rally on me, please."

As the group maneuvered to him, Maddy's faint voice rose just enough to be heard by Lexi and Joe. "Where's Joanna?"

Joe squeezed the diagram he was holding and looked up into her eyes. One emerald and the other onyx. Instead of unnerving, it just made her all the more exotic. With a hard swallow, he answered, "We haven't been able to raise Brandon on the radio."

"I thought they were going to wait for us."

"That's what they said, Maddy," Lexi cut in. The other girls drew closer. "I think whatever's happening to Adeline right now has scared Joanna. She didn't feel like there's time to wait."

"We're so close, though. She'd be stronger with us."

"I doubt she realizes just how strong," said Lexi, squeezing

Zuri's shoulder. "But they're sisters. This is what sisters do."

As emotions rose, their eyes shone brighter, illuminating the group. A faint pulsation rippled through the air.

Justin stepped forward, touching Zoey's back just between her shoulder blades. Gavin grasped Maria's hand while Phil put his arm around Sheila's waist. Aidan stepped to Zuri's side, his arm brushing against hers. Looking up into his eyes, she smiled, grateful for his comfort. It was as if gravity was pulling them all together.

Beneath the vibration, all four girls could feel Joanna's presence. She wasn't far. They could also feel the faint pulse of Adeline, along with an unfamiliar hum.

"What's wrong?" Aidan asked, noticing a change in Zuri.

"There's a lot of pain in there. It's all muddled together," she whispered, shaking her head. "There are a lot more girls in there than just Adeline. I can't...."

Aidan put his hand on her lower back. "Oh!" she yelled, sucking in a deep breath. Her eyes opened wide and bright. It was as if she could see clearly, like looking through a window into the iron prison.

"What do you see, Zuri?" said Zoey, jumping to her side.

"There are twelve others," she whispered as if they might hear her if she spoke too loud.

The vibration intensified, along with the hum.

"Like us?" Maddy whispered back.

"Not like us. Imprisoned. They've been there a long time, and they are..." her breath hitched.

At the same moment, each girl felt pressure pushing at their back. A sensation that wasn't coming from within them. It was coming from the FTA.

"Remember the box. Put the pain in a box so you can see properly," said Maddy, looking to Zoey for confirmation.

"That's right, Zuri. Find that box in your mind where you can put their pain. Don't carry it with you."

The image of Adeline became clear. She was hanging by her wrists. Blood covered her face and the floor around her. And there was Joanna, hiding in a dark room. These images and more flooded her mind, simultaneously looping through the vision.

She watched as Adeline's face rose against the darkness—an evil presence without a clear image.

One by one, the women stepped toward Zuri to grab ahold, partnering in the vision. While they could see, their views were hazy, unable to make sense of what or who they saw. Maddy was the last to reach out. As her fingertips touched Zuri's arm, an explosion of light flooded Zuri's view. A blast of warmth followed. The others witnessed the light, but managed to stay on their feet now that they understood how to better separate themselves. Even Aidan sensed something overpowering him.

They could hear Justin shouting, his voice thin and warbled, as if coming from some far-off location. "Grab them before they collapse!"

"What just happened?" asked Sheila, crawling from one girl to the next, checking their pulses and breathing.

"They're stronger together in every way. They can feel what each other is going through, and right now, whatever is happening to Adeline must be extreme to put them all on their knees like this." Joe had wrapped his arms around Lexi in order to keep her steady. It wasn't so long ago he was doing the same for Zoey.

So much had happened in such a short period he could

barely recall daily life before this.

When the intensity of the vision wound down, and the girls found their breath, Maddy cleared her throat and said, "She did something." The other girls nodded, silently recouping. "This was different. Not something done to her, but something she did to them."

"It's because we're here," Zuri said in her hushed voice. "We're here together and so is Joanna. We're helping Adeline get stronger just by being closer."

Joe, mulling over her words, pulled on the string of an idea. "What if you girls stay out here where it's safe? I mean, if you really can give them strength just by being close, maybe you don't need to get in harm's way. We can go in and get them, with you out here, maybe… uh…." He wasn't sure how to phrase it.

"Heal them from a distance? Give them strength to make it out of there?" Zoey added. "I understand why you're saying this, but Joe, we have to go in."

"No, you don't, though. Zoe, it's going to be beyond dangerous. I read Oakley's face. I heard the evil in his voice. It'll only take one wild connection to put all of you on your knees again," he pleaded, revealing the love he still had for her and wanting to do anything to avoid losing her again. "You know more than anyone that if we have to shield the four of you in a critical moment, any one of us might be lost."

She wanted to argue but knew the validity of what he was saying. Even so, her body language demonstrated her resolve.

Several tense seconds passed in their battle of wills. All the while, Joe's brain filtered through all the cards in his hand until he realized precisely what they needed to do.

His voice felt loud as he broke the silence. "New plan! Doc, you're going to need a bigger med kit."

"How much do you remember about being at VISP after you got out of the lab?" Maddy's question interrupted Lexi's thoughts.

Lexi pulled her eyes away from watching Aidan help Zuri strap on her Kevlar vest. She had been listening to everything going on but was internally trying to figure out how to keep Zuri outside and away from what she knew was coming. "I'm not sure. I remember Grant," she said, mulling over the question. Her heart sank just thinking of what she'd done. Shifting her gaze over to him, his warmth told her he'd never even had to forgive her.

"Do you remember the hallway where we came together? You were running when I called your name, and you turned to look at me."

"I think so," she said, mostly recalling the rage she felt. "It's a little fuzzy. Why?"

"I found you running down the hall. You had this wild look about you. But the most incredible thing was how bright your crystal eyes were. I tried to talk to you—get you to calm down, but you were in another place."

Nodding, Lexi started to recall those moments. "I thought you were there to hurt me. All I could feel was this burning inside. It was… it felt… it just consumed me." Suddenly, Lexi's face sunk and a burning sensation prickled the skin down her arm to her fingertips. "I did the same thing to you that I did to Grant."

Madison put her hand on Lexi's, causing her eyes to

shimmer and her thoughts to become clear.

"You remember," Madison said, sensing Lexi's shift in understanding.

"Yeah, I actually do remember." Eyes wide. "But how did I do it? How did you do it?"

"I have no idea but I think it would be useful if we could figure it out, don't you? Before we find Adeline and Joanna?"

Chapter 37
The Devil Himself

His chest pounded as he surveyed two sets of security monitors. They had made it inside unseen, though not without a few close calls. Brandon had been to the FTA several times before the grid failed and once after. Except for the increased surveillance, navigating the familiar grounds was relatively easy. Once inside, only one guard had been in their path as they descended the stairs from the main floor. Silently choking him off, Brandon restricted his breathing until the man passed out. They secured him under the stairway platform and hoped he'd stay unconscious long enough for them to find Adeline and get out.

Crouched low in a security office on the basement floor, he noted two sets of live feeds. One set had eyes surveilling the rooms in the underground space he and Joanna were hiding in. The other set showed the woods around the facility, along with several cameras on the outskirts of the treeline. Common access points people entered to hike. People like Joanna.

His radio nearly gave them away when it chirped, letting him know Joe and the others had arrived. It was too late, though. Joanna changed the plan shortly after arriving at the rally point. Sensing that her sister was crashing, waiting was no longer an option.

He didn't doubt that Joanna had deep insight into Adeline's well-being. Belief wasn't the issue, which is why he followed along with the dangerous plan. He did, however, struggle to understand how. He also knew that that didn't matter at the moment.

He could see the determination on her face and a subtle glow in her eyes. He'd witnessed it the day he met her out in the woods. A glow that had slowly gotten brighter as the days passed. Now, with the intensity of the mission peaking, the blue embers in her eyes bounced through the crystalline points of her irises. He couldn't help but be drawn to her, though he refused to admit to himself that he loved her. He'd never loved anyone this way before, and the thought terrified him. He couldn't lose her here. Not now. He wouldn't.

She caught him once again with a concerned look staring at her. "We will get out of here," she whispered, her eyes offering a promise. "And we're bringing my sister back with us."

He wanted to tell her how he felt before it was too late. But he was too rational. These emotions, no matter how real, were a distraction. Instead, he simply leaned toward her. She was so caught up trying to figure out where Adeline was locked up that he startled her when he kissed her forehead. "Yes. We will."

She hadn't noticed it before, but now it was unavoidable. This bond that had grown between them was strong.

With a deep breath, he turned away to analyze the images on the monitors. One feed specifically caught his attention. It was the cliff Joanna's sister had disappeared from.

"I know how they took her," he whispered in her ear.

Pointing at one of the squares on the screen, he said, "This is where your sister was taken. It's the bottom side of that dropoff. The camera is pointing toward a hidden tunnel behind the brush. See this image?" He pointed to the one next to it. "It's from inside that tunnel looking out. And this one over here, does this look familiar? Is that where you entered the woods from?"

She stared at both screens for several seconds then nodded. "They saw us coming in. They saw us and sent someone out there to get us."

Placing his hand on her arm he whispered, "They have openings out there in the woods where they can bring people back through underground tunnels. I think these feeds right here," he said, gesturing toward the monitor showing four arbitrary locations in the woods, "these must be where the tunnels open up." Under his breath, he said, "How could I not have seen them?"

"None of this is your fault, Brandon."

He wanted to disagree but knew she'd protest. Instead, he looked back at the feeds and said, "We need to find Adeline. Do you see her?"

One square showed a room with several groups of women huddled together. Their heads were shaved and they were dirty, but they were clearly all women. A few screens showed men walking around, some standing around talking, and nearly all carrying weapons.

"No. I don't… I mean, if her head's shaved too, then any of those women could be her. I don't know!"

"But you can *feel* her, right?"

Closing her eyes, she honed in on a familiar pull she knew could only be her sister. Yet there were others, like threads tugging at her from different directions. Two threads led further into the underground bunker, yet a different group of threads pulled her back outside. She recognized the feeling, but it was all so new at the same time.

"I know how to find her, Brandon."

She started to stand up, but he stopped her. "The problem is you don't know who will be in the way of us getting to her. We can wait. Joe and the others are here. We just need to hold tight."

"But we don't know how long it will take them. Addie's fading quickly. I barely have a grip on her thread now."

Before he could ask what she meant, an odd pressure began to build in the back of his head. Joanna turned toward the door, so he knew it wasn't something he alone was feeling.

"What on earth?"

"It's her… It's Addie." Grabbing her head and wincing, she groaned, "How are you doing that?"

"What's happening?" Brandon asked, watching as Joanna appeared to speak directly with her sister.

"I'm not—" she mumbled as a wave of heat washed over her.

Brandon, holding the back of his neck, fell back as if pushed to the ground.

"It was her! It was Addie!" she sucked in her breath.

Brandon threw his hand over her mouth. Eyes wide, they sat still, muscles tensed, silently listening for anyone that may have heard. After nearly a minute, with beads of sweat forming, he whispered, "What did she do? How did she do that?"

"I don't… I… she was protecting herself."

"How did *we* feel it?"

"I think…" she said, scrunching her nose and rubbing her palms together, "that she… that somehow she attacked the darkness." Her eyes quickly found his. "She sees darkness. Around people. Remember? I told you that?"

Nodding, he waved his hands to keep talking.

"Maybe she's figured out a way to fight against it." A subtle smile broke out but was just as quickly squelched quickly by fear. "Only… only now she's incredibly weak." She grabbed his hand and launched to her feet. "She can't defend herself anymore. We have to get to her n—"

Before she could finish, the door flew open.

Brandon yanked her behind him, shielding her with his body.

The outline of a large man filled the doorway, his features hardened by the light of the screens behind them. Several more bulky men came up beside him and his expression turned from fierce to a smile so grotesque and so memorable Joanna immediately knew who he was.

His Grinch-like smile had been haunting her dreams. Dreams born of the reality her sister was living.

He was the devil himself.

"Looks like my day is taking a turn for the better," he joyfully sang as his gravelly voice cut through the silence. "Hello, Brandon. Haven't seen you in a while. Looks like you brought a friend."

Shackled to the floor, blood seeped from a fresh cut on Brandon's cheek. Joanna was on the opposite side of the room, wrists bound, though uninjured. Addie, nearby, struggled to see, though undeniably recognized Joanna's scream as the two were dragged into the room.

She still wasn't sure how to use her new gift exactly, so instead of trying to see Joanna with one good eye, she closed it and focused on finding the colors around her instead. Tuning out Oakley's voice, she concentrated on the shapes forming behind her eyes. Pressure was building at her temples, along with a singular point in the back of her head at the top of her spine, as if someone was pushing their thumbs into those specific spots. Slow, steady breaths helped sharpen her view of the room and objects within. With her eyes open, the shades of light had always varied by degree between black and white within the shadowy images. Yet earlier, red streams appeared, weaving together within the contours of Long's body.

Did I dream it? No. It happened. The burst and the red.

It was real. It had to be.

I can do this. Focus. Just focus.

The pressure in her brain was so intense she teetered on blacking out. Then her ears popped. It was like a bubble floating high into the air until the atmospheric pressure was too much to bear. The release of pressure left her mind open to seeing everyone and everything around her. The colors were mesmerizing. Not just reds and grays but a palette far beyond the rainbow that seemed to blossom with each passing second.

In the place Oakley stood, she saw an array of black, from onyx to charcoal, along with a deep red. Hurt, fear, vengeance, and anger all swirling. Solid, shadowy tendrils reached from his core toward her, her sister, and Brandon.

Joanna was even more visible now. Teal, grays, and reds prominently formed the contours of her body. While other colors swirled in the mix, Adeline could sense that fear and anger were more prevalent than she initially believed, yet instinctively knew what the colors meant. Teal symbolized love, and it was in abundance. Tendrils of it reached out from Joanna to her. A reminder that she'd never actually been alone. But the tendrils also reached out toward Brandon. Like a winding vine, it crossed the span of the room and intertwined with his own darker shade of teal tendrils reaching back.

"Are you listening, Adeline!" Oakley's voice startled her, whipping her back into the cold, dark present. "Are you imagining your sister?" he whispered. "Hanging on the wall in front of you like all the others? Or maybe I should just put you on the wall and start all over again with her."

She bucked against the straps holding her in place. Gritting her teeth, she threatened, "You won't touch her."

Her eyes still closed, she watched as the grays spiked all around him momentarily before settling back to a simmer.

Oakley knew what she was capable of and that if she regained strength, she would try to kill him at the first opportunity. Yet, there was something else.

He still had the upper hand, physically, anyhow. After all, Oakley could only see her bruised and battered body. The way she sat limp on the chair after putting Long on the ground. Though he was fully aware of her incredible, unseen power, he didn't fear her broken body or her inability to control her power. He was, for lack of a better word, untouchable.

What he couldn't see spinning, weaving, pushing through the air toward Adeline was an intangible strength that far surpassed the healing offered by rest, nourishment, and medicine—the needs of the physical body. With Joanna in the room, just as it is among the other women, there was a sensation penetrating Addie's core that came straight from her sister. As it steadily hummed along, Addie felt the pain in her muscles decrease. The sensation of pins and needles spread through her fingers and toes as strength returned.

Addie could see it all. The shades, the strength, the healing, all of it flooded her entire being with Joanna by her side. Objects couldn't impede their reach. Wisps of it touched her skin. Soon, entire tentacles latched on and began to absorb into her. Shades of green both healed her and gave her strength.

Strangely, it wasn't just coming from Joanna. An overwhelming sense of peace and strength washed over her from behind, wrapping around her body from someplace beyond the room.

Once again, her attention jerked back to the evil in front of her when Oakley's hand gripped her throat.

"I know you can hear me. I know you're afraid!" he screeched as spit sprayed across her face. "I'm not waiting anymore." Turning back, he began to direct Long to grab Joanna but found himself alone. Long, wounded, and in relentless pain, had since left the room, unable or unwilling to continue to do the dirty work. "Looks like I'm on my own," he sneered, creeping to within an inch of Joanna's face.

"NO!" cried Adeline. At her shout, his feet left the ground as his body flew through the air and into the mirrored wall behind him.

Brandon, who had been fighting with the shackles around his wrists, now sat motionless, staring straight ahead—straight at Adeline.

All of them in shock at what they'd just witnessed.

"Addie?" said Joanna, her voice breaking through the reverberating clang of a gong in Adeline's ears. "Addie? Can you hear me?"

Her lips moved without sound. "Yes."

"Addie, I'm right here. I'm here! Tell me what to do." Joanna fought with the zip ties cinched tight around her wrists, drawing blood and making her hands slick.

Both Joanna and Brandon had been working their way onto their knees when they heard it. It started out quietly, a giggle, before turning into a laugh. Quickly it was a full-blown bellow before Oakley exclaimed, "Whoo! Oh, honey. Whatever that was, it was quite the mistake." Pulling himself upright, he stood there just as arrogant as before, unharmed, except for his right arm, which now hung at a grotesque angle by his side. She'd hurt him, just not enough to stop him.

Glancing toward one of the upper corners of the room, he flashed a signal to the camera.

His shoulders still bouncing, with an eerie chuckle quietly escaping his lips, he made his way to the door. Passing Adeline, he couldn't help but stop and physically force open her one good eye. "I'm so glad you did that."

As he opened the door, they could hear the stomach-turning sound of girls screaming.

What have I done?

Chapter 38
The Pull

FTA | August 25, 2029 | 7:25 p.m.

"The Grinch," Madison murmured.

"Grinch?" Aidan repeated. "Zoey, what's she talking about?"

Zoey could see Oakley's face in her mind. The description made sense. His smile was wide, devoid of guilt and shame. *Had the man ever had a heart?*

"Zoey?" Aidan touched her shoulder, which caused her to jump.

"I can see him," she whispered, looking through Aidan. "He's done something terrible."

"Who?" asked Sheila, goading Zoey on. "Why haven't I heard of this before?"

"Oakley," declared Aidan. He and Zoey knew him, just not as well as Joe. Though Sheila had never met him, she remembered Zoey's discomfort back when Joe was working on his security. The hairs on the back of her neck would stand up whenever they were in the same space together. She sensed he was off but couldn't have imagined he was this kind of evil.

"How could I not have known?" A wave of hindsight hit her.

"Zoe, there is no way we could've known what he was doing out here." Aidan's logic went unnoticed.

"But I knew he was wrong. I should've made an effort to find out why." Her cheeks flushed as she thought about how close she'd been. Clenching her fists, she swung at no one in particular.

"Stop. Listen to me," Sheila said, grabbing her shoulders and facing her head-on. "This world has only been for survivors, and that's what you did. We did. Survive. How could any of us ever have imagined the powers you have and the things you can really do."

"*Or* that there was anyone else out there like you, Z?" Aidan piped in.

Zoey wanted to argue, to hit something, but instead put her hands on Sheila's forearms. "You're right. You're right." With a gentle squeeze, she cleared her throat and said, "Let's go."

Joe had assigned them to move in last. Madison had learned to protect herself a little better from the onslaught of her connection with Adeline, but she was still too vulnerable to be on the front line.

Leaving her behind, however, was not an option. Joe was smart. He didn't want any of them to come, but he also knew they needed to be close when they finally found Adeline. Putting them together would only make them stronger, and they didn't know how much strength they'd truly need when they found the girls. So he changed the plan at the last moment.

No longer a hostage rescue, they were taking the place over. Between Brandon's and his surveillance, it sounded like Joe had more men on his side compared to the team Oakley harbored. His plan was to subdue the guards from the outside-in so they wouldn't have time to call reinforcements. Thankfully the lights were already glitching, which meant that disabling the cameras as they moved in might just go unnoticed by anyone paying attention to the monitors.

He sent three operators in a wide berth around the perimeter to simultaneously take out the patrols. Once that was done, he moved in as those operators came up from behind and provided rear support as they broke into the building. The women were sandwiched in the middle for protection.

Zoey, Aidan, Sheila, and Madison followed two minutes behind so the team had a chance to remove any opposition ahead of them.

After the allotted time passed and they hadn't heard any gunfire, they pushed forward to the building. An operator crouched at the entrance which meant it was clear for Zoey's group to enter. Pushing in, they sat Madison against a wall to wait for an update.

Without warning, both of Madison's eyes opened wide. A palpable fear exuded from her.

"Madison?" Zoey called out, grabbing her hand as the electric vibration bonded them.

The terror Madison saw left her speechless. An awful sight Zoey only caught a glimpse of.

So many girls.

So much horror.

Lexi moved as if propelled forward. Joe had his hand on her back, trying to stay with her the whole time. He had initially taken lead, but the pull toward Adeline and Joanna consumed her, prompting her to push past him as if being led directly to them.

Inhuman screams echoed off the walls and down the halls.

"What's up there, Lexi?" Joe said in a low, monotone voice.

Matching his tone, she spoke without emotion, fully aware that she needed to keep it in check, stay focused, and simply keep moving. "They're torturing the other girls. They want to make Adeline pay."

"Pay for what?"

"I don't know… it's not very clear. Like maybe she's not cooperating…."

"Where are we headed, Lexi? Adeline? Joanna? The others?"

Lexi didn't reply. Waving them on, she followed the pull as it led her to an intersection. "Here's where we make that choice," she said, spinning around to face him mere inches apart. "If we go left, we find the group of girls. If we go right, we find Adeline and Joanna—both of them."

"Go for the sisters first," Justin cut in, crouching behind Joe. "Once we have them, we can take out the bastards holding the rest of the women here."

"Something's not right. It's hazy, but I can feel the… fears of the women growing. It's as if they're preparing for death.

None of them may be alive by the time we come back for them."

Joe smacked the cold wall, glancing down the hall in each direction as if hoping to find a sign telling him what to do.

"I'll go," said Gavin, pushing his way forward.

"What? No. Gavin, you have zero combat training," Justin shot back, shaking his head.

"And you do!" Gavin bucked.

One of the operators slipped in behind him. "Two of us will go with him. We can scope it out at the very least and see if an opportunity presents itself before you get down there."

Justin thought separating was a terrible idea, but there was no time for discussion.

Joe gave them a thumbs-up and then signaled each team to move forward.

Justin paused, incredulous at the rapid pace of such a major decision to split up the team. Not particularly a man of prayer, he prayed they hadn't just made their biggest mistake.

Halfway down the hall, Lexi stopped cold. With a gasp, she braced herself on the wall. The devil's presence suddenly washed over her and there was nowhere to hide.

"Oakley!" Joe called out as the demonic figure emerged from a door at the end of the hall.

Frozen in place with a growing smile that chilled each of them to the core, Oakley silently stared at Joe, his eyes bouncing from one member to the next of the entire squad until he caught sight of Lexi. The dark purple lines that traveled like vines up the left side of her face gave him pause. The shock of it, of her, of them all having gotten so far in his fortified bunker, left him equally dumbfounded. "Well, this is a little embarrassing. If you didn't know any better, which Joe ought to by now, you'd think this was amateur hour around here."

"Davis?" Phil's voice rang out in disbelief.

Oakley's eyes flicked to his old teammate. His smile grew.

Sheila stood up at the back of the group. "Davis," she said, her voice barely audible.

"Would you look at this! It's like a family reunion."

"Davis?" Sheila said, stepping out from behind Joe with her hand over her mouth. "It's been you? This is you? But how… but you—"

"Died? MIA? It's better than that. Seems I was left for dead by my own team!"

"But we came back. We searched for both of you. You and the girl. There was no sign. No body. No chatter from anywhere." Her breath hitched in her throat as the realization settled in. "This… this has all been you?"

Staring at her old friend in disbelief, Sheila cautiously walked in his direction—the others followed suit.

"I appreciate the credit, but it wasn't all me. The story is much longer, Doc. In fact, I think it'd make for a great movie someday. Maybe another time if it's alright with you? I wouldn't want to keep my girls waiting."

"Stop!" Joe shouted. His weapon pointed at Oakley's chest. "No one needs to get hurt."

His laugh cut through the air. "Seriously, Joe?" he said, taking another step back.

"Don't you dare move, Davis," Phil growled. He'd grieved for this man. Felt guilty at never having found even so much as a scrap of his uniform. "We just want the girls. This doesn't have to go sideways, Davis."

"Sideways? Look around, Phil. This is as sideways as it gets, man!"

"No one has to die. Just let us have them and we'll be on our way."

"Wow. This is almost history repeating itself. Deja vu, if you know what I mean, except it really is happening twice. In a different world, you know, a world with old-fashioned print newspapers, the headline would read, *Girls Abducted Twice in Lifetime*." He took another step back.

Lexi's heart was pounding out of her chest. "Please. *Please* let them go."

"*Please let them go,*" he whined, pretending to wipe tears from his eyes. "You don't actually think *they're* not going to use you to get what *they* want?" he said, pointing directly at Phil. "I'm just doing what they're too weak to do. I think I'll take my chances." With his last word, he ducked back into the room, slamming the door behind him, but not before Joe managed to fire off a round, grazing his upper arm.

Still sporting his sardonic smile, Oakley hoisted a chair up to the door, tilting it to wedge beneath the handle before clasping three consecutive locks along the door jamb. "Well, it looks like we have visitors," he joyfully sang, as if this was the day of victorious reckoning he'd been waiting for.

The moment of joy passed in a flash as pain shot upward from his broken arm when he attempted to reach for his radio. Screaming in rage, he helplessly left it to dangle, instead using his left arm, now bleeding from the fresh wound, to pull the radio from his belt. "Where the hell is everyone? Long, status!"

Several slow seconds elapsed before he got a response from

a confused yet jovial-sounding voice. Oakley shook his head at what sounded like screams and sobs in the background. "Just having ourselves a little party is all. What's up, boss?"

"Who's in there with you?"

"Bugs, John, and Keeps. Need something?"

"We've got company. Go Delta Red." Oakley didn't wait for a response before snapping his radio back into position. Staring at his three guests, he simply said, "It would be in your best interest not to move."

Adeline had heard Oakley and his team discussing alternate plans earlier. They spoke as if none of the girls were paying attention, but she was. Delta Red meant arming the hallway explosives and moving everyone to the tunnels. She dreaded what it might mean if they followed through with it.

Oakley glared at each of them, debating what to do first. With nothing to precipitate it, he walked over and punched Brandon in the side of the head with his good hand. "I'm willing to take you with me..." he growled, hitting him again, only this time causing blood to spray from Brandon's mouth across the floor. "To use as a bargaining chip if it comes to that..." he huffed, hitting him once again, compelling Brandon to tilt to his side until his elbow touched the ground, keeping him from falling over completely. "But there won't be any fighting back, right, neighbor? Cause then I'd just have to kill you."

With a final kick to the abdomen, Oakley relented.

He took a few deep breaths and, shaking out his hand, headed straight for Adeline. Undoing the handcuffs he'd re-engaged after her earlier attack on Long, he asked, "How'd you do it, Brandon?"

Brandon didn't respond, just spit on the floor and, with great pain, pulled himself back to an upright position.

"Seems like a lot of people are in on this. How did you find our little Addie here? I mean, I'm impressed. With your reclusive lifestyle and all."

"I don't know who they are," Brandon muttered, spitting another mouthful of blood in Oakley's direction. "We didn't come with anyone."

Suddenly, the door took a hit from the other side.

"They're going to break that door down any second. You have nowhere to go. I don't know who they are, but they clearly hate you as much as I do."

"Really? That's hysterical! You don't know who they are. You just all happened to show up at the same time? *And* you included my old teammates in on the fun. Well, that was just downright thoughtful of you."

"Stop," Addie said in what sounded more like a groan.

"Addie, don't," Joanna whispered.

"Oh no, by all means, continue," said Oakley, struggling to release her cuffs with his one good arm. "Clearly, I'm a patient man who has all the time in the world."

Her voice lowered, "I just don't see how you'll get out of this," she said as her good eye pierced his.

"You see the irony in that, don't you? After all, you don't really see anything!" Laughing, he raised his arm as if ready to strike her.

"Shouldn't the rest of your… your goons have stopped them by now? You seem to be all alone down here with us." She was baiting him. Joanna kept whispering at her to stop talking, but just like the good old days, she wouldn't listen to her sister's pleadings. Addie wanted him mad. Wanted him livid. "I think…

I think a moment ago, you thought you had the upper hand. Now… now you're alone in here." She paused, giving him time to process. "With me."

Heat flooded his cheeks. "Fear? Is that what you think you'll get out of me?" His Grinch-like smile reached ear to ear. "Oh babe, I have backup plans on backup plans."

Joanna pleaded with her to stop, unable to see what her sister could see.

Addie had used every ounce of power within her only moments before. But she could see it now. Tendrils flowed toward her, not just from her sister but from beyond the door. She watched as they swirled around Brandon, avoided Oakley altogether, then crawled up her legs, into her chest, and around her head.

I can feel it building. I can feel its power and the control I have over it.

Watching Oakley's face turn sour, her heart sank. His evil smile actually kicked up a notch. While the colorful streamers infused her with hope, he had an unmatchable way of stealing it.

Just a few more seconds….

She saw before she heard. It was as if lightning had struck, crackling and deafening. She winced, not from pain, just shock, as the bullet hit Brandon's chest. The crack from Oakley's gun was like an afterthought, followed by a gut-wrenching scream from Joanna.

Every muscle in her body stopped cold. The kaleidoscope of tendrils pouring in retracted along with the previous confidence in her antagonistic plan.

Oakley grabbed her arm and yanked her off the chair. With a solid kick, he released Adeline's legs from their clamps. "Three of you is overkill anyway," he sneered.

Moving as if underwater, she went where she was told. Her head swam in the chaos while her body felt numb, otherworldly almost. Oakley pushed them to the door next to the long mirror. A keypad hung on the wall beside it. Cursing his painfully lifeless arm, he released his grip on Joanna to punch in the code.

When he did, she immediately reached back and grabbed Adeline's hand. Her touch was an electrical jolt to her system that caused her body to jerk upright.

"Joanna?" Addie questioned, opening her eye as much as the pain would allow. Trembling, Joanna locked eyes with her disfigured sister, whom she hardly recognized. Addie pulled back—she had never seen anything like it. A million glistening cinnamon stars emanated outward.

Follow along, Joanna said, passing the words along to her sister. *The others are coming.*

She let Oakley push her into the dark room. A small glow of muted light shone through the mirrored window allowing their eyes to adjust. Addie had known he was watching her. Day after day. Night after night. She knew he was there, enjoying the torture from this safe space.

"Well ladies, the good news is that…" he began, grunting in frustration as he attempted to move his broken arm, "is that where there's a will, there's a way. And I *always* have the will."

Adeline could feel Joanna's courage encompass her before her once meek sister spoke. "You should just leave us here. If you were smart, you would. We'll only slow you down. Besides, you can't carry two of us with your arm broken." Joanna took a step toward him. "If you want to get out of here with your life, you need to leave us—"

Oakley walloped the side of her face hard, causing her head to ricochet off the nearby wall. "Ah-ah-ahhh. Don't try to be brave. You'll regret it." Pulling out a cache of weapons stored beneath the desktop below the one-way mirror, a voice came across his radio, startling him into dropping a handgun.

Addie pulled her sister into her arms as best she could, helping her to reorient.

"Boss, we've got a problem."

"Where are you? You should've already cleared me a path."

"Yeah, well, they seem to have disabled the surveillance. None of the guards are responding. You ready for Delta Red?"

"Have you emptied the cage yet?"

"They're prepped, sir."

"Set it for five minutes, starting now."

"Done. Meet you at point three."

"Rog—"

Oakley was cut off as the door flew open with a bang. The silhouette of one very infuriated man stood there.

"Brandon!" Joanna's shock turned to uncontrollable joy.

Oakley shoved Adeline to the ground, pressed down on her chest with one foot, then quickly pulled Joanna in front of him in one fluid motion. His eyes flicked to the floor in search of his fallen handgun.

"We're out of time, friend. You should've just stayed dead."

Chapter 39
Please God

FTA | August 25, 2029 | 8:00 p.m.

"We need to go!" Madison, terrified, grabbed Zoey with more strength than she'd marshaled in weeks.

"What happened?" Aidan asked, caught off-guard yet quickly turning in search of who or whatever scared her.

"I… I don't know exactly. Heat. Wiring. Explosives! I can see them in Adeline's mind." As if following Addie's lead, Madison placed her hand on the wall. Noticing a flat square panel, she ran her hand across it, feeling the edges. As she traced the lines, her breathing grew heavier and her movements more frantic. Using her fingers, she started prying at its corner.

"What are you doing?" questioned Aidan, unsettled by her odd actions.

But then Zoey saw it too, like a faded mirage of a device behind the panel. "Oh god!" she cried, furiously scraping to grip the edge.

"IEDs," Sheila mumbled under her breath. "They've placed IEDs in the walls." Her eyes followed the length of the hall, recognizing the pattern from her deployment days. Square panels evident every four feet or so.

Madison and Zoey stepped back from the wall, frozen in place as the metal clang of the panel cover hit the floor. A tied-up block of C4 sat in the open. It looked dormant, however, the moment the thought crossed Sheila's mind, an LED screen lit up with red numbers counting down from 4:59.

"No. No, no, no, no!" Aidan could see a wire from the device disappear into the wall in the direction of the next panel. Grabbing his radio, he yelled, "Everyone out! Less than five minutes and this Death Star is gonna blow!"

With adrenaline pumping, he tried pushing both girls back to the stairs but they wouldn't budge. "What are you doing? This isn't a game. We have to go right now!"

"We can't," said Zoey, calmly. "Aidan, stop. We can't leave." She wrapped her hand around his and stated without question, "We have to get the others." Her eyes pierced his and saw his mind battling their options.

With a deep breath in surrender, he simply asked, "Where?"

Where is she? Oh, god.

"Joe!" Lexi yelled over the thumping of the operators trying to break down Oakley's door. The fear in her voice startled him.

"What's wrong?"

"Something's about to happen. I can feel it, and Zuri's gone."

Spinning in a circle, he stammered, "Where… where did she go?"

"To find the seventh," she said, squeezing his arm tight. "Adeline is struggling to share something with us. I can feel it. Something's barely breaking through, something about time. That we only have a few minutes. I went to grab Zuri but she was gone."

"Can you sense where she went?"

Lexi closed her eyes, attempting to block the chaos. With a gasp, she spun around to run when Joe snagged her shirt. "Where, Lexi? Where!"

Pointing back the way they'd come, "There. Toward the center, there's a room.

"We have to—" she began to yell, but before she could finish, the image of an explosion flashed through her mind. As if aware of her vision, Aidan's voice crackled across the radio, shouting about a Death Star.

The operators, caught off guard by the odd warning, momentarily paused from breaking into the practice room. "Get in there and get those girls. Now! We're out of time!" Joe yelled before taking off down the hall.

Zuri stood over her. They'd passed right by the girl's door, and no one noticed that Zuri didn't follow.

The young woman lay there motionless, staring straight up at the ceiling. Zuri felt a slight vibration between them but couldn't comprehend the connection.

With an undeniable draw, she reached toward the seemingly comatose girl, swiping a strand of hair from her eyes. When Zuri's fingers brushed the girl's skin, a fierce jolt rocked her entire body. The girl's memories rushed into her mind like a kaleidoscope of images and colors swirling and shifting.

Wincing in pain, Zuri collapsed, unable to break the connection between them.

Macie.

The name echoed through Zuri's mind. Despite the pressure in her head and the agony paralyzing her, the mysterious woman's name rolled from Zuri's lips in a whisper like a breath of fresh air beginning to cut through the painful connection.

Suddenly she remembered Aidan's instruction—*separate the pain.* It repeated over and over until the image of a box unfolded in her mind, and she began fighting back the onslaught of horror. She put the scenes in the box one by one until she was physically strong enough to push herself up from the ground.

Macie was no longer staring blindly at the ceiling. She was conscious, present, and wholly focused on Zuri. Her crystalline espresso eyes sparkled dimly, but the light was still there.

Filling her lungs and calming her mind, Zuri gripped Macie's hand. Fighting back the darkness emanating from this woman, she strained to push strength into Macie's frail body.

I can't, she told herself, shaking her head. *I'm not strong enough for this.* Just as Aidan's words began to slip from her mind, she felt the warm strength of familiar arms wrap around her waist and firmly pull backward. The instant Aidan's hand touched Zuri's skin, she caught a clear glimpse of Macie and herself as little girls, holding one another in fear and for strength. Then like smoke, the image dissipated as their hands pulled apart.

That flash of an image woke Zuri up from a fog she didn't realize she had been consumed by. As though she'd been walking around in someone else's skin since her awakening at VISP.

Macie, too, was fully awake, only now her physical body had atrophied, leaving her entirely helpless.

"Zuri!" Aidan said, pulling her back as Joe slid into the room.

"Aidan, time to go! Grab her, and I'll—" Joe's voice cut off at the sight of the figure on the bed.

Lexi raced into the small, cramped space with the others, pushing through until she reached the side of the bed to get a look at the seventh. "Joe, grab her. We need to get out now." She swung around to the others and yelled, "Go! What are you waiting for? Get everyone out!"

Brandon and Oakley looked through the mirror to see the operators force open the door to the practice room.

Undeterred, Brandon took a step closer. "It's over, Oakley. Let them go."

"Over?" He snorted a laugh. Holding his broken arm above a black switch inside a plastic box on the wall, he declared, "All I have to do is hit this. It bypasses the countdown and sets off all the explosives in the building. Then poof. The ones you love are gone."

Brandon's heart beat faster at Oakley's threat. He had every reason to believe the man.

"Oops. Didn't anticipate that, huh?" Oakley's lips turned down in a faux frown as he squeezed his arm tighter around

Joanna's neck. Brandon clenched his fists. "Wait. Is this girl special to you? These woods haven't been kind to you, Brandon. Watching another loved one struggle on the brink of death."

Slowly, the operators crept up behind Brandon, their weapons focused on Oakley. Brandon threw his hand up and they stopped their approach. Sweat beaded on his forehead as he processed their options. "You have nowhere to go. Look around. You can't win this one, Oakley."

"Such heartbreak. I almost felt a modicum of empathy for you, Brandon." A grotesque smile immediately replaced the fake frown. "On the flip side, she was so much fun to play with. Until she wasn't."

"Don't… listen…" groaned Adeline, her voice weak and rough.

Adrenaline rushed to his brain. Brandon knew he was talking about Kristine, and he couldn't help his reaction. His stomach twisted as his face turned blood-red. He longed to slaughter the evil monster in front of him. Squeezing his fists tighter, he knew it wouldn't help Joanna and her sister if he handled this wrong. "If you push that button, that means you die too," he growled, his words pushed through gritted teeth.

"Well, that's the way it is with last resorts," Oakley said with a chuckle, pressing down harder on Adeline's chest and squeezing Joanna tight.

"We'll all get out of here. Together. You too." Brandon's voice was hard. He was desperate, but he couldn't watch the woman he'd come to love die.

"Tick-tock, Brandon. You can either leave now, and the girls will live long and fruitful lives with me, or we all die."

"Dammit, Oakley! Come on! End this now."

Gavin had two operators with him. He wanted to go in guns blazing, but an arm shot out in front of him, stopping him before he could even start. "We need to know how many men are in there, how many women, and what sort of weapons they carry." They assessed as best they could through the dim light of the cage. As they observed, they witnessed several guards senselessly abusing the women behind the iron bars. Without warning, the abuse stopped before they could make their move. They watched one guard cocked his head to the side as if listening intently to something or someone.

Switching gears, the guard commanded the others to round up the girls. One of the men ran to the back of the room where the iron door was situated. As it swung open, Gavin could see a dark tunnel appear.

"Move!" One of the men bellowed. "Everyone up!"

Most of the girls could hardly maneuver without assistance, the men carelessly snatched some of the girls off the ground. Others, they kicked at in order to get them up. Gavin grit his teeth as he watched one man reach down, grab the front of a girl's gown, pull her up to his face, and growl, "Get up, or I'm leaving you behind."

Despite his threat, the woman crumpled to the floor without a sound. The rest stumbled into the tunnel and disappeared.

As soon as the room cleared, Gavin raced in and put his fingers to her neck. "She's alive!" he called out, picking her up and throwing her over his shoulder, shocked by how light she was.

"Do we follow them?" asked one of the operators.

Before Gavin could answer, Aidan's voice rang out over the radio, saying something about explosives. Torn between running back into the hallway or following the rest of the hostages in the hopes they could rescue them in time, he made a snap decision. "Yes. Let's go. The others would've heard that warning too and they'll get out. We can't risk losing all those girls."

Motioning the operators to follow, he stepped across the threshold onto the dirt and gravel floor. Flicking on his flashlight, he faced it straight to the ground before shining it down the length of the mysterious tunnel, not knowing how far ahead the guards could be.

Please, god, let them all get out.

Chapter 40
Delta Red

The operator was in position to take the shot.

"Give me the girls, Oakley, and you can run out of here and live a long and miserable life." Sweat pooled under Brandon's arms and slid down his back. Joanna was too close, too entrapped by Oakley. He knew the bullet could easily miss its target or, worse, deflect, hitting her instead.

Adeline was out of oxygen. Her chest felt ready to implode, and her eyes were closed as consciousness faded.

Unseen by the men in the room, an animated swirl of rainbow cords swept in, weaving between them as if searching for their destination. Joanna, too, could not see it, but the energy itself was palpable. Moving with such speed and power, like a sonic wave, it nearly concussed the sisters though mysteriously went unnoticed by anyone else in the room. Thick ropes of gold and silver split into smaller vines, maneuvering around the bodies of the men until they bombarded Adeline and Joanna. Both women arched simultaneously as strength and healing poured into them.

Brandon noticed their bodies seize and used Oakley's momentary confusion to launch himself forward, knocking the devil to the ground. The operator outside the window took her shot, creating projectiles of shattered glass throughout the small space.

Joanna hit the ground hard in the clash. However, before the pain stunned her, like a kite in a hurricane she and Adeline were whisked away from the brawl by the nearest operators. Blood immediately began to pool on the ground, and neither Brandon nor Oakley moved for several seconds.

Dusty memories flooded their minds of a deeply buried and long-forgotten scene. Being held in the arms of larger-than-life men opened a hidden door to those memories.

Shaking off the chaos, Joanna caught sight of Brandon lying still, "Get up! Come on. Brandon, you have to get up!"

Listening for a response, she held her breath as a light groan emanated from the bodies. The groan quickly morphed into a pain-laden chuckle.

Screaming at Brandon to wake up, Joanna cursed the demon that lay laughing at death's door. Her screams, however, turned to thankful sobs when she saw Brandon begin to push himself onto his hands and knees while Oakley remained on the floor, groaning and giggling as his blood pooled around him.

"Someone grab him. We're outta time," said Brandon, still catching his breath. His command was instantly obeyed as two others pulled Oakley to his feet and held him tight between them, his chuckling growing and fading as blood loss left him drifting in and out of delerium.

"We'll never make it out in time," he mumbled with a heavy dose of gloating. "It's funny how you're trying to save me right now, even though this final act of pithy goodness is absolutely going to kill you. All of you." Oakley's eyes locked onto Brandon's.

Without another word, Brandon spun and ran to catch up to Joanna and Adeline.

"Put me down!" Joanna demanded, not far down the hall, stubbornly fighting with the operator until he set her on her feet. Lights sparked from her crystalline cinnamon eyes as they connected with him in her anger. The shiver that rocked the operator's spine at the sight left him with a whispered apology as he released her arm. She spun back to see Adeline, limp but alive, carried close behind her. "Addie! I'm right here, okay?"

Only steps in front of them were Lexi and the others. As the girls caught sight of one another, the recognition stirred up a relief that could be felt in the air. Adeline, leaning her head back and closing her eye, witnessed a joyful river of turquoise flood the hall, though only momentarily as the purple hues of mauve began to infiltrate when panic set in.

"Joe!" Brandon yelled. "How much time?"

"Fifty-two seconds!"

"We'll never make it," he breathed through his teeth. After all, they still had to get everyone up the narrow, concrete stairs and out the main door. Not to mention a healthy distance away from the building and out of the blast zone.

Lexi didn't have to hear him to know what he was thinking. She knew it too. They all did.

"Go to the prison," Maddy shouted, gripping Lexi's forearm.

"What?"

"Listen, we need to get inside the prison. Trust me," Maddy pleaded with her eyes.

"There's no time to chance it, Madison," Lexi pushed back. "There's nothing down there but…." Finally grasping her point, Lexi cried out, "Follow me!"

"Lexi, up! Go up! What are you doing?" Joe barked, looking back over his shoulder at her, almost speechless at her order.

"Trust me," she said, her tone more than an invitation.

With a nod, his insides shook with fear despite an even deeper trust in her. To everyone else, he called out down the line, "Follow Lexi! Move, move, move!"

They scrambled after her to the exact opposite end of the long hall. Bursting through a nondescript doorway, they found themselves within a large, nasty, terrifying cave. Iron bars surrounded them from wall to ceiling. Despite Maddy and Lexi's confidence, the rest of the team felt like the end had suddenly arrived.

"Twelve seconds. Everybody down!" In a practiced move, the operators shuffled everyone into the middle. They created an outer circle using their bodies as a barrier around the group. Willing to sacrifice themselves if only to save any one of them.

"Lexi!" Zuri shouted from the center of the mass.

Looking up, Lexi could see the fierce expression on her sister's face. She watched as Zuri gripped Madison's hand next to her. Madison jolted up at the vibration of her touch and knew immediately what she needed to do. She reached across Joe's lap and grasped Zoey's hand. The spectral light in Zoey's eyes intensified as she gripped Adeline's hand. The pulsing in the room so strong every person could feel it rattle their bones, not to mention the nerves of some. Joanna, trusting yet anxious, found Addie's and Macie's hands at the same time and gripped them tight.

Lexi watched as each woman instinctively knew what needed to be done. Out of her peripheral vision, she saw Aidan place his hand on Zuri's back for comfort and protection. Lexi grasped Macie's limp hand, closing the circle. Instantaneously a prism of light formed amidst all the women's eyes and above the huddled group. A distinct hum enveloped them. All eyes were now directed at Lexi, with Zuri focusing intently on her before uttering, "The bees—"

The blast of debris shook the building, caving in the central hall as well as the main floor above. Furniture and equipment were tossed around like children's toys. Suffocating concrete and stone debris and dust engulfed them. Water from broken pipes sprayed in myriad directions while sparks from frayed wiring flashed in the dark.

"Oh my god!" Maria said, gasping at the sight.

Grant grabbed her arm. The ground shook under their feet as they watched the building tilt to the side while the earth caved in underneath.

Cupping her mouth with trembling hands, her head began to spin. "This isn't right. What's happening!"

"There are other ways out," Grant whispered, more to himself than to Maria. "Joe said there were multiple tunnels. They found a way out... I know they found a way out..." He repeated the words trying to believe them himself.

The building was swallowed up by a cloud of thick and gritty dust. Their eyes pinballed back and forth, searching for any movement—any sign of their friends. There was nothing.

"Okay, we're going in," Maria said, pulling away from Grant as she snatched up her bag. She had dropped her radio during the blast and was scrambling to find it.

"Gavin? Joe? Sheila? Anyone?" Her voice was harsh with fear. "Someone answer me. Please!" She held it away from her face, staring at it, willing it to make a sound.

Nothing.

"Does anyone copy?"

Placing his hand on her shoulder, Grant said, "If they're in the tunnels, there probably isn't any—"

"Gav—!" Maria started to call out again as Grant pushed her to the ground. The sound of coughing and leaves crunching in the distance meant someone made it out. The question was who.

They scanned the woods in the direction of the sound. Maria finally caught sight of a small group of women in torn and dirty hospital scrubs covered in dust, climbing up a small embankment. The men around them appeared almost military, but with their weapons trained on the women, they were by no means part of their rescue group.

"There are only three men over there," Grant whispered. "If we play this right, we can take them."

Maria's head snapped up. "With what?" she huffed, shocked he thought they could in any way overtake what looked to be professionally trained soldiers as the two of them sat there in the woods with little ammo and even less support.

Crawling back, Grant opened a black box containing

additional weapons, which included a grenade.

"What are you doing?" she squeaked out before dropping her hand on top of the grenade. "You're a doctor! You have no clue how to use this. You'll kill us. You'll kill those girls!"

"You just pull the pin and throw it. I know that much!"

"Stop. Stop! Just one second." Covering her mouth with her other hand, she thought for a moment before asking, "How good is your throwing arm?"

His heartbeat thumped in his ears as adrenaline began to flow. Blinking in confusion at her question, he slowly connected the dots and said, "Uh… I played baseball in high school. Not bad, I guess."

"Alright, you're gonna throw it in that direction," she declared, pointing to a spot about twenty yards in front of the group." Cocking his arm back to throw, "Not yet!"

Grant's eyes were so wide she could see white all the way around his irises. "I'm sorry, I'm just all fired up."

"Seriously, let's create a plan, not a catastrophe! I'm going to get closer to them, just below their position. When I raise my hand, I want you to throw it. While they're distracted, I'll pop up behind them and… hopefully… shoot a couple of them before they know what's happening."

"Do you know how to use a gun?"

"Well, looks like I'm gonna figure that part out in a hurry, now aren't I?" Her sass threw him for a loop in the seriousness of the moment. She watched as his face relaxed and his grip on the grenade softened. In that moment, they both felt the weight of the situation.

"Okay," he said, his voice sober and his mind clear. "I'm ready. I believe in you."

Maria crept through the dead leaves and scraggly brush as quietly as she could. Thankfully, between the girls whimpering, coughing up dust, and the men moving around, they didn't hear her.

Grant watched as she made her way behind a tree, taking note of her position. Maria took a deep breath, locked eyes with him, then exhaled as she lifted her arm.

With a deep breath of his own, Grant jumped up behind a tree, pulled the pin, cocked his arm, then let the grenade fly.

Counting the seconds in his head, he reached six before it hit the ground. He watched as the blast put everyone on their knees, including him.

Sticks and leaves rained down. The crack of a tree trunk preceded the whooshing sound of limbs racing toward the ground as a tree fell to the far side of the group, blocking their movement and placing them between Maria and the tree. All the women remained on the ground as the men frantically rose to their knees, weapons drawn in search of the enemy.

"Hey, guys," said Maria in her fullest voice as she appeared seemingly out of nowhere. She stood one foot up on an old stump, feeling like a female Rambo. As the men turned their weapons on her, three pops from her gun sounded, and each man hit the ground with a thud, groaning and cursing.

She hadn't killed them, just maimed them. And just enough to keep them from making any rash moves. As quick as they fell, the healthiest girls in the group grabbed the loose guns from the fallen guards and stood up.

From back at his perch, Grant watched the million-dollar picture unfold, wishing he had a camera.

Chapter 41
Charlie's Angels

FTA | August 25, 2029 | 8:20 p.m.

As the building stopped creaking from its collapse, the sound of rushing water grew in their ears. Broken pipes had created a flood throughout the basement and about an inch of water had already risen around their bodies.

Huddled in a circle, they lifted their heads one by one as the water washed across their cheeks and soaked their hair. A layer of dust covered them, but only from what fell after Lexi collapsed. The violent percussion of the blast had left their ears ringing, but they were grateful to be alive. The iron bars of the room were twisted, bent inward, and mangled around them from the explosion, creating a half-moon shape as if the inside of the cage had sucked the bars in. The bars remained intact, though, keeping the building above from collapsing onto their little plot of space. Debris from the collapsed floor above filled the doorway into the hall. They would never be able to clear it out of the way to get out.

Zuri stood up slowly, and with the room spinning, she gruffly whispered, "Lexi?" The word sounded muffled in her own head. Her sister lay across Aidan's lap as he sat there holding her. He spoke softly in Lexi's ear, though Zuri couldn't make out what he was saying.

"Is she… Aidan, is she…" she said, her voice soft and trembling as tears welled up, causing her eyes to burn as they mixed with the dust in the air.

Aidan looked up with wet, red eyes, shaking his head. "I don't know."

One by one, each of the girls stirred, caught their bearings, then began to slide or crawl to get to Lexi.

Zoey reached up and took Zuri's hand, pulling her next to her sister. The others moved out of the way as the girls gravitated around Aidan. While no one was injured in the blast, they were, however, in various states of awe, confusion, and fear as they took in Lexi lying there, lifeless, surrounded by rubble, dust, and darkness.

Sheila, feeling for a pulse, confirmed that there wasn't one. Everything seemed to move in slow motion. She put her face right in Aidan's so he could watch her lips move as she said, "Put her down! CPR. We need to do CPR!"

With eyes wide, Aidan immediately laid her on the ground. Everyone pushed back enough so Sheila and Aidan could take turns working on her.

Through chest compressions and breathing into her deflated lungs, the two took turns trying to bring her back. Minutes ticked by without any discernible change. *Not giving up. Not letting go,* Aidan repeated to himself as he pressed down on her chest. All around, the girls' tears fell into the slowly rising water as the pipes incessantly gushed.

Zuri, shifting her weight from foot to foot and wringing her hands, said, "Oh god. Oh please. Lexi, please come back." Usually calm and self-controlled, her feverish energy began to rub off onto the others.

"It's not working!" Justin said as Madison pushed Aidan to the side and took over.

"You can't die, Lexi. Come on! You're the one that pulled us all together. You can't leave us now," Madison cried out through stilted breaths and compressions.

Joe, noting that more than enough time had passed for a healthy resuscitation, reached over and touched Maddy's shoulder.

"No!" Her head whipped around and gave him a look so piercing he stumbled back several steps, bumping into one of the operators.

"This building isn't safe, Joe," the operator said, "We need to find a way out. Soon."

Joe nodded, signaling him to start the search along with two others.

Madison's tears fell onto Lexi as she continued to perform CPR, refusing to give up.

Aidan, unwilling to just stand by, moved over to Macie, who was lying on the floor nearby. She was alive but no better off than when they found her. Carefully pulling her into his lap to keep her head above water, he cradled her as best he could.

Adeline, feeling helpless, closed her eye in an attempt

to process what was happening. At first, she could only see darkness through her despair. Then, without instigation, an image of Joanna and Brandon formed in her mind. It was soft and bright, filled with a tangible love that flowed from one to the other, and it reminded her that she could see through the darkness. Immediately a switch flipped in her mind and the thick, inky blackness was suddenly sprayed with a vibrant array of colors that mapped out everyone in the room. It wasn't anything she'd witnessed before. Bright shades of green, turquoise, pink, and blue eddied around them. Silver and gold strands wound through the air. Color poured forth not only from the women but from *every* person in the room, with the most vibrant colors and swirls emanating from Zuri.

Altogether they were creating a wide band that formed an almost complete circle around Lexi. The strands of color only brushed against her body as if trying to break through but finding a barrier.

Without a word, Adeline's knees and hands took over, propelling her toward the open space in the vibrant circle. As she approached, she could see why it remained broken. Every point of contact between each woman, from holding hands to chest compressions, each connection allowed the strands of color, now forming a thick, braided rope, to wrap and stretch from one to the next.

She knew.

Without hesitation, she placed her right hand into Zuri's left. The colors illuminated the room, blinding her in a world that was hers alone. She could feel the cords of healing, strength, and love move through and around her. It pushed her other arm out as if it already knew its path, and she was just a physical conduit. She watched as her fingertips touched Madison's furiously moving shoulder in her attempt to save Lexi, still lying lifeless on the floor.

As soon as the circle was complete, every point of contact sparked like the arc of an electric current. Everyone felt the pulse of energy and joined with Adeline in carrying the weight of the vibrant movement. The operators searching for a way out were forced to stop and turn in awe. The illumination wasn't just coming from the crystals in their eyes, but from a now visible force that to them looked like a colorful light show pulsing to the rhythm of a heartbeat.

Adeline watched as Madison's hands were met with resistance from the color-filled ropes entangling her, stopping her from pressing down on Lexi's chest. The winding threads then spilled over, finally attaching to Lexi's body. At first, only thin strands seemed to penetrate and adhere, but as she watched, shades of silver and gold, green and gray rapidly intensified their connection. Then faster. Finding new paths through the barrier of death that had engulfed her, reaching deep into her soul. And with sparks and flashes, pulled her back from the dark.

A shockwave of colors reversed, billowing outward through them like a stormfront as Lexi gasped for air. Her body arched upward from the center point of her chest and the women collapsed in unison, once again breaking the circle.

In the silence, Zuri crawled to her sister, lifting Lexi's head into her lap. "You're okay, Lex. We're here," she whispered, gently brushing Lexi's hair. "You saved us, you know that?" Zuri's words were muffled in her ears as she drew air into her burning lungs. Lexi's eyes darted around the room, trying to focus. Amid her confusion, a woman she'd never seen before stood over Aidan's shoulder. Her slight smile was directed at Lexi as she placed a hand on Aidan's arm.

"Lex? Can you hear me?" Zuri put her face right in front of her sister's eyes, drawing their focus onto her.

The clear crystals in Zuri's eyes radiated outward. With a quick look back at Aidan, Zuri followed her sister's gaze with a questioning look. "Are you okay? Can you hear me?"

The space occupied only moments before was now empty. Shaking her her head to get her bearings, Lexi's raspy voice finally broke through the tearful silence, "What did I miss?"

A bubble of laughter rose as Zoey placed her hand on Lexi's face. "Oh, ya know. Just another day of fun in a dark and secluded torture chamber." Their smiles faded quickly as an unspoken fear replaced the joy of her dramatic return.

Lexi shifted her gaze to Joe, whose concerned expression was momentarily succeeded by gratefulness at the sight of her ocean eyes. "Listen, everyone, we need to move. The only thing holding up the building above us are these warped iron bars surrounding us. If you can move, follow Rich." He pointed to the back corner where the commanding operator stood beside the mangled open iron door.

With quietly murmured words, those who could walk rose to their feet, helping one another to the door and disappearing into the dark tunnel beyond.

Aidan, holding Macie in his arms, carried her petite body as he entered the tunnel. Brandon, too, picked up Adeline, and with Joanna, they eagerly made their way through the door.

Joe watched over the group to see them safely out before helping Sheila with Lexi, gently maneuvering her into his arms.

"I'm surprised you're not grunting," Lexi said jokingly. She couldn't see his grin but felt his body relax.

"What, you? Nah, you're like carrying a watermelon."

Scrunching her eyebrows, she said, "Aren't you supposed to say feather?"

"If that was the case, I'd just use a fan to blow you through the tunnel. A watermelon still needs to be carried with care."

"Or rolled," she added with a chuckle. "You're the strangest man, Joe. Thank you." Lexi's smile spread across her face. Her head still swam and her body trembled almost to the point of numbness.

"Where did all of the girls go? The ones trapped here with Adeline?"

"I don't know."

"Gavin?"

He shook his head. He hadn't seen them in the hall or in the prison.

"There's light ahead," Rich said, signaling those behind him to stop. As they drew closer, they slowed down, pausing at the opening. Joe set Lexi down beside Sheila and made his way up front.

"Can you tell if anyone's out there?"

"No. Hard to see through the foliage. I'm going to scout it out." With practiced moves, he crept slowly to the mouth of the tunnel, careful to push aside the plants with as little disturbance as possible. Two others followed close behind him.

Everyone else watched silently as Rich scanned what he could see through the kudzu vines. Then, without saying a word, he slowly stepped through, disappearing beyond into the light. The group waited with pursed lips and squinting eyes expecting the worst. Moments later, however, he returned with an odd smirk and waved them forward.

They emerged from the tunnel as if exploring a new planet, with their eyes slowly adjusting to the most unlikely sight before them. It was almost incomprehensible.

Gavin stood tall and triumphant with his hand on Maria's back. Her weapon was pointed at three of Oakley's guards. With a swipe of dirt across her face, she looked extra tough. Surrounding them were the missing women, several of which held weapons at their sides though clearly ready to fight should one of the monstrous guards make an ill-advised move.

"It's like being in a Charlie's Angels movie!" exclaimed Aidan as his eyes adjusted, struck by the awesome sight.

Chapter 42
Freedom

"You cannot deny it now," Aidan insisted as he sat on their little apartment's living room floor.

"Okay… Yes… I see where you're coming from. There are a lot of similarities." Maddy was trying hard to keep her smile in check.

"It's not like you all didn't see the same thing I did in that prison. A literal dome formed around us!" he said, growing louder and flailing his arms around as if feeling out an invisible dome, straining to get his point across.

Joe couldn't resist. "You're right. You're absolutely right. It was like magic. Turns out they are witches."

"No! Not just magic and not just witches. They were communicating. Like, without talking."

"Like I am right now with you? Look into my eyes and repeat what I'm telling you to do," Joe said.

"No, I won't shut up. Look, they're a mixture, part witch…" he paused for effect, "part werewolf." His face was deadpan as the room fell silent. "See? Your silence tells me you're finally getting it."

"You're right. We're speechless, my friend." Unable to hold back any longer, laughter broke out like flowers bursting open on a warm spring day. The sort of spring day that breeds hope and fosters joy. Not as recently met strangers, but among family.

"What? Werewolves communicate without—" he grunted as a pillow hit him in the face.

The ever-present fear and anxiety had dissipated. There was a freedom in the air that none of them had felt in quite some time.

The operators that Jahnsen assigned to them for Adeline's rescue mission had left earlier that morning. Zoey had offered them rooms in the apartment building if they wanted to stay, but they had jobs to get back to. Rich, who had been their on-site commander for the mission, told Zoey they had plenty more left to do to combat the Breakers, not to mention finding out what VISP personnel were secretly working on in those bunkers in Pennsylvania.

"Well, you know you always have a place to stay if you're ever out this way," she offered.

"My wife and three kiddos are back at LIMIT. Brooke would kill me if I moved us without her input. But hey, if I decide to retire from this life, I'll definitely hit you up," he said with a smile, nodding as he looked across the room at some of the most incredible individuals he'd ever met. "I think she and the kids would like it here."

After a hefty hug, he left with the rest of the men. She sensed that wouldn't be the last time they'd meet. There were still unanswered questions. Not to mention their group history up to this point ensured there would definitely be more trouble ahead before they saw the end of it.

Without a formal police department in Sanford, Joe had reinforced one of the apartments in the building into a holding cell. Bars on the windows, metal doors that locked from the outside, and hidden cameras for monitoring were emplaced to hold Oakley and his men until they could devise a better plan.

Sheila had the group of women they'd found at the FTA set up in rooms on her floor so she could tend to them. Some had years worth of injuries from abuse. Phil spent every spare moment outside of VISP being her gopher, searching for medications, and bandages, even hunting down different plants with medicinal properties. He had missed out on so much time with Sheila that now, with a second wind, he found himself creating ways to visit on official business, check in on the women, and reconnect with the doctor.

Joanna and Adeline stayed, sharing an apartment with Brandon right next door to them. Adeline had gone almost completely blind from the head trauma she received. Her sight was brutally damaged in her left eye though less so in her right. When she did attempt to use her right eye, the vertical double vision gave her vertigo and nausea. Aidan, ever the visionary, saw fit to supply her with a patch for her right eye and a pair of dark-tinted sunglasses. He was convinced that all superheroes wore such things and made sure to let everyone know it. With her eyes closed, she could see far more as it was. Every object was clearly visible. Inanimate objects like furniture showed up as shades of gray, while every living thing was made up of an array of colors.

Joe was working on his fourth cup of coffee for the afternoon as he looked out over the hodgepodge of people across his living room. It had only been a few days and they were all only beginning to recover, but the smiles on their faces as they told stories and shared experiences confirmed what he'd been feeling, that no matter what happened next, they were better together. All of them.

Despite having their own private space, it wasn't abnormal for them to gravitate to Zoey's apartment, often falling asleep in recliners and on floors in the cramped unit. Being together just seemed right. Felt right.

Lexi sidled up next to him with her own cup of coffee. They'd been chatting about renovating, opening some of the apartments into larger units. There were also a few homes on the outskirts of town he knew of. Something with enough property hidden from prying eyes that they could turn into a compound of sorts so everyone had more room. She imagined a shared garden and a clinic for Sheila. If they secured it right, it could be a fantastic place to live and offer the women a more fitting place to test their gifts.

When Gavin saw Aidan carrying Macie out from that tunnel after the explosion, his heart stopped. He hadn't seen her in decades, yet something about her clicked. Aidan, guarded and confused, squeezed her tight as Gavin rushed upon them, pausing as he drew near, taking in the seriousness of her condition. Maria moved beside him and the look on his face spoke volumes. She gave Aidan an encouraging look, after which he hesitantly allowed Gavin to scoop Macie into his arms.

Tears washed over Gavin's red cheeks as he locked eyes with her. Her eyes, the only physical part of her she seemed to be in control of, flicked back and forth across his face and between his eyes, trying to understand. After several minutes of little more than gentle sobs and attempted explanations, her eyes lit up and immediately filled with tears, comprehending their connection.

From that point on, Gavin didn't leave her side. Though Macie hadn't yet spoken, with Sheila's help, and her sisters nearby, her body began to show signs of recovery.

Zuri had become a different person since Macie was rescued. Her sweet and light personality was back in full force. She was singing again. Humming to songs only she knew, melodies that filled her mind. Her smile was soft and genuine, and her laughter was loud and joyful. She was more alive than ever since breaking free of the glass prison. The fog had dissipated completely. Often she would sit and hold Macie's hand for hours, at times telling her stories. Other times she would just quietly nap beside her—their connection so strong anyone within ten feet could feel the hum in the air when they were together.

Sheila told them all that just being with Macie would help her heal. After completing a full examination of Macie upon their return, she believed a spinal injury had severed the nerves in her lower back, leaving her paralyzed from the waist down. She also believed that with time and care, Macie would fully regain the use of her upper body.

Like the others, Macie was a fighter.

Adeline, too, had spent a good deal of time over the last few days checking in on Macie. Once in a while, she attempted to describe to the group what her new sight was like. That she could see their gold and silver ropes winding toward Macie. And that, just as Doc Sheila had said, the more time they spent with her, the faster she'd heal. Though it was up to Macie to remember how to move again and to work at it with all her might, their partnership was vital.

Unlike the other women found at the FTA, Macie stayed with Lexi and Zuri in their apartment. Gavin and Maria settled into an apartment across the hall, though he had yet to leave Macie's side for an entire night.

Maria, on the other hand, spent most of each day in the kitchen cooking. It was her love language, and everyone agreed it couldn't simply be called *food*. Maria didn't have crystal eyes, but no one could deny her gifts.

Besides Adeline, no one knew what Macie's gifts were yet. Adeline could see now that the colors of each woman's gift coincided with the colors of their crystalline eyes. While the rest of the women had ropes of intertwining colors enveloping them, Macie's were still mere threads. But she knew, with Zuri's care, those threads would thicken into colorful cords of twine, on into vibrant and powerful rope, eventually wrapping her up and recreating her into the person she should've been all these years. The woman she was designed to be.

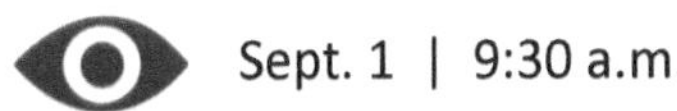 Sept. 1 | 9:30 a.m.

"Hey, guys? You're not going to believe this," Gavin called out. He'd been pouring through the files Zoey and Rich brought back from the hospital over the last week.

With all eyes on him, he walked into the living room

with papers in hand. Tossing them onto the coffee table, his excitement silenced all conversations in the room. "What do you see on all of these?"

Zoey, Maria, Joanna, and Madison each slid onto the floor around the coffee table and began to rifle through the pages to get a better look.

"Not sure. What are we supposed to be looking for, Gavin?" said Zoey, as her eyes scanned each one. "I mean, we already know we were all born at Central Carolina in Sanford. Well… at least five of us were anyway."

"Six if you count me," Aidan piped in, prompting Zoey to roll her eyes.

"Lexi and Zuri are question marks, but we did find what we think is Lexi's file." Zoey was speaking mostly to herself, still looking for the hidden information on each of the docs. "Lexi wasn't the name given, but an *Alexi* was born around the same timeframe."

"Spit it out, Gavin," Justin griped. Gavin's glasses slid down his nose as he nodded. Pushing them back up in his typical manner came off as a silent curse.

"Okay, look at the team that delivered each of you."

Madison saw it first and popped up on her knees to look closer. "Oh my gosh. It's right there."

Maria, not close enough to see, said with excitement, "What is it? Who is it? Speak, woman!"

"It says…" she began, her eyebrows pulled together as she focused on the document, "well… no." She paused. Trying again, she said, "In some way or another, there are three consistent names. Some of us were delivered by the same midwife, coupled with the same doctor, in case of complications. Oh, and one of the nurses comes up frequently as well." Madison pulled the rest of the documents. "Except, not in every situation. Joe, can you grab me a highlighter?"

He was in the kitchen and back with three colors in ten seconds. Maddy snatched them from his hand like a snake on a mouse and pulled all the documents to the floor, spreading them out for a better view. She zipped from one paper to the next, highlighting any information that matched.

As they watched the colors expand from page to page, their mouths dropped in awe. When she finally sat back, they couldn't tell if she'd just made things easier or more difficult.

"So?" Adeline insisted, leaning back on the recliner and wearing her shades. Her body was still a mess of bruises and broken bones.

"I'm missing something," Madison mumbled, sliding pages back and forth, trying to determine what was wrong. "Three of us had the same nurse, Nurse Amee. Five of us had Dr. Harold and a midwife—"

Sheila sat up straight in her chair. "Did you say, Harold?"

Madison nodded.

"Is his first name listed?"

"Uh… yeah… it's, it's James. Does that mean something to you?"

Sheila looked up at Phil, whose shocked expression caught their attention. With a sigh and subtle head-shake, Sheila turned slowly to look at the women before saying, "He was the man that we believed kidnapped all of you. He was a Colonel in the military. Worked in OB on base. But he also moonlighted at the hospital here in Sanford. He took early retirement and disappeared."

"Do you think he did something to us when we were born?" wondered Lexi, asking what they must have all been thinking. "Just because he didn't deliver us doesn't mean he wasn't in the hospital at the time."

"It's possible," Sheila whispered, unsure of what he could've done to them for this to happen. "Maybe we go back to the hospital and see if there are any records on him? What do you think, Phil? Here, hand me one of those. I want to see if there are any other clues."

"Who was the midwife, Maddy?" Joanna asked, unsure of what to make of it all just yet.

Humming to herself, she found the name again, highlighted in pink, and said, "A Josephine Dyson."

Aidan was leaning against the door jamb that led into the kitchen when he heard the name. An exaggerated chill raced down his spine, drawing the attention of others.

Zoey could feel him shift behind her and when she turned to look, she saw the color drain from his face. "What is it, Aidan?"

He just stared as if lost in some unknown memory.

"Hey, buddy, what's goin' on? Do you know her?" asked Joe, grabbing Aidan's upper arms. He could see something significant was going on behind Aidan's eyes and reached up to squeeze his friend's shoulder in hopes of stirring him a bit.

Aidan blinked himself out of wherever he'd gone. His head shook slightly as if clearing the cobwebs of a deep sleep. "It's just that… well… Josephine Dyson was my grandmother's name."

Zuri, who had since made her way to his side, entangled her hand into his. Quietly, Aidan looked down at their intertwined fingers, lifting their hands up as if to acknowledge the connection.

Then he looked into her eyes. The kitchen light reflected off the crystals in her iris', creating a chaotic rainbow effect.

"You never told us about your family," said Zoey, recognizing it was a topic they'd always shied away from. Avoiding their past was a skill they were adept at.

"I, uhh… well, it was before the grid failed. She disappeared one day. Middle of the day." Clearing the dry lump in his throat, he continued, "We were at Kiwanis Park. You know, the one down close to the hospital. She had gotten off early, picked me up from daycare, and so we went to the park, waiting for my mom to leave work. I was on the far side of the playground with some kids when I heard tires squealing. Looking over, I saw two men in black grab her. They pulled her into a van and took off." His eyes glistened as the memory spilled out. "That was it. I never saw her again," he paused, took a deep breath, then, as if realizing there was more, said in a shallow whisper, "Well, I did see her once more. Or I thought I did."

Zoey wrapped her arms around him and squeezed. He barely reciprocated the hug. His limbs felt heavy and awkward. "Why didn't you ever tell us about this?"

"I guess I just sort of buried it. At a young age, I would imagine a box in my mind. Whenever something hurt me, I would shove those memories into that box, I guess to avoid the feelings that came with them. Figured I could always pull them out if I needed to. I guess I'd forgotten the memory was there," he said, knocking on the top of his head with his knuckles.

"So that's where the idea of the box came from? Your own desire to move on from past hurts?" Lexi said, connecting the dots.

Before he could stop them, nearly everyone pressed in for a

great bear hug. He could feel the hum of their love and strength move through him. Madison purposely laid her hand on his shoulder, fostering the sense of calm he was feeling.

Brushing off the emotion, and with some leftover grit in his throat, he yelled the obvious, "Group hug!" Burying the memory beneath his usual obnoxious self, he wrapped his arms around as many as he could, squeezing tight.

"Aidan! Ugh! I can't breathe," choked out Zoey, squished right in the middle of the pile.

Once they settled back down and the shock of the unknown wore off, Gavin chimed in, "Alright, so it looks like more answers lead to more questions. Where to next?"

Sheila was looking at one of the records as her eyes bounced back and forth from the page to Aidan. "Aidan?" she said, clearing her throat.

His eyes swiveled to her.

"You said your mom was still at work?" He nodded as she hurried her next question. "Where did she work?"

Squinting, he said, "The hospital… with my grandma."

"What was her name?"

His throat began to close but he squeezed out her name, "Maya. Why?"

Sheila stepped toward the rest of the records spread out across the floor. Looking them over, she saw the name Maya stand out on each one, plain as day. "What did your mom do at the hospital?"

Zoey grabbed his hand once again and he squeezed until both their fingers turned white. "She worked there for, I think, four years as a pediatric nurse in the maternity ward. She told me her mother used to call her a baby-cuddler because it was her favorite part of the job." At the memory, his chest began to tighten and his cheeks flushed.

It was as if all the air had been sucked from the room. All eyes were on Aidan as they processed the possibility.

A low hum began to pulse through the room. Adeline had been listening intently to every word and behind the darkness of her closed lids burnished ropes of onyx circulated around where Aidan stood. His heart pounded, aching at the mention of his mother. Blue threads of sadness filtered through the thicker onyx ropes. But coming from all around him, as if working to subdue the pain, golden cords of strength along with green vines moving in love, braided and twisted together as they advanced from all the women in the room. The vibrant strands encircled and infiltrated the onyx making up the contours of his body as another set of threads settled faintly behind him. The colors, so out of place, were a smoky purple and difficult to distinguish.

Adeline, noticing Lexi straighten her back as the tight cords engulfed her, was thrown off by the purple haze beginning to encircle Lexi as well. Where Addie had instinctively understood what the colors meant, this particular shade left her confused.

Sheila lifted her eyes from the page in her hands catching sight of Aidan's questioning look. Clearing her throat, she said, "Your mother's name is written on every file."

IRON
PRISON

Epilogue
To Live

Central Carolina Hospital | 2009

"Deep breaths, Veronica. Deep breaths. That's it," said Josephine, soothing her patient as she worked through another contraction. "You're doing amazing. See? Like riding a bike with number two." Her smile genuine.

"Number two," Veronica groaned through gritted teeth between breaths. "Girl, how did I get myself into this for a second time? This one better be a boy!"

"What are you talking about? Alexi was the perfect baby girl. Rarely cried from what I remember."

"She was… until she hit eighteen months," Veronica growled through another contraction, still managing to crack a smile. "That girl is Houdini. Always finding her on top of counters when my back's turned."

"It's not time. Don't start pushing now." Josephine's voice was calming. Every word she spoke seemed to put Veronica at ease.

"All right! How we doin' in here, ladies?" The obstetrician's booming voice preceded him into the room.

"Really good, Dr. Harold. She's six centimeters dilated. We're getting close," she said, her smile stretched ear to ear.

"That's what I like to hear! Baby's in a good position?"

"Head's down. Vitals look good. She still refuses the ultrasound, but…" she looked down her nose jokingly at the mom-to-be and, with a wink, said, "Veronica here is a pro, so I think we'll be just fine."

"And so aren't you, Ms. Josephine." He took a quick look at Veronica's vitals then turned to head out the door. "I'll be down the hall if you need—" he started to say before bumping right into a petite, young pregnant woman in scrubs as she turned into the room."

Stumbling, she let out an "Oomph!" as he grabbed her shoulders. She gripped his arm and started laughing. "I'm so sorry, Dr. H."

"Maya! Holy-moly you scared me, kiddo," he affectionately replied in a fatherly manner. He'd known her since she was in high school after her mother began working at the hospital.

"That was my fault. This belly beats me to the doorway every time," she said as he gave her upper arm a little squeeze before heading out.

"What's up, Maya?" Josephine said, only taking a quick glance away from the baby's heart rate monitor. She thought she had noticed an odd blip in the graph.

"Hey, Mom," she said. Then turning to Veronica, "Morning,

Mrs. Beasley."

"You've seen my cooter too many times to call me *Mrs.* anything."

Maya laughed at her words. Pregnant women were allowed to say anything they wanted. Her mom's favorite line was, "One day, when you're shooting a watermelon out of a peach, you'll realize how much a good curse word yelled from deep in your belly can help." Turns out, that day was coming up quick.

"Everything okay in the nursery?" her mom asked.

"Yeppers. I just got the last little one to sleep. She's been unsettled for some reason." Maya was a pediatric nurse but was back in college studying meteorology. In high school, she'd taken nursing classes for college credit through the school's higher education program. She loved working with babies but realized after the first few months it was too much of an emotional rollercoaster for her whenever there were complications.

Maya decided on meteorology because she loved the weather and the outdoors. She'd probably seen the movie *Twister* twenty times. The study of it, however, involved a lot more math and physics than she imagined. That piece of the puzzle hadn't been told to her when she was deciding on her major. Not that she wasn't good at math, it was mostly that she hated math. In high school, she made this huge pitch to her mom about how it was so dumb, and she was never going to use it.

Then she chose weather forecasting.

Josephine gave her a quick squeeze. "Well, you are the best baby cuddler around, my dear."

A half-smile creased her lips just as her eye caught a blip on the baby's heart monitor. Josephine saw Maya's expression and turned her eyes back to the readout. The baby's heart rate seemed to be slowing.

"Something's wrong, Jo," Veronica said, her hands covering her stomach.

"It's okay, honey. It's just fine. I'm going to check something." She glanced back at Maya, and without words, her expression told her daughter to go get Dr. Harold. Maya gave a quick nod and hurried out of the room.

She could hear her mom's soothing words to Veronica but knew the next few minutes were crucial as she raced to find the doctor. Turning a corner in the hall, she saw him standing outside another room. "Doctor!" yelled Maya, waving her arm to get his attention. Catching her out of the corner of his eye, he immediately headed her way.

"What's going on, Maya?" he said as his long legs quickly brought them face to face.

"Heart rate started falling. I have a feeling it's the umbilical cord."

"Right." Between Josephine and Maya, he'd never known them to be wrong. "Head to surgical and call the team. Prep the room. I'm bringing her straight there."

As they split off, Maya sensed it wouldn't end well. Pushing the feeling of dread down deep, she berated herself for allowing those negative thoughts into her mind. Her mother was an exceptional midwife, and Dr. Harold knew what he was doing.

Within minutes Veronica was in the room with a curtain pulled shut so she couldn't see what was happening on the other side. Maya was holding her hand while Josephine and Dr. Harold considered the best strategy.

"We'll need a C-section. It's the best chance to get them both through this," Josephine said sternly. Dr. Harold looked her in the eyes for several seconds processing any other options. With a deep breath, he nodded and motioned to the surgical nurses to prepare, then to the anesthesiologist to adjust Veronica's position and put her to sleep.

"No! Do not put me out! Just numb me up. I need to see my baby when she comes!" Tears streamed down her face as her voice shook, but her words were clear and fierce.

Maya held one hand while Josephine grabbed the other. "Honey, I think it's best you sleep for this."

Veronica's eyes bore into her midwife's. "No. I can't. I have a terrible feeling. I can't explain it. I just know I can't be asleep when she comes into the world."

Her determination, mixed with a healthy dose of honest fear, was obvious to everyone in the room. "Okay. Okay, V." Josephine looked at Dr. Harold and quickly got everyone started. They were the best at what they did. Skilled and compassionate. In a planned C-section, it can take ten to fifteen minutes. Dr. H. had the baby out in six.

Maya tried not to let her emotions show as Veronica stared at her during the procedure, but she couldn't help feeling just as unsettled about it all. Her fears were confirmed as little blue fingers and toes appeared. There were no cries or gurgles from the newborn as she emerged with the cord wrapped above her shoulders and her neck like a snake.

Usually, Maya would be talking in hushed tones to the mother. Words of encouragement and hope. This time, all words failed her.

Her mother felt the desperation exuding from Maya and pulled Veronica's attention her way. "Hey now, it's alright. They've got her out."

"I don't hear her. She's not crying. Why isn't she crying?"

Josephine learned a long time ago to just provide the truth. Anything else just inflamed emotions and stirred up questions that would lead to hysteria. "Remember, we said the umbilical cord got tangled around her neck. They are untangling it right now and performing—" a weak baby's cry broke through her words.

They all took in a cleansing breath along with the baby.

"Can I have my baby?" whispered Veronica, her voice hoarse and her words heavy with emotion.

"Just a moment, honey. They're still checking her over."

Maya kept her eyes glued to the team around the baby. They still hadn't brought her over to her mom. The tension that had broken for a moment when the baby cried quickly filled the room again. Maya's gaze flickered over to her mom. Josephine caught the almost imperceptible look on her daughter's face. So did Veronica.

"Something's not right, is it? What's wrong with my baby, Jo?"

Josephine squeezed Veronica's hand. "I'm not sure yet, honey. I'm here with you, though. No matter what, you're not alone. Do you hear me?"

She nodded then froze as Dr. Harold turned around with her baby girl wrapped in his arms. He walked over as Maya took a step back to give him space.

"Veronica, the baby is struggling. I'm going to lay her on your chest and I want you to massage her." He placed the tiny warm body on her mother's chest and then stepped back, motioning to Josephine to come speak with him. Maya rejoined Veronica by her side but kept one ear open, hoping to hear what the doctor was saying.

"The baby went too long without oxygen."

"So bring her to the NICU. Why don't you have her on oxygen?" Josephine wanted to grab the baby and run her to the intensive care unit herself.

He put his hand on her shoulder to steady her. "She's not going to make it. Even if she did, her brain will not function properly."

The information, though painful to accept, slowly registered in Josephine's mind. Though deep within, she knew the truth already. Taking a steadying breath, she walked back over to her friend's bedside. Putting her hand on the baby's head, she looked Veronica in the eyes. "Honey, I need you to listen to me carefully. Can you do that?" Her voice was soothing but firm.

Veronica only nodded as a stream of tears followed a winding path down her cheeks.

"I want you to love this baby with all that you have. She's not going to know this world for very long, but what she'll know of it will be the most warm, wonderful, and loving experience any of us could ever know. Her life will be perfect."

Maya touched the baby's head and stepped back. She had to leave. Gasping for air, darkness started encroaching on her vision as she entered the hall.

The cool walls against her back kept her from passing out, but even when the feeling passed, all she could do was lean against the wall, listening to the sounds of quiet sobs coming from within the room. After some time, her mother walked out holding the still baby. Their eyes locked in grief, but both had jobs to do.

Josephine, aware of Maya's struggle, asked in a hushed

voice, "Can you take her to the nursery? I need to stay with Veronica."

With everything inside her, she did not want to hold the baby, but there was protocol to follow. Lifting her arms, her mother transferred her gently, then kissed its tiny head.

Holding the still-warm bundle, Maya carefully made her way to the nursery. The room was dimly lit, kept that way for the comfort of sleeping newborns. At the back of the room were two doors. One led to a room used to care for infants in need of smaller procedures. The other led to a quiet room for nursing mothers and volunteer baby-cuddlers. Maya knew she should go into the first door but found herself shouldering open the quiet room door instead.

The room was empty. She sat in a rocker and held the baby close.

With her own child growing in her belly, she was devastated that the one in her arms would never gain another pound. Tears finally broke free. Her emotions were too high, too intense. This pain was more than she could bear.

Placing her cheek on the little girl's head, she felt the familiar hum in the center of her body work its way out toward the ends of her limbs. It was a feeling that came with any strong emotion, but this time it felt different, stronger, warmer.

After several minutes she knew she couldn't sit there any longer. Taking a deep breath, she went to sit up when she heard the sound of a small hiccup, feeling a subtle bounce in her arms.

Maya held her breath, too afraid to look. When she finally did, a little girl's eyes began to peek out at her. Several long blinks later, her wispy eyelashes opened wide enough for Maya to see a crystal-like brilliance with clear irises like cut diamonds.

She'd never seen anything like it.

Her legs lifted her upright as though no longer in control of her actions. With all other thoughts erased from her mind, and the sounds of the hospital muffled and distant, she found herself moving, walking as if underwater. Maya brought the baby into the room where Veronica was deep in grief, being consoled by Josephine. Even though Maya came in quietly, her mother turned around, having felt the air shift in the room.

Maya's own tears had ceased. Her mouth was open but no words came out. Josephine stood up and frantically shook her head with the unspoken question, *What are you doing?*

Holding the baby close, she went to step past her mother. Josephine put her hand on her daughter's shoulder to stop her but pulled it back to her chest in shock when she saw the baby's eyes were open. Blinking.

Mother and daughter looked at one another. It was impossible to comprehend.

Dr. Harold came into the room behind them. When he saw Maya holding the baby his face flushed with rage. Grabbing her shoulder he turned her around, whispering, "What are you doing, Maya? The baby should n—" His words cut off as he saw the baby's hand open and then squeeze back into a tiny fist. "What?" He set down his clipboard and lifted his stethoscope to listen to her heart. "How? What is this? Is this the same baby?"

Maya unwrapped the baby's right foot showing the little anklet with her mother's information.

"This is impossible."

Veronica had stopped crying, noticing something odd happening among the doctor and nurses. "Is that my baby?" she mumbled between short breaths, her voice barely audible.

Maya locked eyes with the woman and stepped forward. She could only nod because her voice refused to make a sound.

Veronica was shaking her head back and forth in confusion as Maya slowly handed the beautiful, glowing, healthy baby over to her mama.

"Is this real?" Her tears paused as her puffy eyes worked to grasp the reality of this healthy, pink baby in her arms.

Finally, Maya's words came out in a whisper. "She's real, Veronica." Swallowing hard, she touched the baby's head with her fingertips. "What's her name?"

Veronica stared at her baby with so much love the weight of it could be felt in the room. "Her name is Zuriella."

"Gift of God…" whispered Josephine, her voice trailing off.

Maya turned toward her mother, adding, "Or beautiful."

Smiling, Josephine said, "Both meanings are perfect for her." In her peripheral vision, she realized Dr. Harold was still standing there, watching. Only the air of his presence had changed. She put her hand on his arm but he barely noticed, with his eyes glued to the baby. He could see little crystals in her eyes glinting off the light from the overhead fixture.

Josephine and Maya felt the atmosphere shift. The same doctor who, only moments before, demonstrated tenderness like no other was now unrecognizable.

A calculating mind was at work behind his cold expression.

Maya's chest felt heavy once again.

This baby was not safe.

Also by M. J. Thompson

Glass Prison | Prisoner Series: Book One

ABOUT THE AUTHOR

M.J. Thompson is a retired Combat Weather Forecaster who occasionally jumped out of perfectly good airplanes, owns and operates Red Glasses Real Estate, renovates houses, and in her down time writes fiction novels.

M.J., her husband, and four children live in Sanford, NC. Her debut novel, Glass Prison, was born after a jump accident found her with a traumatic brain injury that temporarily plunged her into a dark and silent world in which the only thing she found tolerable was writing with her eyes closed. During those lost days, she occasionally wrote snippets of her experiences. One of which gave life to the women in the debut of her Prisoner Series.

www.ingramcontent.com/pod-product-compliance
Lightning Source LLC
Chambersburg PA
CBHW020337010826

48970CB00012B/1340